The

MINOTAUR
TAKES
HIS OWN
SWEET
TIME

BLAIR

blairpub.com

Library of Congress Cataloging-in-Publication Control Number: 2016026939 (print)

ISBN 978-0-89587-673-7
ISBN 978-0-89587-674-4 (ebook)

10 9 8 7 6 5 4 3 2 1

Cover Design by Brooke Csuka
Interior Design and Illustrations by Anna Sutton

The

MINOTAUR
TAKES
HIS OWN
SWEET
TIME

STEVEN SHERRILL

ALSO BY STEVEN SHERRILL:

The Minotaur Takes a Cigarette Break
Visits from the Drowned Girl
The Locktender's House
Joy, PA
Ersatz Anatomy

For Esmée

with love and

more love

CHAPTER ONE

THE MINOTAUR FALLS DEAD in the Pennsylvania mud. Belly up. Bang. It is April. Mud season. Dying season. The mud is black. The sky is blue. The Minotaur is dead. The black mud pulls hard. So, too, the blue sky. The Minotaur succumbs. The Minotaur falls dead belly up. Maybe one thick horn tip gouges the earth. Maybe it doesn't. Either way the Minotaur falls dead. Belly up. As planned. A gut full of grapeshot. Or maybe a musket ball. Doesn't matter. It is dying season. Mud season. Late April, maybe. The Minotaur's calendar is imprecise. Doesn't matter. The Minotaur falls dead, as planned.

"Pour it into 'em, boys!"

"For God and country, boys!"

"This war will be over by Christmas, boys!"

Cannon fodder. The Minotaur takes the hit, snorts through his bullish nostrils, and goes down in black muck. The black muck splatters across his gray wool jacket. The regiment clanks and rattles through the field, toward noon. Lunch break. The Minotaur is among the first to die. Doesn't matter to him. The battlefield looks better with bodies. Always. He waits for the first volley of rifle shots—insipid, arrhythmic little bursts of smoke from the opposing side. From the Union. Then he dies. Like a good Confederate. A good Rebel. He dies.

The rest of the regiment bumbles ahead—the hardcore, the starry-eyed dilettantes, history piddlers, triflers, all stumble toward their own deaths. Or victories. Doesn't matter.

"Rally round the flag, boys!"

"Give 'em hell!"

The Minotaur falls dead, belly up. Welcomes death. The sweet release. The absence of unending life. Bang. The end. Gravity's unrelenting grip on his snout, his horns, finally, once and for all, conquering. Falls dead, the Minotaur, belly up. Willing and able to let it all go. The wars, and the humans who make them, will rage on with or without him. Clamor and clang. The battlefield looks better with bodies. They all do. Always. The Minotaur falls dead on this battlefield, belly up. Belly up, because he wants to see. Wants, in death, to watch. The Minotaur grunts when he falls.

"Unngh," he says, falls dead.

CHAPTER TWO

THAT VERY MORNING, NOT DEAD YET but getting ready to die, the Minotaur, in his motel room, dressed with care. He put on the rough trousers, the wide and supple belt, and its bulky cartridge box. He wet a paper towel in the tiny sink and dabbed the mud from an earlier death off the woolen jacket. He licked a fingertip and rubbed each brass button so that, even in the wan fluorescent light of his cramped bathroom, even in that light, the buttons glinted. The Minotaur shrugged his big shoulders into the coat, straightened his side knife on the belt, and stepped out into the cool dawn. The blue-black passage. He paused there, remembered something, and looked toward the motel office, the dark of the windows fractured intermittently by the flashing *Vacancy* sign.

The Minotaur returned to his room, sat on the edge of the narrow bed, rifled through the nightstand drawer to retrieve a nearly empty pad and a pen. He cocked his big head and made a short list. A handful of necessary things. The old bull is graceful when he needs to be. He walked quietly to the office door. They were asleep. He didn't want to wake them. The Minotaur knelt on the walk and thumbed open the mail slot's thin brass door. The hinge protested loudly. The Minotaur poked the note through and closed the slot. But before he could rise, the brass flap slammed back open. Topple, Minotaur. A giggle brought him back to his knees. The Minotaur peered, as much as one with such a cumbersome noggin can peer, into the mail slot. Saw her face, those wide eyes holding all of the night's fiery black. She wrinkled her nose, stuck out her tongue. The

Minotaur nudged his big snout up to the opening and gave a snort. She ran away into the dark room. It's called pitter-patter. The Minotaur arose, started down the walk toward the road, toward this day's inevitability.

. . .

Alive and dead. The Minotaur takes the hit—a belly full of grapeshot, or a musket ball. Falls dead to the Pennsylvania earth. Finds himself on a battlefield, yet another battlefield, feigning death. The gut shot make-believe. The bloodlust real enough. The black mud real. Too, the sky's hard blue and its burning eye. He contorts a little, this way or that, to suggest suffering and pain. But really he's positioning his horns to block the midday sun. The Minotaur wants to see. To watch, from his cockama-mie angle, the boots and legs of the other soldiers march over the ersatz battlefield. To let the black disks of his eyes scan the visible plain, crisply defined in the span between his horn tips, less so beyond. The Minotaur's wide snout is sometimes a problem. It blocks the view.

The Minotaur doesn't wear a soldier's kepi hat. It won't stay on. He keeps the cap tucked in the waist belt and wedged behind his canteen and side knife. The Minotaur drops his rifle. He's dropped it so often it surely wouldn't fire.

"Unngh."

The Minotaur grunts when he falls to the Pennsylvania mud. The gray wool frockcoat wicks the damp to his skin. The Minotaur welcomes the cool. He cocks his head one final time and begins the long wait for the battle's end. It's Friday. The Union always wins on Friday. Nobody is in a hurry. The Minotaur likes the dying season, its rituals, its leisure.

The Minotaur can see a pale blue swath of the April sky. It is cloud-less. All of it. From where he lies, the Minotaur sees more. Sees the rusted water tower's legs rising over the tree line, sees the moonlike tank. He's seen the looping lime green graffiti often enough to know what it says: *Boo–Dah!*

Dead or alive, the Minotaur finds himself neck deep in a new millennium. Dead or alive, the Minotaur struggles for the moment in some place called the Rust Belt, the metaphor cinched tight at the waist of a waning empire. The Minotaur knows none of this to speak of, but lives and dies the central Pennsylvania reality day in and day out. The Keystone State. Humans, he knows, like to name things. The Minotaur finds himself, a willing Confederate, above the Mason-Dixon line. The Minotaur understands divide, division. Rebellion. He finds himself on yet another battlefield.

Cannon fire. Three thunderous blasts from the Union battery. From behind the earthwork. The Minotaur feels the percussive wallops rise up through the black earth and stir in the crevices of his spine. Feels them before he hears them. No matter. The Minotaur always trusts the tactile over the aural. Though he couldn't say so, or why.

On the periphery of the battlefield, just at the edge of his vision, the Minotaur sees the chain-link fence surrounding the electrical station. As if power is so easily contained. Through the fence, sees the massive transformers and their impenetrable green, the crisscross skeletal towers that carry the charge into and out of the station, the heavy atrial lines that split the narrow valley, that run right up and over Scald Mountain.

The skirmish line ebbs. The skirmish line flows. It is Friday. The fortifications will hold. The Minotaur smells the gunpowder. Everybody smells the gunpowder. Though the Minotaur doesn't see it, blocked no doubt by his thick snout, he knows there are bleachers—a pair of them, old pipe-and-plank things, likely scavenged from a junior-high sports field—on the opposite edge of the battleground. It is April, and warm enough. The bleachers are full. A ragged canvas lean-to shelters the fifer, the drummer, and the pimply horn player whose sputtering ditty will signify the battle's closure. Nobody is in a hurry.

The Minotaur snorts through his bullish nostrils. Softly. He's been watching a bluebottle fly circle. The fly lands on the bridge of the Minotaur's nose. Paces the bony expanse. Circles again and comes to rest inside the Minotaur's nostril.

"Unngh."

The bluebottle fly thrives on decay. On death. The Minotaur thinks we all do. It's not the fly's fault. It has been deceived. Trickery is afoot. This death is, alas, a ruse. The Minotaur snorts the fly back into flight, watches it plot its next move. It's nobody's fault.

"Unngh."

The Minotaur is happy enough in his ersatz death. Make do. Make do. Comes back again and again, to die over and over. The Minotaur dies Friday, Saturday, and Sunday.

A crow swoops in from up the mountain, cocks the black wings back to slow its descent. The bird is on its way to pluck bits of potato chips and cheese puffs from beneath the bleachers. The Minotaur knows it for a fact. Facts are sometimes important. The bluebottle fly lights briefly on the Minotaur's tarnished belt plate, walks the rim of the embossed lettering, the *C* and the *S*, takes flight, then hovers over the Minotaur's wellish nostrils.

"Unngh."

"Hey?"

Somewhere in the preplanned distance, sabers rattle. Bayonets clink. A hearty surge of overly sincere grunts, yips, and growls. Watered-down bloodlust, and out of sight, but bloodlust nonetheless. Farther off, the steady traffic on Business 220 lulls the afternoon toward drowsiness.

"Hey?"

"Unngh."

It's a girl's voice, maybe. Nearby, surely. The Minotaur can tell that much. But he can't see the source without moving his head, and the Minotaur isn't quite ready to break the role of Confederate dead yet.

"Hey?"

Closer this time. She pokes him with something. The Minotaur can't see what it is without moving his head. So he does. Yes, a girl. The second of the day. The Minotaur ponders this welling theme.

"Hey," she says. "Hey."

The Minotaur is on the earth. Grounded. She looms over him, though her looming is tiny. It might be a girl. It might be. But there's a single horn and a glittery mane. What rough beast is this? What? Few things surprise the Minotaur. He is hopeful this time. But when he finds focus, when he sees from his upside-down perspective the unicorn on the girl's T-shirt, it is disappointment the Minotaur feels. He looks again. Scrutinizes. Longs. The girl herself, a little thing with translucent and chestnut-colored skin and a head of tight brown curls, a mashup of race and lineage, could easily be part unicorn. Easily.

The Minotaur's lament is brief.

"Hey," she says again, wagging a half-eaten corndog in his direction. "Want a bite?"

The Minotaur cannot smile. He's tried, but the result is usually terrifying. He does not want to frighten this girl, even though she has disappointed him. Nor does the Minotaur want a bite of her corndog.

"Mmmnn, no," he manages.

The girl smiles. A battle is ending somewhere out of sight. Rage abates. No matter. Other battles will follow. Always. The girl smiles. There is more than meets the eye here. The Minotaur thinks it but keeps his hopes at bay. The black mud. The blue sky.

"Hey?" she says again.

No, it's a bigger voice. More insistent.

"Hey! Braylynn! Get away from there!"

The father's brief command betrays much: *Get away from there*, not *Get away from that*. But certainly not *Get away from him*. Braylynn. The unicorn-cum-girl.

Braylynn sticks out her tongue, wiggles it at the Minotaur, then turns and runs toward her father. As she gallops across the field, the Minotaur watches the red and white lights in the soles of her shoes fire with each step. Magical. She'll take flight any minute. He has no doubt. Look, there she goes, up over the treetops. Glorious in flight. Peeling back the veil of the here and now. To reveal what? The Minotaur's wishful thinking. The Minotaur lets his fat tongue loll out just a bit, just over the tops of his tarter-caked teeth, just between the rubbery black lips.

"Mmmnn," he says.

Nobody is in a hurry. Especially the Minotaur. The spectators head back down the gravel drive to Old Scald Village. Some will stick around and hammer moon and star designs at the Tin Punch Cottage, or maybe dip rows of dangling candlewicks into a vat of beeswax. Most will just go home, their souvenirs more intangible.

The Minotaur lingers, there at the end of this day's death. The Minotaur dawdles. The Minotaur takes his own sweet time. He finds himself in a moment of stasis, of relative calm. But *moment* itself is a relative word. The Minotaur's time is endless, and as such potentially meaningless, empty at its ticking core.

This day marched into being like hundreds of other recent days. He's been here for a while. But niggling there in the murky sloughs of the Minotaur's awareness is the sense of impending change. That girl. That little corndog-wielding unicorn girl. A portent. Something is coming down the pike.

The Minotaur takes his own sweet time getting up but eventually rises to his knees, orients himself between the horn tips. The Minotaur gathers his rifle and empty haversack. The April sky over Scald Mountain is a deep azure blue. All of it. Tomorrow is Saturday. The Confederates win on Saturday. Always. The Minotaur takes his time, brushes the twigs and dust from his gray wool trousers, and joins the uniformed stragglers, the other risen dead.

• • •

March he does, back into life. And remembering the list of necessary things and his obligations back at the motel, the old bull picks up his pace. Time is a fickle beast; its ticky-tocky heart hammers on with utter disregard for any and all in its path. The Minotaur recalls his list and what he has to do this afternoon, now that the dying is done. Breaking from his normal post-dying routine, he skirts the mishmash of period-correct hoopla in Old Scald Village and hurries past the crowd of soldiers and spectators. Hurries along dirt streets full of living history. Through the parking lot that contains a herd of dirty yellow school buses, the kids, shepherded by harried teachers, fresh from the killing. Hurries through the covered bridge, hurries up the road, up Business 220, toward the Judy-Lou Motor Lodge. Home. It is Friday. It is dying season. Tomorrow brings a new death. Tomorrow the Minotaur will linger, will wallow in his role as casualty. Today other things occupy his mind.

He keeps his snout down, his black eyes cocked on the road. Looks only where his boots land. Tomorrow is a different day. Today the Minotaur can be of use. Today the Minotaur reins in his focus, keeps it tight all the way back to Room #3, his room, where he finds, arranged neatly on his crisply made bed, the spackling paste, the shelves and necessary hardware, a new light fixture, and everything else on the morning's list. There is a key ring with a peacock-feather fob, and a single key. Room #7. Too, the Guptas left a small foil-covered plate, a snack for the Minotaur, and a note explaining that they will be home in late afternoon, that they are off to the outlet mall to get some pillows and curtains for the room, nice things, that they are grateful, deeply grateful, for his help. The Guptas, Ramneek and Rambabu, are the proprietors of the Judy-Lou Motor Lodge. Their daughter takes classes at Allegheny Community College. Bavishya is rarely home. Bavishya answers only to Becky.

"Our Bavishya is coming home to live, Mr. M," Ramneek said earlier in the week.

"We must ready her room, Mr. M," Rambabu said.

"You will like her, Mr. M. And she will like you as well."

"Our Bavishya," they said. "Our Becky."

Becky's little out-of-wedlock daughter, Devmani, a dark-eyed sprite full of grinning mischief, peeked from behind her grandmother's swaddled legs as she spoke.

Mmmnn," the Minotaur said, following the Guptas into the vacant room beside the office.

Devmani stuck out her tongue.

That was earlier in the week.

Here stands the Minotaur in service. In the door of Room #7, he plans the afternoon. Gets to work. The Minotaur spackles and sands. The Minotaur changes the gasket in the dripping faucet. Replaces a switch plate. The Minotaur sets about assembling the shelves.

The Minotaur has never met Bavishya. Becky. What did they mean, Ramneek and Rambabu, when they said, "You will like her," when they said, "She will like you as well"? What does she do, this Becky, this young mother of Devmani? What does she study at the community college? Where does she hope that study will take her? These are the questions that swarm the Minotaur's mind as he works. And he should be paying more attention. He should not touch that bare wire while swapping out the light fixture. What did they mean, the Guptas? The Minotaur is not one to get his hopes up. Nor, however, has he ever been able to fully let go of hope. And it is hope's slippery little tail that the Minotaur is trying to grab hold of when his screwdriver touches the wire.

The jolt knocks him back to Becky's bed. The whole of the Judy-Lou Motor Lodge goes black.

"Unngh," the Minotaur says.

"Unngh," he says again, more embarrassed than in danger.

It takes a full hour to get all the fuses replaced and the Judy-Lou's *Vacancy* sign flashing again. By the time the Guptas return, their plastic shopping bags stuffed full, the Minotaur is pretending to be asleep in Room #3. He peeks through the parted curtains to watch Rambabu carry his sleeping granddaughter from the car.

CHAPTER THREE

SATURDAY. THE DEAD, THEY RISE, always, to join the march toward Old Scald Village. The village welcomes all the conscripts home with equal fanfare. Zero. Everybody—the bloodied and the bloodless, the valiant and the cowardly, the victorious, the defeated, too—meanders down the hundred yards of gravel road, past the wooden ticket booth that's used only in high season, toward the parking lot. Old Scald Village promises living history. Promises to "bring the past to the present." The Minotaur slogs along almost hopefully. He likes best the moments of silence, when nobody talks, when the gravel crunching beneath the shuffling brogans and ankle boots is all the song they need.

"Pretty good one today, huh, M?" Biddle says.

The Minotaur would be hard pressed to tell the difference between any of the battles. Any of the days.

"Unngh," the Minotaur says.

Biddle is the cooper. When he's not cannon fodder, Biddle makes barrels two doors down from the Tin Punch Cottage. Biddle is pink and sweaty. Too fat for the gray wool uniform he wears. But he wears it with gusto. Biddle offers the Minotaur a drink from a wooden canteen. The Minotaur shakes his big head no.

They're halfway to the Welcome Center. A gaggle of battlefield nurses walks ahead, their satchels full of wound-dressing supplies, laughing loudly about something. Behind them, the drummer keeps an uneven rhythm with the trumpeter's human beat-box routine.

Biddle looks nervously up and down the line of returning soldiers. He fishes in the leather cartridge box on his belt, takes out a cell phone, and taps at the screen. High above, the turnpike traverses Scald Mountain. Few heed the *Falling Rock* signs.

"Look at this one," Biddle says, handing the phone to the Minotaur.

The Minotaur holds the phone up to one eye, then the other, turns it this way and that, but in the midday sun, and with his ocular challenges, it's hard to tell exactly what he's looking at. Biddle snaps and unsnaps the cartridge box. Snaps and unsnaps. Sweat trickles down both temples.

The Minotaur can make out the breasts—incredibly large breasts—but not much else.

"That one's so sweet she probably poops Milk Duds," Biddle says, sucking air between his teeth.

"Unngh," the Minotaur says. What else can he say?

Old Scald Village promises to preserve the past. Promises battles and craft exhibitions, Christmas festivals and murder-mystery evenings and more. And more. The Minotaur likes Biddle, flawed as he is. The Minotaur sees in Biddle kinship. The Minotaur respects the fat man's willingness to be fully himself. Transgressions and all. Out of kindness, he looks again, trying to see what Biddle wants him to see on the cell-phone screen. The breasts, yes. In motion. A fleshy rump. The Minotaur squints, cocks his head. A crow gets caught in the angle delineated by his horn tips. The Minotaur tries to focus. Is focusing. Then he feels the pinch on his backside.

"Tssss!"

It's Smitty.

First the pinch, then the accompanying hiss, meant to be a sizzle. Meant to be the sound of burning flesh. His flesh. A brand on the Minotaur's human haunch. A hot stink fills the air.

"Tssss!"

The pinch and hiss. The burn. The stench.

All of the moments that unfold in a life—any life, human, animal, mongrel—almost never arrive ready made with predetermined outcomes. Each moment that wriggles and shrugs down the birth canal of time does so under the burden of every single other moment that's come be-fore it. And at the instant of unfolding, of awakening, of awareness, that moment—every one—is at the immediate and perfect whim of mindless happenstance. There are always other choices, other possible outcomes. Better or worse is always in the eye of the beholder.

"Tssss!"

Smitty, the blacksmith, his callused fingers a make-do branding iron, pinches the Minotaur. As if the Minotaur's past means nothing. As if.

The Minotaur throws back his bullish head. Bellows. The roar fierce, the rage so primal it blackens the sun. Shrivels the moon. Lightning sears the sky. The river boils its fishes. Rank and file—the soldiers, the nurses—faint dead away, not wanting to bear witness. The horned beast roars, and the brass buttons of his jacket give way, pop and hiss in the air as they fly. The Minotaur, ravening, thrashes his heavy head. The horns whip the sky into froth. Smitty, beneath the smudges of black ash, weeps. Wets himself. Begs for mercy. None comes. The Minotaur looms over all. Smitty flees. Runs, as if he could actually escape his self-made fate. The Minotaur stomps his booted foot on the graveled earth, and all the pines drop their needles and, sapless, wither where they stand. Smitty runs and runs, weaving among the picnic tables, through the river's mucky bed, runs up the steep bank, through the black trunks of the dead pines, runs looking backward, runs hoping for escape, runs right into the barbed-wire fence surrounding Old Scald Village, the blacksmith's tender neck flesh succumbing without protest, a hot wing of blood fluttering to the ground, steaming for the briefest of moments.

No.

"Tssss!"

The pinch and hiss. It could happen just so. It doesn't.

When Smitty, the blacksmith, pinches the preoccupied Minotaur and hisses in his ear, the bullish soldier startles and drops the cell phone to the gravel.

"Don't look like standard issue to me," Smitty says, then spits on the road by the phone.

Smitty is hardcore. Smitty is a stitch counter, in constant pursuit of a past perfected. Smitty is a living historian, and committed to the role. Devoted, even. Every detail of his uniform, his Blacksmith's Shoppe and the tools there, his behavior—everything about Smitty is perfectly re-created. Accurate. There are a handful of hardcores at Old Scald Village, looking down their period-correct noses at the mere pretenders. The Minotaur finds it all both intimidating and mildly amusing.

"Tssss!"

Smitty takes ingots of raw pig iron and transforms them. Smitty makes hinges and horseshoes. Plowshares and bullet molds. Smitty makes trouble for anyone who isn't period correct. Smitty makes trouble for the Minotaur. But the Minotaur knows this man, this kind of man. Knows what his forge is capable of. The Minotaur has withstood such petty brandings countless times over the long span of his life. Knows he will surely endure more.

"Unngh," the Minotaur says.

The Minotaur lets the moment pass, releases the potential for rage. Release serves him well. The Minotaur takes his time.

Biddle scrambles for the cell phone, blows the dust off the screen. The nurses and other soldiers go about their business. When the trio of young musicians walks by rapping some vaguely obscene lyric, Smitty follows and thumps the fife player on the ear.

"Unngh," the Minotaur says.

"Here," Biddle says, handing the Minotaur the phone once again. "These are my babies."

The Minotaur has been here before. The Minotaur has been here a long time.

The Minotaur positions the phone just so. This time, he can clearly see Biddle sitting on a couch, a big goofy grin, three bug-eyed pug dogs clutched in his arms.

Old Scald Village promises much. The price of admission is sometimes high.

CHAPTER FOUR

THE MINOTAUR HEARS THE ANVIL RING three times. Smitty, in the Black-smith's Shoppe at the far end of the lopsided figure eight that defines Old Scald Village, is driving out the devil. The Minotaur stands at the Welcome Center door and listens for all three hammer strikes. With each, the redwing blackbirds lift off from the cattails circling the manmade pond; they flit, then settle. Flit, then settle. Flit. Settle. The Minotaur waits for the metallic hum to die away.

Biddle is headed toward the Cooper's Shack. He's trying to get one of the nurses to look at something on his phone. The girl ignores him, flicks at a cricket climbing up between the faux bloodstains on her apron. He tries again.

"Aren't you married or something, Biddle?" she asks.

"Something," Biddle mumbles.

He gives up and skulks over to the Minotaur. "You know she lives on the island of Lesbos, don't you," Biddle says to the Minotaur. It's not really a question. "Her and that basket maker."

"Mmmnn," the Minotaur says.

"The dark-haired girl, the one with the nose ring and all the Band-Aids on her fingers."

"Mmmnn," the Minotaur says. It's a quiet day. He hears a semi Jake-braking on the steep turnpike descent. "Mmmnn."

"They caught 'em one time in the church, up in the choir loft. She had her—"

"Mmmnn, no," the Minotaur says. No. He's not interested. Besides, he has vague memories of being there, on the island of Lesbos.

"Suit yourself," Biddle says. "See you tomorrow."

Three times the ball-peen hammer strikes the anvil's face. Legend has it that Satan himself was duped by a clever blacksmith. That the smithy hammered the devil into a pair of shoes so tight and painful. Legend says so, or maybe it is rumor. What the Minotaur knows for sure is that when the anvil rings three times it means that the Old Scald Village blacksmith is deep in the heart of his shop, cranking the bellows, stoking the forge, its fiery eye pulsing. Smitty will be there for a while. The Minotaur can go about his own business unmolested.

The Minotaur watches some of the other soldiers who aren't working in the village shops that afternoon load gear into their cars at the far edge of the parking lot. It is Saturday, early in the dying season. The Minotaur doesn't like to carry his rifle or side knife on the walk home. It's hard enough to lug the horns through his days. The manager of the Gift Shoppe lets him tuck the weapons behind the mops and brooms in the closet near the cash register.

"Hey, M," she says when he triggers the electronic bell. "How'd it go out there today?"

She always asks the same questions. She might be middle aged, whatever that means in human terms. She looks up from beneath the deep brim of a crisp white bonnet, and the big round rims of her glasses magnify the green eyes, and the kindness therein.

"Did you die good?"

"Mmmnn," the Minotaur says.

Her name is Widow Fisk. That's what they all call her, anyway. That's what the Minotaur knows her as. Middle aged, maybe. Content in the body she carries. The Old Scald Village Gift Shoppe is her domain. The Minotaur admires her commitment to the role. Always has. She rules, with beneficence, the cadres of elementary-school kids who, left to their own, would crumple all the Declaration of Independence scrolls, pocket without paying for all the authentic Civil War bullets, dump the wicker basket of handmade doilies, likely even try to eat the cakes of artisan soaps, made three doors away. The peppermint, the honey, the vanilla especially.

"Ain't nobody going to pay that much for a bar of soap," Widow Fisk sometimes says to the Minotaur. "I don't care how many pretty leaves and colors inside it."

She was here in the shop way back when the Minotaur came in looking for work. She didn't flinch at his horns, his snout. Registered, even, something akin to kindness when she looked at him that first time. Widow Fisk made a joke about her bloomers; they were white and silky and draped across the drying rack in the cramped office. She winked at the Minotaur and pointed to a narrow staircase. Told him to see Mitch in Personnel. Told him to visit again on his way out, all those years ago.

This Saturday, after the day's dying is finished, Widow Fisk closes her eyes and sniffs at one of the soaps. She offers it to the Minotaur, holds the fragrant bar close to his snout. Widow Fisk is his touchstone, of sorts. His go-to for gossip and guidance. The Minotaur trusts her.

Occasionally, the Minotaur sees a fully human face and knows something. He makes judgments accordingly. In Widow Fisk's soft open eyes, the fine web of wrinkled flesh around them, in the fullness of her bottom lip and the two crooked teeth betrayed by every smile (all of them), the Minotaur sees the whole spectrum of life experience. Sees both want and resignation. This Widow Fisk has known misery and pain. But this Widow Fisk is not afraid of joy.

She smiles, and the tiny fleck of tomato peel stuck to her bottom tooth glows like a beautiful ruby.

"Mmmnn," the Minotaur says.

In the far corner of the Gift Shoppe, two boys tussle over a coonskin cap and a wooden pistol.

"It's mine!"

"Boys," Widow Fisk says, and that's all it takes.

Widow Fisk. She is the one human in Old Scald Village the Minotaur can imagine himself talking to. Even more than sweet fat Biddle. The Minotaur could tell her things. She is the only person there who he's told anything about his journey, about his coming to the village. How he left behind kitchens and concessions, a different life, below the Mason-Dixon line. How he found himself in uniform and followed the battles north. Dying and dying again. He didn't tell her everything. He didn't have to.

Widow Fisk. The Minotaur can imagine telling her other things. Telling her what he knows. A clear plastic jar sits by the cash register. It's half full of souvenir key chains, all of them cast-resin anvils. The Minotaur knows a thing or two about anvils. He could tell Widow Fisk these things. The Minotaur could mark the weight. Nearly four hundred pounds of steel. The Minotaur could name the parts, one by one. The bick. The table. The face. The shoulder. The throat. The hardy hole. The pritchel hole. The hanging end.

The Minotaur will not tell Widow Fisk everything. He will not tell her that sometimes he imagines her into his darkness. That gingham dress pulled up high. Dreams the Minotaur, Widow Fisk at her most animal.

"Mmmnn, I did," he says. "Die good."

The Minotaur would get very quiet and almost whisper the anvil's last part, the horn, and Widow Fisk would understand why. She is the only person the Minotaur makes the effort with.

"Stay away from the Tavern," she says.

"Mmmnn?"

"That old hussy behind the counter is on a rant," Widow Fisk says. "She cornered me this morning, talked for ten solid minutes about her diarrhea."

The Minotaur grunts something like a chuckle.

"Grab a piece of horehound on the way out, hon," Widow Fisk says.

She's already plucked a couple pieces of the hard candy from the little tin bucket on the counter and is reaching them toward the Minotaur. When he takes them (and he always does), her fingertips graze his palm (they always do). The Minotaur occasionally sees the fully human in a face. Sometimes, though, he can detect the animal. Widow Fisk winks when she gives him the candy. Maybe. With her enormous glasses and his own struggles with seeing clearly, the Minotaur can't be certain.

"Mmmnn," the Minotaur says, and is poking one of the bittersweet lozenges deep into his mouth when he opens the Gift Shoppe door.

"Hey!"

The Minotaur looks up.

"Hey!"

Up and into the eyes of the little unicorn girl, her beautiful hazel eyes. The same girl from the battlefield, from yesterday. She's in the pillory. Her family has come back to see the dying two days in a row. It's not uncommon. She's in the pillory, the stocks, perched tiptoe on a stepstool. The girl cranes the scrawny neck and wiggles the birdlike arms jutting through the pillory's three rough holes. A boy, probably a brother, chops at her feet with a rubber-bladed tomahawk from the Gift Shoppe. The lights in her magic shoes blink madly with each whack.

"Hey!"

She's speaking to the Minotaur. A woman, probably her mother, sits—exhausted or bored—on a wooden bench between the *Chickens* and *Roosters* bathroom doors. The woman barely looks up from the cell-phone screen she's tapping at. The unicorn girl's father, struggling to focus his own cell phone on the squirming kids, looks fully at the Minotaur. His paternal hackles rise instantly.

"Hey!" he says.

The pillory. Medieval. Simple. Little more than planks and chains and humiliation. There are three, maybe four pillories in Old Scald Village, and always lines at every one. Always someone shrieking, "My turn!" or "You next!" And the ceaseless photographs. The Minotaur is perplexed by humans' obsession with, love of, punishment. The Minotaur knows, too, that nothing in Old Scald Village could hold that tiny beast against her will. Not really.

"Hey!" she says.

And the whole gathered throng looks at the Minotaur.

The Minotaur is stunned by her presence, by her reappearance. Not exactly spooked, but so surprised that he gasps. He gasps and sucks the horehound lozenge deep into his throat. There it plugs his windpipe tight, seals it, guards against any breath, out or in.

A choking Minotaur is a sight to behold. Or maybe not. The Minotaur isn't quite sure what to make of the airless moment. Thinking back over the millennia, he's surely been in this situation before. But for the life of him the Minotaur can't recall. He scuttles backward into the Gift Shoppe, mostly to get away from the scrutinizing eyes. In his haste, trying to dislodge the candy, the Minotaur dips his head low, and his horn tip plows through a bin of sock puppets. George Washington. Betsy Ross. Ulysses S. Grant. When the Minotaur rears his head Abe Lincoln dangles, impaled on the horn.

Much about the Minotaur's life is ridiculous. He accepted that fact a long time ago. He tries not to dwell on it, but sometimes . . .

Widow Fisk, on the other hand, is a pragmatic no-nonsense creature. She doesn't judge. She acts.

Widow Fisk rounds the counter, steps up behind the breathless Minotaur, encircles him in her capable gingham-clad arms, snugs him tight against her ample and aproned bosom, and yanks her balled fists into his gut. One time. The Minotaur's cavernous diaphragm is no match for Widow Fisk. Neither is the horehound lozenge. The hard candy fires from deep in the Minotaur's throat. It flies across the room. It pings and plinks in a "Union States of the Civil War" shot glass display, coming to rest in Ohio.

"Mmmnn, thanks," the Minotaur's says. His eyes water. Faces may be pressed to the glass door, looking in, but he can't tell.

"Sit yourself down, hon," Widow Fisk says, leading the Minotaur into the tiny office behind the register. "Catch your breath."

The windowless room is warm and smells of running computers, smells of lanolin from the open tin of Bag Balm by the keyboard, smells of cinnamon mouthwash, smells like her. Like full-grown fully human woman. The office is cramped. The Minotaur moves his head slightly and almost knocks a framed poster from the wall. The poster reads, *One Monkey Don't Stop No Show.*

The computer screen flickers on the desk. Widow Fisk is working on the flier for The Encampment, Old Scald Village's biggest reenactment event of the year, two weeks away.

Widow Fisk goes out to make a sale. The Minotaur thinks about what just happened, about the unicorn girl. Can't help thinking her reappearance is somehow linked with the electric shock from yesterday, the sudden blackening of the Judy-Lou, the stopping of all the clocks. Change is coming. Change. Change threatens to overtake the plodding old bull. The Minotaur knows it. For better or worse is in the eye of the beholder.

Without really planning to the Minotaur snaps the lid on the Bag Balm and slips the tin into his jacket pocket.

"Catch your breath," Widow Fisk said.

Sometimes it really is just that simple.

CHAPTER FIVE

THEY SAY THAT, IN THE OLD DAYS, bridges were covered, were built to resemble barns, so that farm animals would feel more at home and not stampede as they were driven across streams and rivers. They say that bridges were covered to keep snow off, to keep the oiled planks of the roadbed from becoming dangerously slippery in the rain, to cover up unsightly trusses, to provide shelter to travelers caught in storms. Shelter. They say—some of them, the hopeful—that bridges were covered to secret away one's love. To kiss there unseen. Shelter. They say.

The Minotaur comes and goes. He has for centuries. And there have been many bridges.

The Minotaur pauses, as he walks, midway through the covered bridge that serves, in more ways than one, as the entrance to Old Scald Village. He rests his heavy snout against one of the wooden trusses. The Minotaur likes this portal, both ingress and egress, a breach in the terribly human construct of time.

"Mmmnn," he says. The Minotaur likes this bridge.

Music—or something like music, anyway—drifts into earshot from somewhere in the village. The Minotaur considers going back to see, to listen. Ponders it. But his history with music, that very human endeavor, is itself ponderous. He is drawn in. He is kept away. After the day he's had, the portentous little unicorn girl, the lozenge in his throat, the Minotaur cannot fathom navigating his big horned head back through the village and the people. No matter how much he'd like to track the song to its source, to be in the presence of sound shaped by human intent.

"Mmmnn," he says.

He likes this bridge. He liked it the first time he ventured through. Though the timing has to be right. He tries to wait until Biddle and the rest have left, or are occupied somewhere deep in the village. The Minotaur doesn't want either the generosity of an offered ride or whatever comes with a passing stare.

The single-lane bridge spans the weed-choked banks of Mill Run (when the upstream paper mill is in high production, Widow Fisk calls it Stink Creek). No lights are inside the bridge, and though there are gaps at the roof gable, there is, at nearly a hundred and twenty feet, a very real into-and-out-of-the-shadows experience for all who pass through.

"Mmmnn," the Minotaur says, and with his horn resting against the plank wall feels the ghosts of the old traffic, hoofed and otherwise, in the wood grain.

To get anything from Old Scald Village, you have to cross this bridge, to move through, to let go of something behind and be willing to accept what's ahead, no matter your direction of travel.

Timing. It's often all about timing. The day has been strange. Portentous. There in the bridge, shadowed, sheltered, the Minotaur feels time careen. Past, present, and future roil. He can feel it in the planks at his feet. They vibrate. They rumble. No. It's a vehicle, a pickup truck, leaving the village, its coming felt through the wing walls of the abutment. The Minotaur hurries over the boards, out of the bridge's squarely gaped mouth. He turns, pretending to see something interesting, maybe even important, flopping around down in the murky water of Mill Run.

As the truck passes, the Minotaur hears it slow, feels the soft impact on his back, feels a sudden damp, then sees the empty McDonald's soda cup bounce at his feet, down the creek bank. The Minotaur is torn. He wants to watch the cup float downstream and out of sight. He doesn't. He looks back at the truck that is now spinning its wheels in the gravel and barreling toward Business 220 a few yards away. It's an unfamiliar truck. No. He's seen it before. It is April, late afternoon. Dangling from the truck's trailer hitch, a pair of bulbous chrome testicles. Bull's balls. Huge. Truck nuts. They swing madly, glint madly, in the afternoon sun.

"Catch your breath," Widow Fisk said.

"Unngh."

. . .

Business 220. The Minotaur knows this stretch of road well. Business 220 lies keen along the base of Scald Mountain, running north and south all the way to Homer's Gap, its two lanes a precursor to the turnpike high above. The truck peels out of the gravel drive and fishtails to the left. The white stench of burning rubber hangs in the windless moment and dissipates slowly. A mile, maybe less, up the road, the Moonglo Roller Rink struggles to stay in business; Battery Boyz: Batteries for Everyday Life fares only a little better. Beyond that shopping center, a turnpike junction and the commercial enterprises that fester around it. The Minotaur never ventures left. The Judy-Lou and the Guptas (all of them, maybe) lie to the right.

The Minotaur pauses at the turnoff to Old Scald Village and looks directly across Business 220. Looks at the fifteen-foot-tall plaster Union soldier standing with a *Welcome* sign dangling from his musket. The plaster soldier is a weatherworn but commanding presence. The blue paint on his jacket and trousers, faded and chipped. The bayonet snapped off long ago. Behind the statue, a steep bank dense with rhododendrons. The white flowers splay obscenely. It is spring. Rut is in the air. The Minotaur looks up and down the road. There is no traffic. The soldier stands tall, cocky, his cap askance, and mute; his unyielding silence is too much for the Minotaur.

The Minotaur slips a finger between the buttons of his army coat and scratches at his scar, his transition. That thin ridge where bull flesh gives way to man flesh. Every day the Minotaur touches this harsh divide, certain that it moves. Some days—some years, decades, centuries, even— he is sure beyond doubt that the line is falling down and down his lean belly. That he is becoming more fully bull. That eventually thick gray hide will cover his legs. And his hands, his feet, will be cloven hooves. Other centuries he knows that the scar is creeping up his ribcage. That he'll wake some morning, in some distant future, almost man. Fully human. Both scenarios are terrifying.

The Minotaur reaches into his pocket, tapping the tin of Bag Balm. The Minotaur is not a thief. The Minotaur stole the salve. Both facts are true. Every balm has its antithesis. Though he hasn't driven in a long while, the Minotaur knows this stretch of road well. He knows the soldier well. Knows the silence.

"Unngh," the Minotaur says, expecting nothing in return.

So when the plaster soldier retches a response—"Arrrwk"—the Minotaur is more than surprised.

"Unngh," he says again, shaking his big bull head.

"Arrrwk," the soldier replies.

The Minotaur's ears are dwarfed by his horns. Hearing clearly is sometimes difficult. He lifts the pitiful gray flaps of skin and wiggles a fat fingertip into each ear canal. With very human palms, he rubs hard at his wide-set eyes. The Minotaur has known monsters of all sorts. Has known that sages and soothsayers crop up where you least expect. The Minotaur is ready to accept the voice of this monstrously patient creature he's passed daily for year after mute year. It means nothing more than rethinking. Change is at hand. The evidence is everywhere.

The Minotaur looks up at the newfound oracle, ready to follow.

"Mmmnn," he says almost eagerly.

"Cawww."

When the crow pokes its insidious black head overtop the plaster soldier's cap and caws again, disappointment is swift. The moment is rendered. No augur, this. More harpy than haruspex, the crow caws again. Laughing. Surely laughing.

The Minotaur throws a piece of horehound candy at the crow, misses by a wide berth. It was a halfhearted gesture anyway. The crow flies off. A car speeds by on Business 220, a percussive bass thump momentarily filling the air. The plaster soldier bites his tongue. And the Minotaur is left alone with his shame, that most human emotion.

• • •

A life as long as the Minotaur's—that half-man half-bull, and fully scapegoat—a life that long doubles back on itself from time to time. Caves in. The miniscule tectonics of being alive, among the wholly human, always unsettling. The world shifts continuously beneath his feet. The Minotaur came from misspent want, from the planked birth canal, came from blood-drenched stone walls, from yellow thread. Belayed by desire, the beast pulled himself along. Pulled himself through centuries, through zeitgeists and kitchens, through paradigms and junkyards. Pulls still. Home.

• • •

The Minotaur walks home. Home. Walks without rifle or side knife. Walks in his Confederate gray wool uniform. Walks with both horns. Both horns, always. Home. For the moment, for the past few years, with the Guptas at the Judy-Lou Motor Lodge, a mere quarter-mile from Old Scald Village, down Business 220 where the road pulls away from the mountain just enough for Chili Willie's Soft Serve to stake its paved claim.

It is April, and the ice-cream stand across the road from the motel opens in May. The windows lack shutters or blinds; the interior of Chili Willie's is stark, sterile. The parking lot is empty. Almost. In the corner nearest the road another kind of army stands guard around a painted cargo trailer and its canvas portico. The regiment in a loose semicircle, all products of, results of, *Pygmalia-Blades: Danny Tanneyhill, CEO (Top Dog, Kingpin, Head Honcho, Guru, Overlord, and Emcee)*. It's emblazoned on the trailer. Danny Tanneyhill is a chainsaw carver. An artist. That's emblazoned on the trailer, too. Danny Tanneyhill is nowhere in sight, but signs of fresh cuts abound.

Danny Tanneyhill sets up shop in Chili Willie's parking lot every spring and fills the air with the smells of sawn wood, of gasoline and two-cycle engine exhaust. The Guptas are by and large indifferent. To-day Danny Tanneyhill is nowhere in sight, and the Minotaur looks for footprints in the sawdust that blankets the macadam. He's never actually met the overlord of Pygmalia-Blades, never had an up-close interaction, but Danny Tanneyhill, the way he sits in that folding chair in his trailer, surrounded by paints, saws and blades, cans of oil, gasoline jugs, and God knows what else, the way he just sits between cuts and thinks, ponders, studies—it puts the Minotaur on edge. Danny Tanneyhill seems always to be eyeing him. Scrutinizing. Judging. Sizing up the Minotaur, it seems.

The Minotaur straddles Business 220's fading edge line—one booted foot on the pavement, the other on the grassy shoulder—and plots his next move. The day has taken its toll. The old bull can feel change well-ing up from the muddled core of his consciousness. There is a path just beyond the Chili Willie's lot, a path nearly hidden by a thick bank of honeysuckle. The Minotaur knows the path well enough. It leads to a secret place. Secret enough. But not today.

The Minotaur looks around. He sees no Gupta. Danny Tanneyhill is nowhere in sight, but his herd, his flock, his congregation, is ever pres-ent. The grizzly bear, its wicked claws and odd near-smile, standing a full eight feet tall, closest to the road. A couple of black bears, consider-ably smaller but no less threatening in their dark crouches. The avocado green Hulk's gargantuan shoulders push against the canvas roof and its guy lines. There is more. So much more. And the chainsaw is present in all of them. A fish-and-eagle thing that the Minotaur can't quite figure out. A totem, maybe. A woman towering over a line of angels and busts of Beethoven, SpongeBob SquarePants, and somebody in a cowboy hat; she's scantily clad, wooden hands on wooden hips, and puckering as if to kiss. The Minotaur is never one to question issues of scale. There is more still, and the ragtag menagerie makes him just as anxious, if not more so, than Danny Tanneyhill himself. But the stacks of logs waiting to be cut, the stumps, and the most pitiable, the rejects, the mistakes—headless, limbless trunks—these are the most troubling.

The Minotaur steps lightly but hastily those last few feet and into the custodial, albeit stubby, arms of the Judy-Lou Motor Lodge, right across the road from Pygmalia-Blades.

Home. The Judy-Lou Motor Lodge. The marquee promises much: *Clean & Quiet Rooms; Family Owned and Operated Since 19--* (other numbers long gone); *Weekly Rates; Free HBO; Free Wi-Fi; Free Coffee & Mountain Views.* A baker's dozen of tiny American flags rising in as many odd angles from the plantless concrete planter by the office window offers a drooping testament to all that free-ness.

The crux, the heart, of the Judy-Lou Motor Lodge is the central office and the unseeable apartment behind it. A rakish awning, cocked skyward, juts out to the road's edge. The office sits at the vertex of ten rooms, five on each side, angling ever so slightly north and south. Or south and north. So much depends on one's perspective. Even the Minotaur knows this.

He sees Ramneek Gupta, wife of Rambabu Gupta. Watches as she goes from room to room.

"Good afternoon, Mister M," she says.

She stands in the office doorway. Stands in her saffron sari. Ramneek Gupta looks at the Minotaur and smiles, that blood-red bindi and those black eyes open all the way from antiquity to the present moment.

The Minotaur feels welcomed in her gaze. "Mmmnn," he replies.

Too, he'd find it impossible to pick between the rich and complicated scents of masala wafting out from behind her and the manic soundtrack from the Cartoon Network that plays all the livelong day on an out-of-sight television. Each gives comfort.

"The clocks, Mister M," she says. "They all stopped. The electricity serves a mysterious god."

"Mmmnn," the Minotaur says, and his fingertips tingle from yesterday's shock.

"Did your day pass pleasantly at the Old Scald Village?" Ramneek asks. "Did you die well?"

"I did," the Minotaur says.

He likes the Guptas. He likes the little cluster of bells that tinkle every time the front door of the Judy-Lou Motor Lodge opens or closes. He likes the dusty and diminutive Ganesh statuette tucked into the small grotto over the *Things To Do In The Area* brochure stand. Likes, too, the Pack 'N Play wedged into the tight cranny between the check-in desk and the wall, right beneath the fax machine, as well as the crib's occasional occupant.

Rambabu leans out from Room #7. "Come see, Mister M," he says.

And the Guptas show, with abundant tenderness, how they've readied the room for Becky's return. The boxy space transformed by color, by fabric, by love and hope. Incense curls a smoky finger beneath the Minotaur's snout. He almost sneezes.

"Thank you so much for your help today, Mister M," Rambabu says.

"Only a few more days," Ramneek says. "Our Bavishya comes home to us in only a few more days."

The Minotaur, not knowing what to say, nods his bulky head. Bavishya studies at the community college. Becky. She studies health and human services. Or maybe public safety. No, something called new media. No. The Minotaur cannot remember, though the Guptas have kept him abreast of their daughter's moves.

"We will make an exquisite dinner," Ramneek says. "And you will be our guest of honor."

"Mmmnn," the Minotaur says. "Okay."

Rambabu wants the Minotaur's help with another project. He shows him how the downspout has come loose from the awning's gutter. The Minotaur sees the rusty coat hanger from which it hung, and where it finally broke. Rambabu tells the Minotaur that his gout is acting up. He can't climb. The Minotaur likes listening to Rambabu Gupta speak. It's as if the words that come from his mouth are tiny sculptures, carefully whittled and polished smooth before their release.

The Minotaur also likes being helpful. And the Guptas are generous in their gratitude. It's one of the reasons he's stayed at the Judy-Lou for so long. Barter this, barter that.

He gets a ladder and tools from a shed in the back of the property, spends the afternoon crafting a bracket, then fixing the downspout back into place. The Minotaur takes his time, up on the sloping roof. His horns provide good balance. The mountain air is nice. But all the while, he keeps his eyes peeled for the return of Danny Tanneyhill.

When the gutter is repaired and the ladder put away, the Minotaur steps into, tinkles into, the office. He loves that the smells fill his cavernous nostrils. He touches, because he can't not, the Ganesh. Sometimes he touches the single tusk. Sometimes right where the head and body meet. The Minotaur has encountered this beast, in one form or another, many times over the centuries. Yet every time he is moved by those beneficent black eyes, the inquisitive trunk. All those hands. Measure for measure, they are more alike than different. It may be affinity the Minotaur feels. Or envy. Whatever the impetus the Minotaur can't help reaching out.

"Finished," the Minotaur says.

Ramneek comes to the counter. "I have something for you, Mister M," she says, offering up a small plate covered in foil.

"Unngh, thanks," the Minotaur says. She offers frequently; he always accepts, and rarely knows what it is he's eating.

"It will be quite a hot one tomorrow, Mister M," Rambabu says. "You must take liquids, before the dying."

There in the Judy-Lou lobby, the Minotaur feels cared for. He also feels something at his feet. The Minotaur doesn't have to look down to know that Devmani has snuck from behind the counter and now sits astraddle his boot, clinging to his calf. She did this the first time he ever came into the Judy-Lou, when his car broke down in the parking lot all those seasons ago. She was just crawling then. Though toddling now, the girl is no less excited. He knows, too, that she's grinning. That she expects the Minotaur to pretend not to notice her presence. He knows that she'll giggle all the way as he drags his foot, and her, from the counter to the door.

Barter this, barter that.

"Mmmnn," the Minotaur says, working hard to make it sound like surprise. Devmani giggles.

Back in his room, #3, which shares a thin wall with the Guptas' apartment, the Minotaur eats. The food is yellow. The food is delicious. Hunger comes and goes for the Minotaur. Sometimes he is indifferent. This time he licks the plate. It's been an odd day. Something nags. Something gnaws.

What is there to say about Room #3? It houses the Minotaur well enough. The double bed takes up most of the space. If he lies in the center of the two thin pillows, both horns fit. Against the other wall, a low dresser with three drawers. The Minotaur uses only two of them. A fat old television set commands the far end of the dresser. Inside it the free HBO bubbles away unused. In the corner between the dresser and wall, an exposed shelf and hanger bar made of chromed tubing provide closet space. There are periods of time in the Minotaur's life when he needs little, wants less. This is one of those times. A clock and a telephone are on the nightstand, and a lamp with a base made to look like a mountain lion fighting a buck. The lamp works. The Minotaur doesn't know about the phone.

The Minotaur has turned the single wooden armchair with cracked vinyl cushions so that he can look out the window at Business 220, at the night or the day. Two cars were in the Judy-Lou parking lot when the Minotaur left for the battlefield early this morning. Now only one, at the far end. Probably Room #10, where the view of Scald Mountain is best. It is not yet high season for the kind of guest who chooses, or ends up at, the Judy-Lou Motor Lodge. Most, these days, prefer proximity to the turnpike and all that is promised by the more beaten path. The Guptas don't seem to mind. Nor does the Minotaur. Beneath his sole window the rattling fan of the air conditioner can sound almost oceanlike if he pretends hard enough. He does.

Nobody is watching. The Minotaur licks the plate, then takes it into the cramped bathroom to rinse in the sink. The bathroom door is narrow, and the tiled walls are close on all sides. With practice the Minotaur knows just how much to turn his massive head, to dip his horns. Two vertical florescent bulbs flank a mirror over the sink. A few days after arriving the Minotaur fixed the constant drip from the hot-water tap. Then he checked the plumbing in all the other rooms. As for the lights, it takes several minutes for the old gasses in the tubes to warm up, to sputter to life, and when they are finally lit fully what is cast can barely pass for light. The silver backing is peeling away from the mirror's edges, leaving a lacy pattern of black webs that refuses reflection. The Minotaur doesn't need to see himself.

The Minotaur looks in the mirror anyway. The florescent bulbs pulse faintly, washing his incomplete reflection in surges of pinkish light. He's there. He's not. He's there. The Minotaur unbuttons his coat at the top, reaches in to touch his scar. He's there. He's not.

"Unngh."

The Minotaur fishes the square tin of Bag Balm from the jacket pocket, hangs the coat neatly on the bar just outside the bathroom door. He stills the coat in its sway, then returns to the mirror and uncaps the salve. The Minotaur likes best that brief moment just after he peels back the green lid with its wreath of red clovers and—he can't not see—the cow, when the scent of lanolin fills his nostrils. His bullish nostrils. He uses the middle two fingers, circling the tips just once on the oily yellow surface. The Minotaur takes his time in attending to the scar. The rift. The balm does as promised.

Through the thin wall the Minotaur hears the Guptas talking. Listens as they stack their syllables higher and higher until toppling is inevitable. The Minotaur puts his hand to the cool tile, thinking to offer some kind of support. He cocks his head, lowering the snout. Finds a spot in the mirror that almost reflects. Looks at his bifurcation. Looks and looks. Out of the blue, out of the pink-hued flickering, he thinks of Widow Fisk. Her kind eyes magnified by the glasses and hidden by her bonnet. He thinks of Widow Fisk in her bonnet and in her apron. The Minotaur thinks of her out of her bonnet, her apron. Those bloomers billow in his mind. The Minotaur is about to keep thinking, about to imagine Widow Fisk doing things, when he hears an engine strain under load, then backfire. And though there is no clear need for stealth, he does his best to creep to the window, to pull back the Western-themed curtain, the crisp silhouettes of bucking horses and cacti losing their form, to part the venetian blinds slightly with lanolin-scented fingers, to look.

Dusk has fully claimed Scald Mountain, but the Minotaur knows it is there, thick with rhododendrons. What he can see is Danny Tanneyhill across the road. The man has backed his pickup truck to the front of the Pygmalia-Blades trailer. The rear of the truck sags under its payload. Its burden. Its burden is a tree trunk, as big around as . . . or bigger, the Minotaur can't decide; metaphor is often out of his grasp. The fat end of the trunk pushes against the cab; its length spans the bed completely; the other end rests on the lip of the tailgate, where the trunk splits into two thick limbs, outstretched, reaching.

Danny Tanneyhill is a lean, sinewy man. Danny Tanneyhill climbs into the bed of the truck, slings a leg over the trunk like he's going to ride it into submission. He loosens two fat straps. The Minotaur watches. There is moonlight now, and the scent of honeysuckle. The tree will not budge for either, despite Danny Tanneyhill's efforts. He circles the truck, climbs over and around the trunk, wrapping his arms here, shouldering there. He grunts and curses. The tree, pronated or supinated, remains stoic in its bark. It is hard to tell how other wooden entities feel about the moment, the intrusion. But the Minotaur's scar grows hot and throbs.

Just across Business 220, Danny Tanneyhill grapples with his burden, with potential, grapples and grapples. The Minotaur watches. Watches for a long long time.

 *CHAPTER SIX*

NIGHT COMES, AND AS IT IS WONT TO DO, drags behind its entourage of demons and fools.

The Minotaur dreams of concession.

Dreams the concessionaire. A past life, maybe.

Everything orbits. Everything.

Dreams that past. Dreams plank and paraffin. Harness and hyacinth. The whetstone. The conch shell, blown. The sound itself. There is kudzu in summer, a deep green insistence. There is kudzu in winter, the gray leaves like paper, then dust. There is the belly of the ship. The hold. The bilge. The bulgine's run. The hog-eyed man. There is stump and root. And riding the donkey. Stamp and go. The ravaged acre, pulp boiled and pressed. And every letter ever written. There is hubris: shape shifter and time traveler, in his holy robes. And the corndogs. The sno-cones. Elephant ears. Funnel cakes. Gigumundus pretzels. Affy Tapples. Paper mills. We all stink of sulfur. The chef's toque. "Soldier's Joy." "Black-eyed Suzie." "Speed-the-Plow." Pickett's Charge. Bull Run. Appomattox. The absurdity of uppercase and flags and fifes.

The Minotaur followed the battlefields north.

The Minotaur is good at dying. Who'da thunk it?

A thing to do.

The spleen is always the spleen. Catechism or catawampus, it's all the same. Everyone wants something. Everything gets egged on Halloween.

The Minotaur dreams it.

"It ain't right," somebody once said, pointing an angry finger at the Minotaur.

The Minotaur could not agree more.

CHAPTER SEVEN

THE MINOTAUR AVERTS HIS EYES. It is Sunday morning, and he is on his way to another death. He averts his eyes, unprepared for what he might see across Business 220. The Minotaur averts his eyes. It means turning his whole head. There is no other way. But it doesn't matter. The Minotaur knows without seeing that the massive tree trunk is standing there in the Chili Willie's parking lot, its two heavy arms reaching toward, what? Heaven. No. The Minotaur is not convinced.

He knows, too, that Danny Tanneyhill, that self-confessed demigod, sits, watching and waiting, inside the Pygmalia-Blades trailer. Just sits and looks. Chainsaws at the ready. The Minotaur feels caught in the blades.

The Minotaur hurries toward the morning's death. The Guptas are quiet. It is Sunday. Warm already. Unseasonably. The April sunshine is rolling down the slopes of the Allegheny Mountains, pooling in the valleys. By midday everything will be musky. Everything will be hot. Bothered. The Minotaur hurries into the mad peal of church bells from Old Scald Village First Anabaptist, just down the road. The clatter, the sacred claptrap, snags in his horns.

Sunday morning, there is music in the church, often. Sunday morning, the soldiers come ready to die. Always. To kill. And the bleachers fill with spectators. Usually. The Minotaur crosses the bridge over Mill Run. The water is clear and ready. He cocks a bullish ear, finds only birdsong. He makes his way to the Welcome Center, keeping watch for anything wayward. The pillory is empty.

"Hey, there, sarge," Widow Fisk says from her office when the Minotaur comes from the closet with his musket. "Is that thing cocked and loaded?"

"Mmmnn," the Minotaur says.

Widow Fisk teases. She's often sassy, though on Sunday morning her sassiness is restrained.

He steps into the cramped room. Cocked and loaded as he'll ever be. The Minotaur catches the faint whiff of alcohol. Widow Fisk sits at the desk. Widow Fisk wears her bonnet and apron. The knots are crisp and tidy. Always. Even when she's hung over. She comes in early. She leaves late. As far as the Minotaur knows she may actually never leave. The Minotaur likes her understated sass. She's working on the poster for the upcoming reenactment weekend. The Encampment. He leans over her shoulder to read.

"You going to be here?" she asks.

"Unngh," the Minotaur says. "Hope so."

Widow Fisk forks something out of a little tin pan beside the computer monitor. A warm buttery scent fills the deep wells of the Minotaur's nostrils.

"Mmmnn," he says.

Once, a long time ago, Widow Fisk asked the Minotaur how long he thought he'd be staying. The question confounded him. Time being what it is. She asked him if he ever thought about settling down, and where, and with whom. Once, a long time ago, Widow Fisk reached out and touched his jowl.

"Maybe you'll get a promotion," she says from behind her desk, and from behind a faint cloud of whiskey scent. "Maybe they'll make you general."

The thought gives him pause. The Minotaur works up a faint smile. Maybe the coming weekend does hold something for the Minotaur. Maybe the signs, the cut-rate prophesies, the modest omens of the past few days, have pointed there.

"Mmmnn," the Minotaur says again.

General, of course, is out of the question. Any officer's role, really. But change is in the air, for sure. Possibility, though, is hard for the Minotaur to conceive. He can barely think, with the smells of whatever it is Widow Fisk is eating filling the air. Delicious. Delicious. He's eyeballing the tin pan. Anybody could see so.

"Butterscotch pie," Widow Fisk says, and so deftly pokes a forkful into the Minotaur's mouth that he can do nothing but let the heavenly dollop dissolve on his fat black tongue. The Minotaur's knees all but buckle. He remembers. He remembers hunger. It has been a long long time. The butterscotch pie in his mouth might be the best thing the Minotaur has ever tasted. In his life. Widow Fisk. Widow Fisk.

"I made it last night," she says. "Made the crust and the meringue, too. You like it?"

"Mmmnn," the Minotaur says. "Much."

Widow Fisk is facile with piecrust. Widow Fisk in her bonnet and her apron. She knows things. The Minotaur doesn't mean for his mouth to hang open. But it does. Widow Fisk teases his black lips with another forkful of pie.

"You want this?" she asks, keeping it just out of reach. "You want this?"

The Minotaur smells butter and salt and flour on her skin. "Mmmnn," he says. The Minotaur could take her entire hand into his mouth. He wonders if Widow Fisk knows this.

"What'll you give for it?" she asks.

The Minotaur sees a tiny fleck of dried pudding on her bonnet. The Minotaur hadn't imagined the bonnet when he thought of her in the kitchen.

"What do I get out of the trade?" she asks.

The door to the Gift Shoppe opens, to a prickly digital rendition of "Dixie." Widow Fisk puts, lays, inserts the fork into the Minotaur's mouth. He lingers before closing, then senses the barely there resistance at the surface of the peaked meringue, tastes that butter, the brown sugar, the vanilla, perfectly balanced. Flakes of crust stick to his teeth.

"Yep," she says. "I bet they're gonna make you a five-star general."

"Unngh."

"Get you all decked out in a gold sash and those epaulettes, get you two rows of brass buttons. You'll be so damn sexy none of us can . . . "

Widow Fisk doesn't finish her sentence. The Minotaur wishes she would. She looks up—her eyes magnified—blinks twice, then turns back to her work.

"Should I put this Confederate icon here?" she asks, clicking away with the mouse. "Or does it look better there?"

The Minotaur doesn't have an opinion, but he leans close anyway. And when his horn, by happy accident, bumps gently against her bonneted head, Widow Fisk doesn't flinch. Doesn't pull away. No. She leans back ever so slightly.

"Mmmnn, there," the Minotaur says, pointing nowhere.

Widow Fisk straightens her bonnet. The Minotaur turns toward the battlefield.

"Maybe I'll make you one," she says without looking. "Maybe I'll make you a pie. Maybe I'll bring it by. Maybe tonight."

"Mmmnn," the Minotaur says, possibility once again confounding him.

As he leaves the Gift Shoppe, the Minotaur's side knife snags in the barrel of whittled walking canes propping the door open. They rattle against the staves and almost tip over.

• • •

From the Gift Shoppe, there are two ways the Minotaur can go. The thirty-some cabins, barns, and sheds that make up Old Scald Village are laid out with intent. There is something algebraic about the pinched curves, the denial of horizon line. A forced perspective. You can't see the Blacksmith's Shoppe for the wattle and daub walls of the Dumpert House, where the candles are made. But the Minotaur knows it's there, right across the narrow dirt road from the Old Jail, where, months ago, Smitty cajoled or coerced the Minotaur into one of the two damp cells and hung the *Gossip* placard on the door. Kept him locked in for the rest of the afternoon. Folks just assumed it was part of the show.

The Minotaur goes the other way around the loose figure eight. Passes the Old Round Schoolhouse, a striking anomaly in more than its architecture. Made round, they say, made without corners, to keep the spirits, the haints and ghosts, from getting trapped therein. The Minotaur knows that some spirits aren't so easily duped. The Minotaur knows, too, that some of the soldiers like to get high in the schoolhouse before the battles. He smells the cannabis in passing. In passing, the Minotaur understands the impulse.

He passes Sprankle's Tailor Shoppe. It's been closed for a while. Its spindles and needles and thimbles, its bolts of muted fabric, shut away and padlocked. Some say that Sprankle got born again. The Minotaur has no reason to doubt. He passes.

Pauses, though, at the open window of a church. One of two. Used to be three, but an unexplained fire took the wattle-and-daub Presbyterian last summer. Biddle said there was talk of another church building coming in but had neither real proof nor details.

The Minotaur has made this pause before. He likes the moment— Sunday morning before the battle, at the church window, the service coming to an end—though it troubles him in other ways. The Minotaur's horns are too wide for the old window, but he wouldn't look in anyway. He doesn't have to. He knows the bare walls—no tortured effigies, no gilded icons. He knows the cushionless pews, their upright and unforgiving backs. But it's not those things he finds troublesome. Most of the time a girl is in the church. It's the girl who makes candles in the candle shop, who dips the wicks over and over and smells of lanolin. Sunday mornings find her in her secondary role, up by the stark altar, chugging and banging away at a wheezy pump organ and singing at the top of her questionable lungs. "On Christ the solid rock I stand." The congregants, if there are any, sing along: "All other ground is sinking sand." The congregants, if any, may be paying visitors to the village, or they may be something other. A few of the Old Scald Village living historians reenact civilian lives. A mayor here, a drunkard there. Too, this early in the season, nearly every-body does double duty. Plays multiple roles. The Minotaur can never be sure who's who or what's what. But he knows the candle maker's nasally song, part yowl, half caw. He leans his head against the plank wall and listens. A paean to discord, for sure, and though the Minotaur is moved by her sincerity, every time, it is the music that rankles. The music seems somehow hobbled. Fettered. As if the very notes are trapped, boxed in, as if they hurl themselves to bloody pulps, verse after verse.

The candle maker is there most Sunday mornings, and most Sunday mornings she gives the Minotaur pause. But not this day. Something different is happening up on the altar. He cocks his head. Hears. Hears more than he bargained for. There is utterance, for sure. Many voices. Sounds emitted from human mouths, human throats. But try as he might the Minotaur cannot find words in the babel.

"Unngh," he says to no one, and leans closer to the window.

Confused. Compelled. The song, whatever it is, draws him in. But the absence of words unsettles. Language is troubling enough. Words do not pass with ease over his fat tongue. Words crash and burn in his mouth. But hearing is not usually so hard. This morning something has rent the fabric of his understanding. What is happening? Where are the words?

The Minotaur wants to see for himself how those sounds spill from those human mouths, but just as he is about to put his horns through the window things change.

"And am I born to die?"

The cacophony takes shape.

"To lay this body down?"

Each syllable is drawn taut, to the point of breaking, by layers of voice.

"And must my trembling spirit fly . . . "

Harmonies pitch and heave. The song lumbers into sonic existence. Into the present moment. For better or worse.

"Into a world unknown . . . "

He wants to look but can't. Old Scald Village rattles and clanks itself awake. There is dying to be done. The Minotaur closes his eyes, leans one horn against the church. The song worms its way through the boards.

"A land of deepest shade, unpierced by human thought . . . "

What can it mean? The smell of butterscotch lingers in the Minotaur's nostrils. The taste, even deeper. The Minotaur tastes the hymn.

"The dreary regions of the dead, where all things are forgot?"

Fits and starts. Fits and starts. Understanding is a dubious Braille. He's not looking.

"Soon as from earth I go, what will become of me?"

What?

He's not looking.

He's not looking when Smitty comes by.

"Tssss!"

Smitty gooses the Minotaur hard in the ribs. The brand, oh so familiar. Torment.

"Tssss!" Smitty says.

The Minotaur startles. His horn tip digs a six-inch gouge in the plank wall. By the time his frayed wits are gathered the song is over and the bodies, the worshipers, are spilling from the church's open doors.

"There's words for your kind," Smitty says.

Of course there are. Always have been. The Minotaur knows what to expect.

"T-bone," Smitty says. "Ribeye."

• • •

Widow Fisk and her confounding questions. To settle. Down. The Minotaur knows only come and go, parsed out by eons. The beast has lugged his cumbersome head across continents and centuries. Pausing here and there to catch his breath. The Minotaur finds it best not to question. But simply to be.

For the time being he finds himself dwelling peacefully at the crumbling edge of a particular history, finds himself in a faux soldier's uniform on a make-believe battleground, fighting enemies that never die.

• • •

The Minotaur falls dead. Falls dead. Falls (ad nauseam) dead. Rises. This Sunday is a Confederate day for victory. The Minotaur dies regardless. It's hot. Sweltering already. He falls dead on his side, to keep the sun out of his eyes.

On the way to the battlefield, the Minotaur walked with his regiment past a tractor pulling a wagonload of sweaty onlookers en route to the bleachers.

"Look, Mama!" he heard a boy say. "Look at that!"

The Minotaur didn't claim ownership.

The battlefield is a rectangular glade that spans the hundred-plus yards between a hillock called Gobbler's Knob (in the brochure) and a cedar brake called Dead Man's Wood (in the brochure). Humans love to name things. It's likely that the battlefield, before Old Scald Village, was just somebody's boondocks. But the grassy plain made for a natural arena. The founding fathers dragged in some bleachers and bulldozed up a line of earthen breastworks at the far end of the field.

The armies take turns. Charge or defense.

"I think I'm gonna die," Biddle says on the way up the path toward the field. The man, sweatier and pinker than normal, slogs along with a hand over his face, the butt of his musket dragging a rut in the dirt. "Curse the son of a bitch who invented Jägermeister."

The Minotaur doesn't respond. One of the girls, one of the field nurses, does.

"Serves you right," she says.

"I hope you puke your guts out," she says.

"Aren't you married or something?" she says.

The Minotaur hopes that Smitty doesn't see Biddle in this sad state.

The Confederates are charging the battlements today. When the ragtag company rounds a copse of black alder trees, the Minotaur sees the boy, the same one from the wagon. He stands with his toy pistol—little more than a piece of stained pine, bought that very morning from the

Gift Shoppe—raised and aimed. Stands bravely, resolutely, facing down the entire marching battalion.

He fires nonstop. The Minotaur can see clearly. The boy makes little shooting noises with his mouth. Nobody hears them. But the boy gets an enthusiastic round of applause when his mother leads him away from his post and back to the bleachers. Everybody cheers his valor.

When the army is in formation, Smitty walks up and down the line barking orders. Biddle's eyes roll, more than once, back in his head. Biddle tries to position himself away from the stand of cannons on the south flank. He'll go down long before the fire from the Union battery can assault his booze-weary noggin. When the Confederate drum and fife corps rat-a-tat-tats by, it musters an insipid little (semi-mandatory) war whoop from the soldiers. The Minotaur watches Biddle grimace into the discord. But even through his hangover misery, the pink man eyes up the horn player (whose fat rump bobs and sways freely beneath her black skirt) and the piccolo player (a skinny short-haired girl who passes for a boy even off the battlefield). The Minotaur sees it all, and who is he to judge?

The band does its best to keep the beat. It drags its crippled melody all the way to the edge of the field, where it will mill about until the fight is over.

Somewhere along the Union front a tall flag waves. The battle commences with a volley of cannon fire. Everybody on the bleachers oohs and aahs over the gigantic smoke rings. The sharp scent of burnt gunpowder lingers even after the smoke dissipates. Smitty calls out something. The Confederates shoulder their muskets. In a slender moment of military silence the Minotaur hears a truck way up on Scald Mountain, on the turnpike. Then a crow. Then the sound of booted feet on the move and rattling sabers.

Biddle drops early. Doesn't even time the fall with Union fire. Just lies down on the hot dirt and starts calling for the nurse. "Nurse! Nurse! Nurse!"

The Minotaur trudges on.

There are nurses on the field, then and now. Their billowing skirts hang to their ankles, then and now. Bonnets halo their faces. And their aprons? Then, stark white canvases ready to be marked by the humors of men. Now, all the stains are prefab. Then, the nurses carried leather satchels full of comfort to the wounded and dying. Comfort that ran the spectrum of need. Roll after roll of bandages. Laudanum. "Soldier's Joy." Scripture. Maybe even the sweet tincture of martyrdom. Nowadays the field nurses of Old Scald Village carry very little. Sometimes the satchels are empty. The nurses come and go among the, what? The sham, the pseudo, the feigned injured. Mostly they just chitchat quietly. Nobody on the bleachers knows the difference. On hot days like this one the field nurses carry ice in their satchels, so that none of the living-history reenactors has a heatstroke.

"Nurse!" Biddle calls out.

But none of the nurses will attend to his cry. They've all suffered the indignity of approaching Biddle where he lay. And regardless of where he lay the Confederate casualty would lift their skirts, poke his head beneath their petticoats, look up, and cry out, "Good God, Gertie, what a gash!"

Biddle can't be trusted, even dead. Even hung over.

"Nurse!"

The Minotaur hears some acceptable fire from the Union army. He takes his gut shot and drops to the ground. He stays, content among the bugs. The taste of butterscotch pie is all but gone. What was it Widow Fisk said? "Maybe tonight." The Minotaur lies content on the battlefield. Anemic volleys of make-believe gunfire pock the aural landscape. A jet plane tracks silently high above; its white tail striates the blue sky.

"Nurse!" Biddle cries.

"Fuck you, Biddle," somebody says. It's the broom maker. She hates playing field nurse. They make her do it anyway.

"Bite me, Biddle," she says, stepping up to where the Minotaur lies. Her shadow covers him. Cools him. Soothes.

"You want a sliver of ice, M?" she asks, kneeling.

"Mmmnn," he says, and listens as she fumbles with the satchel's clasp.

The Minotaur can never remember the broom maker's name. Makayla or Madison? Something like that. She slips the Minotaur an ice cube without hesitation. Her fingers smell of sorghum, taste of sorghum. Twice in as many hours he's taken from a woman's fingers. O blessed day! Widow Fisk and her fingers made the Minotaur yearn for complicated things. This girl, with her rough touch on his tongue, stirs something more animal in the Minotaur. He wishes he could remember her name. He remembers that she talks a blue streak. Talks up a storm. Talks a mile a minute. He remembers her chipped front tooth. Shawna? No. Bailey? No. The Minotaur gobbles her up.

"Destiny!" Biddle calls in a failed stage whisper. "Bring me some ice!"

"No!" the broom maker says loudly. Then whispers to the Minotaur, "The fucker can die, for all I care."

"Mmmnn," the Minotaur says. He can't see her face fully. Can't turn over, this late in this death. He cranes his veiny neck just a bit. "Mmmnn."

"Hey, M," the broom maker says, snapping the satchel shut. "Can you come by the Broom Shack after lunch? I need some help moving the—"

She doesn't finish the sentence, and the Minotaur doesn't answer, the request stopped, truncated, amputated by cannon fire from the Union battlements and the expert dying of Sargent Haberstroh. Sarge dies better than anybody. He takes his hit loudly, with gusto; he contorts in death like a dancer, flings his scrawny arms wide, hurls his haversack willy-nilly; he calls out heroically, "For God and country, boys" or "Rally round the flag, boys" or "I'm coming home, Mama!"; then he falls and lies more still than stone, and for longer. He's perfected the look of belly bloat, that gathering of gases in the body cavities of the dead; some say he even dabs his neck and behind his ears with the putrid drippings of road kill. They say. After a few well-timed leg spasms Sarge doesn't move, doesn't make a peep, until the bugler signals the battle's end. And he does it all as close to the spectators and their cameras as possible.

The field nurses love tending Sarge's death throes. So convincing are the man's demises that the Minotaur is duped every time. Almost. Every time the Minotaur feels it, the bitter pang of envy. Everybody loves a good death.

"Got to go," the broom maker says.

In her haste the hem of her full black skirt snags on the Minotaur's horn, pulls at his head, turns his snout. And there it is. The Minotaur wouldn't look up this dress uninvited, and even then. . . . He looks. It's okay. She can't tell that he looks, what with the pitch of his horns, the angle of his snout. He looks. And is so stunned by what he sees that he doesn't know how to respond. He didn't expect it, the tattoo. The black-and-white portrait. The walleyed portrait of a little boy smiling from within the razor stubble on the broom maker's round calf muscle. *In Loving Memory*, it says over the top of the boy's head. There is more beneath, but the broom maker moves too fast. The Minotaur misses the full view. She giggles and trots over toward Sargent Haberstroh. She giggles, for sure. But the Minotaur can't say whether it is about, or for, him.

"Destiny!" Biddle calls out.

"Go fuck a barrel," the broom maker says.

. . .

The crowd is sparse, and a sparse crowd makes the hardcores pissy. After the battle, after the pitiful applause, Smitty barely waits for the spectators to load onto the wagon before he starts in.

"I heard you running your mouth," Smitty says to one of the soldiers.

"If I catch you smoking dope before we fight again . . . ," to another.

He rarely completes an angry sentence. Fact is, Smitty has no authority outside his own imagined rank. The majority of folks just ignore him, but the Minotaur knows all too well that this is the most dangerous kind of man. He rants. He rails. And his charges are usually trumped up. Smitty never misses an opportunity to berate a fellow living historian.

He steps up to an unwitting victim and cuts loose. "You want to come out on my battlefield, you better strap them titties down better next time," he says.

The girl flushes, instinctively clutches her breasts and presses inward.

"Ain't nobody wants to see that mess," he says.

The girl soldier—period correct in the whole fraudulent endeavor;

brave young women even then fought amid the men—may be crying. The Minotaur can't tell.

"Unngh," he says.

"You got that right," Biddle says, stepping up and leaning on the Minotaur for balance. He keeps talking, but the Minotaur pays no attention. He's watching the girl and Smitty. He hopes to get out of the village unscathed, back to the Judy-Lou, and then to wait for Monday. Mondays are quiet in the village.

"I'm going to the Tavern," Biddle says. "Need me some Diet Coke. To hell with barrels."

"Unngh," the Minotaur says.

"You want to come?"

"No," the Minotaur says.

"Suit yourself."

Biddle slogs toward the parking lot without even trying to show any of the nurses porn on his cell phone. Only the Minotaur watches him go.

"Mmmnn," the Minotaur says to no one in particular, then heads for the Welcome Center, half hoping to get another bite of pie.

Instead he gets mired in the seething herd of kids outside the Surgeon's Cabin. Doc stands in the doorway, a bloody saw held aloft, over the young heads. He waves it back and forth until the Minotaur looks in his direction. Doc gives a knowing nod. Doc always gives the Minotaur a knowing nod, and the affinity, the allegiance, implied brings the bile up in the Minotaur's throat.

Doc stands in the doorway, his apron bloodied. By the stoop, on a table made of sawhorses and planks, one of his patients lies draped in a wool blanket. The mustache is peeling away. One of the glass eyes has rolled far left. And the paint is chipping off the cheekbones. The mannequin has seen better days. But the kids don't mind. They're not paying any attention to it. Not to the mannequin outside the cabin, or the two even more battered and bedraggled specimens inside, by a wooden cask of vials with moldering or missing contents, by the tableful of rusting scalpels and horrifying probes, scopes, ligatures, and more—the gorget, the bistoury cache, the cranial drill, the catlin, the Roman director and spoon, the trephine, the bone chisel, the kidney dish. Doc could name each instrument, and fairly swoon while doing so. But the kids don't care. What the kids like, every time, is the squat barrel full of rubber amputated limbs. Doc uses it to prop the door open, then has to spend much of his time on duty keeping the kids from beating each other with the floppy props.

The Minotaur likes the kids, their energetic presence. Their goofy bodies and giddy babble. Old Scald Village has much to offer them. And much of it the doing of the broom maker. She runs the Hands-On Program, bringing underprivileged youth in by the busload for the living-history experience. The broom maker does a good job of it. It's a steady source of income for the village, and the administrators see her worth. They turn a blind eye to her other occasional unsavory proclivities.

But not Widow Fisk. More than once, in the Minotaur's presence, Widow Fisk has badmouthed the broom maker.

"Slut," she said.

"Trailer trash," she said.

"Unngh," the Minotaur says to the boy who jumps up to swat his horn with a plastic femur. Unscathed. The Minotaur wants to escape the village unscathed.

"Yo, M," somebody says. It's a girl. The Minotaur doesn't know her name. She is in transition at the moment, half foot soldier, half tavern maid. "Destiny's looking for you."

"Mmmnn, who?"

"She needs help in the Broom Shack."

The girl walks away, putting her black hair up in a bun. Her side knife bumps against her behind with each step.

"Oh," the Minotaur says. "Okay."

The Broom Shack sits tucked between Weinzerl's Pottery and the Tailor Shoppe, an apt locale (though probably happenstance); the movement from clay to straw to cloth seems right in many ways. The Tailor Shoppe, Sprankle's, has a full front porch and rocking chairs and a second story, where the smug tailor and his prickly wife are meant to sleep. But there's nothing up there except two rope-slung beds shoved on either side of the chimney. So the Minotaur has been told. The brochure offered up in the Welcome Center numbers and describes all the buildings of Old Scald Village. Details the "turn-of-the-century" construction: log or stone or frame. The brochure identifies the structures that have been relocated to the site, as well as those re-created on the grounds. The brochure fails to mention that nearly all of the two-story buildings have perilously steep, walled-in staircases that are inaccessible to the handicapped, to the top heavy, to anyone with wide horns. Too, the brochure hasn't been updated since a more recent century's turn. The Minotaur tries not to think about it.

The Minotaur has no small skill with needle and thread. He is well versed in thimble. But those skills he keeps secret at Old Scald Village. He avoids the Tailor Shoppe and its cheerful signage:

> *A stitch in time saves nine*
> *Dyed in the wool*
> *Sewing mends the Soul*
> *Make do and mend*

At the moment, there is no tailor in the village. Some say that Sprankle up and died in the parking lot of Adult World, in Joy, PA, two towns over. The Minotaur also heard that Sprankle moved to Joy and opened a lawnmower repair shop. Either way the Minotaur keeps his sewing kit out of sight.

It's hot. Unseasonably so. The sun is high and unforgiving. The Gift Shoppe will likely deplete its stock of paper parasols and straw hats. The Minotaur likes the heat.

He heads to the Broom Shack. The Broom Shack is little more than that. A single story of vertical planks. A cedar shake roof. The paint on the exterior a faded and chipped eggy yellow. A tattered old broom is propped by the front door. It's an inside joke. It means the broom squire is looking for a wife. There is no porch, only a rough stone stoop. The floorboards creak when the Minotaur steps inside.

The broom maker cuts loose right away. "Hey, hey, M! It's hotter than a popcorn fart out there, isn't it?"

"Mmmnn," the Minotaur says, unwilling to commit to either yes or no.

"Not much cooler inside," she says.

Then the broom maker just keeps talking, but the Minotaur doesn't listen. He leans against a high workbench, steadies himself against the surge of her words. The Minotaur waits to hear what she wants. It's dry in the small building despite the warm Pennsylvania day. All that broom straw sucks the moisture from the air. The Minotaur's skin begins to itch, especially at the seam. He can't reach into his coat to rub at it. Not in public. The purplish ridge of flesh tightens, cinches the Minotaur's chest.

"Unngh," he says.

"I know," the broom maker says. "I told the son of a bitch he'd better quit while he was ahead."

The Broom Shack has two windows, one by the front door, the other on the opposite wall, looking out at an unused part of Old Scald Village. Looking out over the marshy ditch at the back of the property, through the drooping cattails with their fat brown stamens to some unnamable detritus stacked along a chain-link fence. If you look, if you pay attention, you can see the trout. It's massive, big as an old sedan, and made of plaster. A pale green motionless leviathan abandoned, propped pinkish belly up, mouth agape, against the fence. The Minotaur refuses to look into that black hole. No good could come of it. On a far hill, on the other side—and there is always an other side—a *Jesus Is Lord* billboard faces God knows where, aims at God knows who.

" . . . thicker than banjo players in hell," the broom maker says.

"Unngh."

The Minotaur likes the shop's efficiency. The winder and the iron vise are where they ought to be. The foot treadle and the rack of knives with hammered blades, too. The Minotaur respects order. And the broom maker knows her way around. *Besoms*, she calls her brooms, because that's what they're called. When an audience is present, of any size, any makeup, the girl is all business in her role as living historian. She never breaks her version of character. But if it's just her and the Minotaur (or any other village employee or volunteer) in the cabin, the broom maker—plump, filling up her floor-length calico (sometimes red, sometimes green) dress—gabbles and jabbers without ceasing. She'll talk her way through round brooms and flat brooms. The Turkey Wing. The Cobweb Chaser. She talks and works. Her fingers are deft, quick, and sure.

"Howdy!" she says to a soggy-eyed couple in matching American flag T-shirts. "Welcome to the Broom Shack."

In most of the Old Scald Village shops and buildings visitors are confined to a narrow patch of floor just inside the doorway, from which they watch and ask questions. Sometimes they're corralled by a strand or two of dusty hemp rope. In the Broom Shack a low rail fence demarks the space. Separates worker from watcher. The Minotaur hasn't yet crossed over, and now the old couple is in the way. He tries to blend in, somehow, with his horns and his Confederate uniform.

"Oh," the wife says to the Minotaur. Or at the Minotaur. She forces a smile and moves behind her husband, who makes do with a scowling nod.

The Minotaur picks up a ball of stitching twine and pretends to do something with it. They'll stay for bit (out of genuine interest or heat-driven indifference), and the broom maker will bandy about terms—*head spray* and *binding* and *suitable tail*.

"Can't forget the spick," she'll say, "or the head will just twist right off."

They seem the type, so the broom maker tells them the joke. "Don't be a besom," she says, winking at the wife, then explains that *besom* means *broom* but can also mean *disagreeable woman*. "Don't be a besom, always sweeping up dust."

Sometimes they laugh. This couple doesn't. But before leaving the wife buys one of the broom maker's little Guardian Angels, splintery talismans made of husk and straw and jute twine.

"Won't it look nice on the Christmas tree?" the wife says.

The Guardian Angels always sell.

"Hey, big boy," the broom maker says when the coast is clear. "Bring those horns over here and put them to some good use."

The Minotaur isn't sure what she wants.

The broom maker sees his confusion. "Can you help me move the shave horse?"

"Umm?" the Minotaur says. He heard her the first time but wants to hear those words again from her mouth: *the shave horse*. It's a foot-operated vise.

"I want to look out the window," she says.

The shave horse is heavy, its narrow bench made from a split log planed smooth.

"I asked Biddle to help yesterday. Fucker came in and started telling me about a website called 'Ass—"

"Booooring," a voice interrupts. The voice is followed by, drags in, perhaps, the head of a boy, eight, nine, ten years old. He pokes his noggin through the Broom Shack's door, cocks his crisp new Rebel cap back on his head, and repeats his charge: "Booooring."

"Bender!" a mother shrieks. "Get over here!"

The boy waggles an Indian spear—its rubber head flopping back and forth—at the Minotaur, then retreats.

"—hole Worship,'" the Broom Maker says. "'Asshole Worship'? What the fuck?"

You have to straddle the shave horse. To make it work. Straddle it.

"'Asshole Worship.' Tried to show me pictures."

"Mmmnn."

"Of assholes! And—"

"Bender!" the woman yells, somewhere out of sight. "Take that out of your mouth right now!"

"Ready, set, go," the broom maker says, and they lift together.

"Unngh," she says.

"Unngh," he says. The Minotaur had never noticed the broom maker's freckles. He's always noticed the splinters in her fingers and palms.

"Yeah, baby," she says after giving the shave horse one final shove. She pulls aside the burlap curtain and looks out. The Minotaur wonders what she sees. "You know what I think, M?"

"Mmmnn?"

"Men are stupid. That's what I think."

The Minotaur agrees, mostly. Sometimes, in those rare moments of clarity, the Minotaur understands that people usually do the best they can in any given moment. But the standard, the bar, the broomstick over which people must jump, is low. It's nobody's fault. It's everybody's fault.

"Mmmnn," the Minotaur lows. He laments.

The broom maker's face is dotted with freckles, nut brown against her pale flesh. She talks and talks and talks, and the freckles move. They swirl—oceanlike, constellation-like—over her cheeks. The Minotaur wants to look at that face. Wants more than anything, there in the Broom Shack, to find the monsters and the heroes (even the lesser beasts) among those stars. But you have to straddle the shave horse, so the broom maker does. Sits with her back to the Minotaur.

"Hand me a stick," she says.

The Minotaur rattles around in a bin of cut birch saplings, does as he is told.

"Sit yourself down," she says. "All them horny horns make me nervous."

The only option is a low three-legged stool roughly crafted from a split tree trunk and some thick branches. The Minotaur does as he is told. The stool wobbles beneath him. The broom maker, astraddle the shave horse, presses the treadle with both feet, clamping the stick tight in the vise's wooden jaws. She leans, stretches, reaches onto the workbench for her draw knife.

"My mama always told me . . . ," she says.

The Minotaur doesn't hear the advice. He's too preoccupied with the broom maker's movement.

"Did your mama ever . . . ?"

The broom maker bends forward over the shave horse, steadies the draw knife in two hands, and begins scraping the bark away in thin curlicues. Back and forth, draw and scrape.

"You ever stick anybody with one of them . . . ?"

And every time the broom maker bends forward, the two heavy mounds of her backside flex, rise, and divide, big as upturned bushel baskets inside her gingham dress. And when she pulls the knife, little tongues of wood, tiny flightless birds, drop at her feet. And her fat ass settles back into place.

"Unngh," the Minotaur says.

"Speaking of asshole worship," she says, "did you see Sarge out there today?"

"Mmmnn."

The Minotaur is not above his animal self, or his man self. The broom maker doesn't seem to need his responses.

"You know what I heard?" she says, reaching back without looking to tug the fabric of her dress from the cleft of her behind. She gives a wiggle. "I heard he's hoping to take it to the next level."

"Unngh."

"They say he's working on shitting himself, every time he dies out there on the battlefield. Can you believe such a thing?"

Yes. The Minotaur can. Human behavior never really surprises him.

No. The Minotaur cannot imagine himself into the fully human moment.

Moments. All of them, human and otherwise, ushered in under escort, flanked on either side by liminal space. There is always room for chaos to blossom. The broom maker yaps away and scrapes the bark from the birch stick. Body. Not body. The Minotaur can smell her. He can't not. Outside the Broom Shack it is spring. Dying season. Rut season, too. He thinks he hears Smitty pounding at the anvil. Thinks he hears the dragonflies winging over the pond, the pump-organ bellows gasping for breath.

"Hunky-dory," the broom maker says, rising, releasing the newly shaved broomstick from the vise and sighting down it as if it were a gun barrel.

"Bang," she says. "Bang bang bang."

The Minotaur knows his limits. Knows his own leanings. Allows himself from time to time to clamber over the wall of guilt and wallow in nonsense. The Minotaur knows his limits. This doesn't mean he is in control. The broom maker chooses, with some care, a whisk broom from among others hanging on the wall over the workbench. She squats and begins sweeping the birch shavings into a neat pile. The Minotaur knows. Knows his limits. He wants to see. Just the tattoo. *In Loving Memory*, it says. The Minotaur wants to know who the wall-eyed boy was. That's all. The broom maker squats, her back to the Minotaur. Close enough. The Minotaur leans forward on the low three-legged stool. Reaches for the hem of her gingham skirt. The transgression ever so slight in his bull brain.

She squats. She sweeps.

"Hey, M," she says. "What do you get when you cross a broom maker with a—"

That's when the stool topples.

There are places the Minotaur and his big old horns cannot fit.

That's when the stool topples.

There are places where the Minotaur and those horns should not fit.

Then the stool topples. Then the stars of outrageous fortune align. Then the Minotaur falls forward and in doing so drives his thick snout all the way up the broom maker's dress, shoving hard against her crotch, shoving her bodily beneath the table and scattering bobbins of stitching twine hither and yon.

It doesn't surprise the Minotaur that the broom maker isn't wearing panties. There's no time for guilt. No time for thoughts of Widow Fisk, or the Guptas' returning daughter. The broom maker wears no panties. Nor do her damp earthy scents surprise. Not at all. But that hair. What horns its way most insistently into his state of mind is the thatch of hair between the broom maker's legs. And how it tickles the deep black wells of his nostrils. The Minotaur sneezes instantly. A full-on, wet, rubbery-lipped sneeze. Right between the broom maker's legs.

They are both profoundly surprised. The Minotaur tries to scramble backward, to extract himself from the unmeant cave. No, more muzzle than cave. Scrambles backward nonetheless. The broom maker begins to scream. No. More auctioneer's cry. More, still, a glossolalia. A sacred, albeit loud, utterance. No words. Pure syllables. A train wreck of tongue against teeth. The broom maker, wailing, upends the table. The Minotaur shakes his big head. The broom maker, wailing, picks up a broomstick, begins to hit the Minotaur. The Minotaur tries halfheartedly to defend himself. The broom maker, wailing, tires of hitting the Minotaur. She runs out the door, wailing. By the time he rights himself and stands, the Minotaur can barely hear her cry.

"Mmmnn, no," he says.

• • •

The Minotaur skulks out into the madding crowd. Dumbstruck. No. There is no crowd. Only the gawking handful of stragglers trying to wring every last second of experience out of their Old Scald Village admission fee. Only the others employed by the village or merely volunteering, the Minotaur's fellow living historians, costumed reenactors, historical inter-preters. Call them what you will, they all gawk.

The candle maker stands on her listing porch, mouth agape, twining a wick tightly around her finger; the tinsmith, too, is there, ball-peen hammer in hand, his punch still, on the bench, awaiting the strike; a mother ushers her children into the Old Jail when the Minotaur passes, their faces clotting the open window. It is spring. Advent and blasphemy.

"Mmmnn, no," the Minotaur says. But the bits of broom straw he trails are a grave incrimination.

The Minotaur pretends not to see any of them. The Minotaur, feeling fully his monster, keeps his big head low, one thick horn gouging a rut in the well-trod earth. Walks watching each step, as if his small very human feet belong to someone else. The Minotaur, a graft gone horribly awry, wonders where they'll take him, those feet.

Advent and blasphemy. It is spring. The gods snigger as they play. O nasty happenstance! The Minotaur pretends not to see any of it. Pretends most not to see the face of Widow Fisk. Widow Fisk, her kind face, her buttered fingers. Widow Fisk, who fed him pie. Who said they'd make him a general. Who stands in the doorway of the Welcome Center clutching a handful of ticket stubs. He pretends not to notice her look of utter betrayal. The Minotaur wonders if his feet will lead him to her. Widow Fisk retreats into the Welcome Center and hangs the Closed sign on the door handle.

The Minotaur drags his musket through the grass, down the drive, and over the planks of the covered bridge. The Minotaur pretends that the water in Stink Creek isn't running red. A deep rust red.

CHAPTER EIGHT

THE TRAFFIC ON THE TURNPIKE, high above on Scald Mountain, is heavy with people rushing toward or away from other kinds of worlds and lives. And all that sound—of metal, plastic, and rubber in motion on pavement, the noise of come and go—it all tumbles down the mountainside, surges over the more languid Business 220, drenches its travelers and dwellers, and slams against the dam that is the Judy-Lou Motor Lodge, with its brick walls and closed doors.

"Mister M," Rambabu Gupta says when the Minotaur hurries into the motel office, "you are looking not so good today. Was the dying unsatisfactory?"

"Unngh," the Minotaur replies. "Not so . . . "

There is more to say. Much. It is late on Sunday afternoon. The Minotaur has much more to say.

"Mmmnn."

Just across Business 220, at the edge of the Chili Willie's parking lot, the overlord of Pygmalia-Blades yanks the pull cord, and the chainsaw engine revs furiously. The Minotaur shivers. Rambabu Gupta looks at him long and hard.

"Please, Mister M, sit down."

Rambabu goes into the Guptas' apartment. The Minotaur sits in a tattered armchair to gather his wits. Coming up the road, the Minotaur saw Danny Tanneyhill out of the corner of his bull eye. The man was standing at the newly procured tree trunk, gesturing, making imaginary cuts. Rambabu and Ramneek Gupta speak somewhere out of sight. The Minotaur can barely discern between the Hindi and the rattle of pots and pans. He leans his horns back against the wall—papered with a repeated print of a stag, a doe, a fawn, in a glade, all monochrome ocher—and eases the curtain aside. Wonders what nascent beast Danny Tanneyhill is after in that massive trunk.

The Minotaur fingers the bumps on his head from the broom maker's stick, a futile and haphazard phrenology. Back in the Guptas' kitchen, something chops away. A grinding mechanical sound. The air is suddenly sweet.

Rambabu Gupta returns with a glass of cloudy yellowish liquid. "Assimilation, Mr. M," Rambabu says, handing the Minotaur the glass. "It is a dubious enterprise. Dubious. Drink up, Mr. M. *Ganne ka ras.* Cane juice. It soothes."

"Mmmnn," the Minotaur says. Guzzles half the glass. Nearly swoons over the purity of the viscous juice. He will sip the rest. The Minotaur has much to say. About the broom maker. About what happened in her shack. About assimilation. About Widow Fisk and what she saw. Or what she thinks she saw. Pilloried as he is by his past, the Minotaur says nothing.

"Just another day, maybe two, Mister M," Rambabu says. "Then our Ba . . . our Becky will be with us. We will celebrate. You will join in."

"Unngh," the Minotaur says at last.

That's when Devmani bursts into the room. The Guptas' granddaughter has escaped from the bath. She is naked, dripping wet, giggling and glorious in her tiny body. She has a bright yellow tub crayon clutched in her little fist.

"*Dohiti!*" Ramneek says, coming into the motel lobby with a towel outstretched. "Come back here right away." Ramneek is smiling. She chooses her words—"You scoundrel, you scalawag"—for their deliciousness.

Devmani Gupta rounds the counter, laughing, and jumps up into the Minotaur's lap. Laughing. He has no choice but to catch her. Devmani Gupta cocks her tiny face and leans close, eyeball to eyeball with the Minotaur. She giggles. She lays the tiniest of hands under his jowly chin, lifts his head. Devmani Gupta reaches up with her bright yellow crayon and makes two long marks on the Minotaur's wide and bony forehead. Right between his eyes. And just before Ramneek plucks her away, wrapped and giddy in the towel, Devmani plants her damp little lips on the Minotaur's snout, that sullied snout, and kisses.

"Hooligan," Ramneek says. "*Upadravi.*"

Ramneek carries the wiggling girl into the apartment. The Minotaur hears the laughing. Sees the damp geometry on his trousers, left by her wet bottom and legs. "Mmmnn," the Minotaur says.

And there is more to come, but it is interrupted by the bells dangling on the door, by the entry of a skinny man with exceptionally close-set eyes and his companion, a skinny woman with an exceptionally wide mouth.

"Y'all got any rooms?" the man says.

The Minotaur recognizes the twang, a Southern thing. The Minotaur recognizes the flash of disdain in the man's eyes, directed at both the Guptas and at him.

"Welcome to the Judy-Lou Motor Lodge," Rambabu says. "We are pleased to offer free Wi-Fi—"

"Get them bags honey," the man says.

The Minotaur, deciding he's seen enough, holds the door for her on the way out. She smells like hairspray. And beer. She pauses a long time before accepting the Minotaur's courtesy, but passes closer than necessary when she finally does. Time stands still for an instant—the Minotaur trying to hold on to Devmani Gupta's joyous puerility, the mouthy woman trying to hold tight to the battered pair of matching Samsonite suitcases (and all they contain)—until Danny Tanneyhill (guru, top dog) rips the moment apart with his chainsaw. The Minotaur looks across Business 220. Sees Danny Tanneyhill drive the tip of the blade into the flesh of the tree trunk, woodchips filling the air around him.

The Minotaur closes the door to Room #3 and wriggles the safety chain into place. The new guests enter the room at the far end of the Judy-Lou. The Minotaur watches the woman lug the heavy suitcases inside. The door slams but opens again almost immediately. The man drags a chair out and shoves it against the brick wall, in the little chunk of space between the doorframe and the wide and clattering air conditioner that sits beneath the shaded window and dribbles constantly onto the sidewalk. The man sits. Looking out. Or not looking at all. It's hard to say. The Minotaur waits for the woman to appear in the doorway, or for the door to close. Neither happens.

The Minotaur's head hurts; the mountain range of lumps and bumps on his noggin throbs. Trouble storms the horizon. The Minotaur isn't afraid of Danny Tanneyhill. Not exactly. Rather, it is the thing that Danny Tanneyhill is pulling out of the fat trunk that bothers the Minotaur. Troubles the Minotaur. Haunts. The Minotaur watches, through parted blinds, to see what will be revealed. Watches. Could it be that this rough-hewn man is hacking loose, is setting free, the change that has haunted the Minotaur's past few days?

The carver, the artist, cuts, steps back, cuts some more. The man is not happy, the Minotaur can tell. Danny Tanneyhill cocks his human head one way, then the other. Sits down to study his work. Legs are emerging at the base of the tree, that much is clear. But higher up, where the two fat branches reach out, the creation is unformed, ill formed, as if the tree itself is resisting.

The Minotaur understands struggle and disappointment. The Minotaur removes his uniform coat. He gets the Bag Balm from the bathroom, returns to the window, and stands, rubbing the salve into his throbbing seam. Thinks back to the Broom Shack and what happened there. He didn't mean it. The Minotaur's nostrils twitch at the memory. He sniffs and finds her still present at the tip of his snout. The scents of her body, what it makes, what it eliminates. The Minotaur licks at the spot until she is gone.

Widow Fisk saw the broom maker run. The smell of lanolin will not go away. Widow Fisk saw the broom maker run screaming, saw the Minotaur exit the Broom Shack. Widow Fisk came to some conclusions. The Minotaur wishes things had gone differently. Butterscotch.

He is about to abandon the window, thinking that maybe Danny Tanneyhill has given up for the day, but there is a commotion at Pygmalia-Blades. It's a customer. A green pickup truck skids to a stop in the gravel. A customer. Sometimes people want what Danny Tanneyhill has to offer.

Two blond kids stay in the cab of the truck. Their bald daddy steps up and starts manhandling a chunky Bigfoot carving. The statue is painted brown, is scowling, is hunched as if in midstep. The man tilts it this way and that. Looking. Assessing. Imagining possibilities. The statue comes up to the man's weak chin. He seems about to drop it at every turn. Danny emerges from the trailer. They haggle; the Minotaur can tell by the gestures. The man turns his attention to a carving of the Ten Commandments, Moses's two slabs hewn from a fat cedar trunk turned on its side. The man struggles with the choice. The Minotaur understands conundrum, is at home in quandary. The man seems less so. His kids sit so still in the truck, the Minotaur isn't sure they're real.

Eventually the man and the artist reach an impasse, and the man leaves. The Minotaur thinks ahead, but only to the weekend, only to the coming Encampment, to what might be his big chance. The Minotaur imagines himself in general's garb. He tries to imagine Widow Fisk into the equation. Her there and proud of his accomplishment. The Minotaur reaches to finger the brass medals that might hang at his breast pocket. Touches only his bull flesh. It isn't the first time, and it won't be the last.

An hour later the truck returns, and the Minotaur watches Danny Tanneyhill help the man load both Bigfoot and the Ten Commandments into its bed. The trio of bungee cords, stretched obscenely tight across the weighty pair like rogue overworked ligaments, seems inadequate for the task of keeping it all from toppling to the road, but the Minotaur isn't willing to go out and say so. Not wanting to witness the almost certain catastrophe, he turns from the window as the truck drives away, spitting and churning the gravel.

The day wanes. The sun has already dropped over Homer's Gap and will not return from there no matter how hard the shadows pull. The coming evening drags with it the sulfuric stink of the paper mill. It is familiar—comforting, even. Danny Tanneyhill has droplights strung around the Pygmalia-Blades tent. He works into the night, sawing and cursing by turns. The Minotaur pushes his bed against the far wall. Puts a pillow over his aching head. Makes no difference. Doors slam all night long. All night long the chainsaw whines. No. Succumbs. It is the hatchet, biting all night long into wood. And the cursing. All night long. The Minotaur's stomach turns. And turns. And turns.

CHAPTER NINE

NIGHT. THAT NIGGLER *EXTRAORDINAIRE*.

Night comes nonetheless, an apparition in slinky black. The Minotaur is on the run. Run.

The Minotaur traces and retraces his steps. Looking for what? Butterscotch?

The Minotaur is at Bull Run. The Minotaur is at Manassas, at Appomattox, at Antietam, at Shiloh. The Minotaur at square one, and at the pearly gates. The Minotaur strikes up the band, pays the piper. The Minotaur keeps his nose to the grindstone. The Minotaur lets sleeping dogs lie. At the eleventh hour the Minotaur burns the midnight oil. The Minotaur has an ace in the hole but cries over spilt milk. The Minotaur beats around the bush, beats a dead horse. The Minotaur knuckles down.

North, south, east, west. The topsy-turvy earth. The Minotaur swaps one life for another.

After the cock-and-bull story the Minotaur hangs up his fiddle. The Minotaur gets down to brass tacks, hits the nail on the head. The Minotaur knows the ropes and knocks on wood. The Minotaur makes no bones about it. In the china shop there is no rule of thumb. The Minotaur bears his cross, leads the blind, has the devil to pay. The Minotaur tastes the salt of the earth but not the laudable pus.

The Minotaur cuts his eyeteeth, chews the fat, clams up. The Minotaur guards his tongue, is down in the mouth, is long in the tooth. The Minotaur on shank's mare. The Minotaur and his monkeyshines under siege. The bonnyclabber. The catawampus. The windbag. Nearly fifty-one thousand humans died at Gettysburg alone. Three thousand horses. It's all Greek to the Minotaur. In the bulrushes. In the breadbasket. The Minotaur gags, retches, and the banjo falls from his gullet. The banjo, spumy, bilious, radiant, cantankerous as hell, rears its scrawny neck and heads for the hills.

CHAPTER TEN

MORNING HACKS THE CURTAINS WIDE, and the Minotaur opens his eyes. Morning. The Minotaur doesn't know what to expect. He puts on his best costumed interpreter face and opens the door of Room #3. Is the sun up there where it's supposed to be, bearing down hard on Scald Mountain and the turnpike? Yes. Are the rhododendrons holding tight to that steep slope, offering their obscene blossoms to any and all? Yes. Does Business 220 still thread Homer's Gap somewhere down the road? And just up the road does Old Scald Village march drearily in place? And do the Minotaur's horns barely clear the lintel, his Confederate soldier's woolen trousers itch incessantly? Yes, and yes, and yes. What, then, is different about this day?

The Minotaur sees it. The Minotaur is no sleuth. He can't tell what happened, who went where and when, though clues abound. Danny Tanneyhill's truck is gone. The tree trunk he'd labored over all day, laid waste. Chopped to splintery bits. Woodchips and sawdust litter the parking lot, clot around the bases of the other statuary. And in the blanket of sawdust, footprints. Multiple. Coming and going across Business 220, back and forth between Pygmalia-Blades and the room at the far end of the Judy-Lou Motor Lodge, where the guests checked in yesterday. On the sidewalk, by the door, a paper bucket has tipped and spilled its grisly contents. Enough gnawed chicken bones to feed a small army. Beer cans, crushed and not, the cardboard case, crumpled napkins, other unnamable detritus, all form a haphazard shrine to some elusive god, right outside the door. The world of the fully human regularly confounds the Minotaur, but nothing here surprises him.

"Unngh," the Minotaur says.

He should clean up the mess before the Guptas stir. It is Monday morning. Ramneek will be sweeping the sidewalks first thing. It is Monday morning. Rambabu will sit with his granddaughter while she watches cartoons. It is Monday morning. The Minotaur's work in the village will be menial, tedious, soothing. There will be no dying. He looks again at the footprints in the sawdust, at the litter—an aftermath of sorts, the scene of something crimelike—and the Minotaur can't face it.

"Sorry," he says aloud, intending it for the sleeping Guptas.

He wishes things were different. He wishes Danny Tanneyhill would pack up his trailer and his monsters and drive away. He wishes the skinny woman at the opposite end of the Judy-Lou didn't have to drag so much around in her Samsonite suitcases. He wishes he'd gone to the secret place last night. He wishes he hadn't been up the broom maker's dress, accidentally or otherwise. And he wishes Widow Fisk hadn't witnessed any of it. He pockets the Bag Balm—used or not, he'll return it. Slip it unnoticed back in her drawer.

The Minotaur cannot face the trash at the opposite end of the motor lodge, nor its makers. Hangdog, then, he trudges down the road. At the mouth of Old Scald Village, the giant plaster soldier takes him to task. Clucks his lifeless tongue. Chides. The Minotaur looks for the crow, finds nothing. The Minotaur musters just enough gumption to throw a rock at the plaster head. Misses by a mile. Maybe more. The Minotaur galumphs over the planks of the covered bridge and, as promised in the brochure, steps back in time. But not enough to make a bit of difference. Not nearly.

He's not the first. Biddle is there. In the pond. Hip deep.

"Unngh," the Minotaur says. "What?"

"Goddamn teenagers," Biddle says. The brim of his leather cap casts a shadow on his face. "Doped-up little shit-pinchers."

Biddle's leather apron, his cooper's costume, lies in a heap on the bank, a shape-shifter asleep, waiting. Biddle wears rubber waders that barely contain his girth, the straps stretched so taut over his shoulders and rotund gut that the Minotaur can almost hear the threads popping.

"They threw a picnic table in, and one of the pillories," Biddle says.

It happens often enough. On weekends, spring or summer, in the tumult of night, in the torrent of rut, rowdy teens from the KOA campground across the river (or maybe even local kids from Joy township, just through the gap) sneak, giddy and heroic in their vandal boots, into Old Scald Village and toss things in the pond.

"Ought to shoot the little fuckers," Biddle says. "Get me some night vision and a thirty-ought-six, do a stakeout in the church tower, pick the fuckers off one at a time." Biddle, increasingly wet from the hole in the toe of his wader, and hungover as usual, is more envious than outraged. "Give me a hand," he says.

"Unngh," the Minotaur says, and heads to the small shed behind the Welcome Center. It's where the lawnmowers and leaf blowers hide. Weedeaters, too. Anything that smacks of the here and now. The *Come Again* sign guards the front door of the building. He can't tell if Widow Fisk is inside or not. The Minotaur takes the long way around; the grass lanes and gravel paths that weave through the village are empty, still, quiet.

The shed door stands ajar. The Minotaur finds the wading boots hanging on a peg against the far wall. The Minotaur takes a long moment to breathe in the smells of gasoline and motor oil. They comfort. When he steps out of the shed, back fully into Old Scald Village, the Minotaur is deafened by the roar of the bellows stoking the forge in the Blacksmith's Shoppe. The massive leather lung sucks in, blows out, breath after furious breath. And already Smitty is pounding away at the anvil. The Minotaur has never heard him strike with such determination.

"Let's get the pillory first," Biddle says. "It's lighter. Closer to the bank."

The Minotaur looks across the pond. No sky is reflected on its surface. The forge rages beyond the opposite bank; the spume of hot air from its chimney stakes its small claim, rankling and refracting the morning sunlight. The Minotaur slogs into the murk, his muddy trail rising up from the lake bed.

"Remember when they found that dead kid?" Biddle says. "Floating in here with his pants down?" Biddle giggles like it's a really funny joke.

"Unngh," the Minotaur says.

"Remember when that dog—"

The Minotaur interrupts. "Unngh."

They lay the pillory on the bank; mud sloughs from its plank base. They go back for the picnic table. It rests on its side, one wide bench jutting from the water. Righting the table is easy enough, but when the Minotaur and Biddle go to lift it they come up against a truth.

"Gooooddamm it. This son of a bitch is heavy."

"Unnnnnngh."

The big man cannot walk backward. The Minotaur and Biddle switch sides, sloshing the pond water into a brown soup in their slow circumnavigation. They grunt into the task. Biddle, overweight, unfit, bearing even a portion of such a burden, can move through the water only a few paces at a time.

"Let me . . . catch . . . my breath," he says.

The Minotaur can wait forever. Biddle babbles nonstop. Talks about nothing. So far he hasn't mentioned the previous day. The Minotaur wonders if luck is on his side. Maybe so. Maybe not. Sweat drips from beneath Biddle's brim. Two cars slow on Business 220 and enter the village. It's time for the rest of the employees and volunteers to arrive. Maybe everybody will pretend nothing happened.

"Did you hear?" Biddle asks. "Did you hear about Gwen?"

"Mmmnn," the Minotaur says.

"Gwen?" Biddle says again, straining against the table's bulk. They've moved it less than halfway to the bank.

"Who?" The Minotaur gets the word out.

"Gwen," Biddle says. "The old bat who runs the Gift Shoppe."

"Unngh?" the Minotaur says, then works hard for the rest. "Ff . . . isk. Widow Fisk?"

"Yeah, yeah," Biddle says. "That's her. Gwen."

The half-bull's imagination goes to a fully human place. He sees

Widow Fisk dead in a handful of scenarios, each bloodier than the last.

"Mmmnn, no," the Minotaur says.

"Yes it is, dumbass. Her name's Gwen. Gwen Harschberger, or something like that. Widow Fisk is her character. She plays Widow Fisk. Did you really think—"

"No," the Minotaur says as decisively as possible, but is clearly embarrassed by his stupidity.

"She got busted last night," Biddle says. He takes his cap off, fans his face. "Got busted for DUI. They say she was so drunk she couldn't even get out of the car."

"Who?" the Minotaur asks.

"Everybody," Biddle says. "They say she spent the night in jail."

The Minotaur lifts his end of the table and pulls. Biddle nearly topples.

"Whoa, big boy!" Biddle braces himself and laughs. "First I heard she was buck naked in the car. Then somebody said she had on that goddamn costume. But everybody said she fought tooth and nail till they dragged her ass to the station."

Biddle yammers away. The Minotaur's mind reels. At the far end of the village the weathervane on top of the barn cants downward and refuses to pivot. The Minotaur had planned to repair it later in the week. The barn, a small timber frame thing with a gabled tin roof, holds a meager herd: a couple of goats, a bony and swaybacked heifer, and (inexplicably) a llama. Half a dozen chickens peck around in the dirt pen. Once, just after the Minotaur arrived at Old Scald Village, they asked him to strip off his shirt and join—mingle with—the livestock. To act like an actual bull, a whole bull. It was a mistake. He took care to position himself so that only his horned head and fat snout were visible. He wasn't afraid of bloat or black leg or foot rot. The Minotaur was unconcerned about lumpy jaw or wooden tongue. Pride is a tiny little human worry. And dignity is present even in the thick, the heart, of the muck. As for the cow, the Minotaur imagined her bovine consciousness and his place in it. Then the kids saw more than his snout and horns and, spooked, ran to their mamas. It was a short-lived experiment. In fact it was Widow

Fisk who came and told him to get dressed, to come up out of the stable. She brought him a pan of warm water and a towel.

"You know, don't you?" Biddle starts. "You know what we're all wondering?"

"Mmmnn," the Minotaur says.

"We're all wondering if you got a picture of Destiny's butthole while you were up there."

The Minotaur is slow to anger. Few things rattle him to the point of action. It wouldn't take much to push Biddle over. But the Minotaur doesn't get the chance.

Biddle screams. Biddle, a look of utter terror peeling his lips back from his gums, beats at the water by his thigh and screams. The Minotaur can make out a word or two, but mostly Biddle just shrieks and pounds.

"Arrhhhh . . . after me . . . oooooob . . . "

Biddle tries to run. Biddle, on dry flat land, would find running difficult. Biddle, in tight rubber waders, hip deep in a pond with a thick muddy bed, takes two steps and falls. When the fat man breaches, dirty water spews from his mouth. His hat floats away.

"It's after me, M! Please help me! Please!"

With Biddle chopping up the water as he flops and flails to the bank, the Minotaur can't see anything. The fat barrel maker is still caterwauling when he crawls out of the pond and onto the grass, and keeps it up as he quick-waddles, dripping, around the Tailor Shoppe and out of sight.

When the water stills the Minotaur sees something bobbing just beneath the surface, something bumping against the picnic table. He reaches in.

It's the trout. The trout he's seen propped against the fence. A secret part of the vandal's endeavor, revealed by Biddle. The fish knocks its big plaster head against the underside of the picnic table, as if trying to get to the surface. A sonorous thud if there ever was one. The Minotaur wonders if they thought they were returning the big fish to its home. The Minotaur wonders if the fish knows the difference. It would not surprise him. The Minotaur hooks his arm through the caved-in eye socket and lifts. Muddy water gushes from everywhere. The black mouth gapes.

What now?

"Hey! Chopped steak!"

It's Smitty. He stands on the bank, hammer in one hand and what is clearly a branding iron in the other. The very air pops and sizzles. It would not be hard to imagine the man spitting nails.

"Hey, T-bone! Mitch wants you in his office. Now!"

Smitty doesn't wait around, though it seems like he wants to. The Minotaur gives the trout a shove toward deeper water, then sloshes out of the pond. He pauses at the bank, fishes the Bag Balm from his pocket, and tosses it underhanded at his own muddy wake. The can of salve doesn't sink. The can of salve floats. The Minotaur considers, for the briefest moment, going back in after it.

Mitch runs Personnel. Whatever that means. The Minotaur has seen him maybe three times total since coming to the village. As far as the Minotaur can tell nobody sees him regularly. But everybody knows that Mitch's office is upstairs in the Welcome Center, and he's likely right behind the narrow rectangular two-way mirror near the ceiling in the center's lobby (the one overlooking the ping-pong-table-sized scale model of what Old Scald Village would look like if money were easy and more people really cared).

The Minotaur knocks lightly.

Mitch hems. Mitch haws. His nametag is shaped like the state of Pennsylvania. Mitch fiddles with the tag the whole time he speaks. When Mitch eventually comes around to the point, it is that the Minotaur has to leave the village.

"Not forever," Mitch says. But he won't be any more specific.

The Minotaur sees the schedule for the upcoming Encampment Weekend spread out on Mitch's desk. There are circles and red X's everywhere. The Minotaur smells like pond water. Mitch smells like hot dogs. His office, his desk in particular, sits right over the Welcome Center's concessions counter.

"I know Destiny is trouble," Mitch says. "I know it for a fact. And between you and me, I don't blame you for what you did, M."

"Mmmnn, no," the Minotaur says. No.

"I've been tempted myself," Mitch says. And then he makes like he's squeezing an ass with both hands.

The Minotaur offers to stay in the Old Jail. To spend his days in the pillory.

"Put yourself in my shoes, M," Mitch says. "Destiny can mess things up for all of us."

No, the Minotaur says, but says it to himself.

He walks back to the Judy-Lou Motor Lodge slowly. On the way he picks a strand of honeysuckle vine. If Devmani Gupta is done with her nap he'll teach her how to pluck the threadlike stamens from the pale yellow flowers. He'll show her the droplets of clear sweet nectar.

CHAPTER ELEVEN

WHAT TO DO? WHAT TO DO? The Minotaur is in something of a pickle. He has moved countless times through the centuries. Been booted right out of one era and grafted himself onto the next. Made do. Trudged along dragging a (less and less) blood-drenched history behind, pushing a tepid eternity before. The Minotaur is, after all, part draft animal. Part beast of burden. The Minotaur will lean into the yoke when necessary. Dray. Dray.

He didn't mean the trespass with Destiny. Didn't mean to put his snout up her dress, didn't mean to have her broom maker's scents on his face, her tastes on his bullish tongue. He didn't mean to steal the Bag Balm. He didn't mean to think Widow Fisk was really Widow Fisk. He is not prepared to go just yet. He was still grappling with her questions. Was almost considering possibilities. But the horn sometimes has a mind of its own. He was willing to spend day after day locked in the stocks, willing to accept the ribbing, the ridicule. But Mitch said no. The Minotaur needs a plan. The Minotaur likes plans. Even flawed plans. It's one of his more human traits. He likes process and order. These things help him to navigate his eternity, to break down *forever* into tolerable bits. Tolerable.

The Minotaur keeps some things in a cardboard box under the double bed in Room #3 at the Judy-Lou Motor Lodge. Some things gathered over the years to help with transitions. The contents change over time—the container, too. For now the Jumbo Corndogs Bulk-Pack box holds a coiled orange extension cord, a crescent wrench, a pair of channel locks, screwdrivers. There's a sewing kit in a small leather case. And a full set of kitchen knives in a canvas roll. The tools are clean. The knives are sharp. These things are remnants from recent pasts. They may be useful again. But he is not ready to make use. Nor, for the moment, can he bear the Guptas' kindness.

Traffic is light on Business 220. The Minotaur clutches the honeysuckle vine and stands by the roadside, looking down an overgrown path. He knows where it leads. It is Monday morning, but that no longer matters. The Minotaur wishes it were night. In the free market of breath, the commerce of daytime can suffocate. It is sometimes easier to breathe, to wait, at night. The Minotaur envies the plaster trout, finally at home at the bottom of the murky pond. At night the Minotaur knows where to go. It is day. The Minotaur decides to go there anyway.

• • •

Joy Furnace. It says so on the information kiosk. It doesn't matter to the Minotaur that there are hundreds of other abandoned limestone kilns in the state, each with its own red dot on the plastic map; Joy Furnace is the one he stumbled into those few years ago. It doesn't matter that the furnaces fired all day and all night, cooking quarried limestone down to its powdery essence. Dozens of men huffed the toxic air all day, all night—mules, too, and horses.

Joy Furnace. Gone are the eight-story-high exhaust stacks, the steel cylinders lining the core of each furnace. Nothing is left of the narrow-gauge railroad track that ran along the skinny space carved out of the hillside overhead, where the hopper cars fed chunks of limestone into the fires. Nothing left. There may be some mule bones buried in the grass.

It's not important to the Minotaur why he left the highway that day years ago. No official vine-covered *Historic Site* sign jutted up from the ditch. The rutted dirt road that led into the woods was blocked by a thick and sagging chain, from which hung the cautionary *No Trespassing, PA Department of Conservation and Natural Resources.*

The Minotaur is nomadic by default. An intuitive vagabond. He may have been drawn, he may have been compelled, or he may have simply stepped over the chain and wandered up the dirt path for no good reason at all. Nevertheless he did walk off the road, step over the chain, and wander up the dirt path to the remains of Joy Furnace—the stacked-stone foundations of five massive kilns in a row, perfectly aligned, each base twenty-plus feet wide, twenty-plus feet deep, each wall rising two full stories, the front and rear walls pierced by arched portals high enough, wide enough, for even a Minotaur to come and go with ease. It took the Minotaur's breath. The tomblike beauty of the structures, each capped by crumbling brickwork, looking parapet-like from below. Or maybe they are plinths waiting patiently in the woods for whatever they're meant to bear. Abandoned. All abandoned now. They took his breath.

The Minotaur stumbled on, those years ago, past the sole information placard mounted on waist-high posts in the grass. He did not see the faded photograph of the scale model of what Joy Furnace probably looked like in the industry's heyday. Didn't read the paragraph about Henceforth Joy, the namesake of the village that grew (just down the river) around the success of the business. Henceforth Joy did not survive the voyage across the ocean; her father never recovered from her death. But Joy Furnace thrived for decades, then in its ruined glory drew buffs and hobbyists for another ten years. The town itself struggles. The Minotaur missed, too, that last paragraph, the one staking the claims: "Lime is a key ingredient in other industries that touch our lives—making steel, paper, and glass, refining sugar, and tanning leather." Though most of this text was obscured by a Sharpie drawing of an overly endowed stick figure and its own claim: "Tommi has the biggest dick of all."

The Minotaur ignored it all and walked right through the arched doorway of the center kiln. Walked onto the cooling floor, where the quicklime was spread before being shoveled into wheelbarrows. The Minotaur looked around. What architectural black magic was this? The kiln's foundation, from the outside, was square. Exactingly square. But inside, eight uniform walls surrounded the Minotaur. The octagon. The geometric dance between circle and square. The give-and-take between heaven and earth. Liminal and everlasting. That day the Minotaur stood in the center of the holy space, his heavy boots crunching on the black pellets of coke, the crumbled rock, and looked up. Eight uniform walls of stacked stone rose high over his horned noggin. Skinks and beetles scurried in the cracks. Weeds rooted in the crevices. Up the Minotaur looked to a perfectly round disk of blue sky.

"Unngh," he said that day, and sat down.

• • •

"Unngh," he says this day, and sits down. Presses his back against the mortared stone. Lets his horns touch there, too. A few generations ago, humans stoked the fires overhead; two thousand degrees stormed and raged, belching black smoke high into the sky, vomiting chalky white lime onto the earth. Men and animals labored and died in the process. Lifetimes. A drop in the bucket of what the Minotaur knows.

The fire is gone. The stone was stone before chisel, before hammer, and after. Mortar is only wishful thinking. The stone walls keep all the secrets. The Minotaur cut his eyeteeth amid stone. He knows well its loyalty. The Minotaur comes to Joy Furnace when he wants to remember nothing. To foresee nothing.

This day, his life in pending upheaval, Old Scald Village and all its people likely behind him, the Minotaur wants nothing. Nothingness. For the moment. The Minotaur sits, his bull head at rest in the ruinous kiln, this mouth of rock, and lets the torrential silence overtake him.

Sits. And sits.

The day does as days do. And in passing leaves the Minotaur alone.

• • •

Alone, that is, except for the stinkbug that lumbers over his pant leg as if it were a veritable mountain. Alone, that is, except for the hive of busy wasps coming and going from a hole in the far wall, perfect in their industry. Alone, except for the king snake and the copperhead staking out territories in the kiln's nooks and crannies, waiting for the field mouse, waiting for the fledgling robin to topple out of its nest on an overhead ledge, not quite sure what flying means yet, is yet—could flight be the mouth of this reptile, its binding hold? Alone, but for the shadows that slice the blue circle of day overhead from time to time. Here a titmouse, there a hawk, a buzzard. Alone. Except for the beast that crawls up out of the noonhour.

The Minotaur hears it first. A creature on approach, coming from the highway. What rough beast is this, slouching up the sloped path to Joy Furnace? A labored grunt, then a squeaking and creaking; the thud of something not quite foot; breath heavy, shallow, constricted; some dragged thing, then a pause.

The Minotaur is not afraid. The grunt, the rattle, the thud, the wheeze—everything gets louder as the creature draws nigh. But drawing nigh takes its toll on the clock, in the universe of near-silence inside the abandoned kiln. The Minotaur listens long into the day. A small-scale clamor and clang. A manageable din. The Minotaur refuses to speculate. Clunk and scrape. Crank, wait. The Minotaur is not afraid. Really. The Minotaur is, however, human enough. Man enough. He looks, after all.

It is hard to peek, what with those horns, that snout. But the Minotaur tries. He cocks his head along the arch of the kiln's portal. The horn tips emerge first; there's no other way. Whatever makes the sound, whatever comes, is close.

Is close. Is closer. Is—can it be?—something of a man. The Minotaur sees him. The man (manlike) doesn't see the Minotaur. The man is too busy struggling up onto the low slab of stone at the mouth of the far kiln. He struggles because of the prosthetic leg, a booted apparatus that telescopes from beneath his pant leg just below the knee. He struggles because of the absent arm, the uniform sleeve pinned at the shoulder. That arm, that missing arm, flails in its immense void. The man, the soldier, struggles. The fat cylinder of oxygen weighing down his backpack.

And the face, the remnants of face. All this, though, merely glimpsed. The manlike creature enters the far kiln. The Minotaur hears him settle in against the stone wall. The Minotaur listens as the soldier's breath slows, eases into peace. The Minotaur breathes his own breath. The Minotaur and the man sit together, apart, and breathe long into the night. They share a rancorous kinship. The worn-out scapegoat of an ancient tale and this modern-day myth. The hero-soldier left to rot after his duty is done. The furnace stones bear these manifest burdens stoically.

At some point the Minotaur looks up. The moon is making its rocky and yellow sally across the black circle of night sky. The Minotaur hopes the man is looking up.

CHAPTER TWELVE

IT IS DAWN WHEN THE MINOTAUR comes back down Business 220. His woolen pants and jacket—those telltale signs of his status as a living-history reinterpreter—are dew damp. Cold and scratchy. The other soldier, the damaged man, may have left Joy Furnace earlier. Or he may still be there. It's not the Minotaur's place to question. To pass judgment. To grant salvation. It is not the Minotaur's place. It is not the Minotaur.

He walks the quiet roadway. The mountain comes to life slowly above him, shouldering up the sun, tucking in and rolling out the shadows. He is in no hurry. It is only Tuesday, and the rest of his murky existence lies ahead. Just beyond a bend in the road the Judy-Lou Motor Lodge comes into view. Its pitched metal roof, painted a leafy green, beckons. *Come home.*

The Minotaur will slip into Room #3, will close the curtain, the blinds, will strip out of his damp uniform, will make whatever contortions necessary to fit into the cramped tub. It is only Tuesday. He will soak for as long as it takes. The Minotaur focuses. He will not be distracted. He will not look across the macadam. He will not look over the Chili Willie's parking lot at Pygmalia-Blades, at Danny Tanneyhill's pickup truck and the gargantuan tree trunk (so much larger than the last) that seems to have toppled from the truck bed and cants precariously, looming overtop the wooden bestiary. He will not look.

"Hey."

"Unngh," the Minotaur says, not in answer. Rather as a deflection. He will not hear.

"Hey."

Slightly louder. No matter. The Minotaur will not hear. He stoops to pick up some litter from the mouth of the Judy-Lou's drive. The blackest crow in existence takes wing from a hemlock bough high on Scald Mountain, hurtles down the slope, pulling the rest of the sun up over the ridge line. The crow lights on the peak of the Pygmalia-Blades tent. Caws its nasty caw. The Minotaur has no choice.

"Unngh," he says, and crosses the road.

The Minotaur approaches the truck with caution.

"Hey," the voice says, "can you help a brother out?"

It's Danny Tanneyhill. He's pinned between the massive log and the truck's tailgate.

The Minotaur can be decisive when necessary. He decided to leave behind what he left behind back in Joy Furnace. Here in the Chili Willie's parking lot, the suffering is more acute. It is not in the Minotaur's nature to overthink. He decides, for the moment, not to leave the man trapped beneath the tree. In the night the chainsaw artist had returned with an oak too big for his own good. He had grappled with its girth and lost. The tree is limbless. The fresh cuts where the branches were removed glare like pale little suns frozen in orbit around the trunk. Everything stinks of sawdust and motor oil. Smells, too, like trespass. Like ill-gotten gain. This pinning may very well be an act of revenge. But there is no visible blood.

"Yo," Danny Tanneyhill says, "there's a pry bar over behind my G.I. Joe."

It takes the Minotaur a minute to understand, but he finds the thick iron rod easily enough. The carved army man offers no resistance.

The rudiments of physics come easily to the Minotaur, and his strength is what it is. He eyes the situation, drags a low stump into place to serve as fulcrum, wedges the pry bar between the stump and the fat oak trunk at just the right spot, and heaves.

"Unngh," the Minotaur says.

The oak rises, enough. The bare-chested chainsaw artist slithers out, as if he were simply resting.

"Damn," Danny Tanneyhill says, shaking his booted foot.

Something around his neck rattles. The Minotaur can't help looking. Doesn't try not to look. It's a chainsaw blade, polished up, worn as a necklace. Behind the teeth, a long scar swoops down along the ridge of Danny Tanneyhill's ribcage.

"Damn," Danny Tanneyhill says again. "That was close. Thanks, man. I owe you one."

One what? the Minotaur wonders. "Mmmnn," he says.

"You want a beer?" Danny asks, fishing in a cooler.

"Mmmnn, no."

Danny Tanneyhill takes a small pot from an unlit camp stove, reaches toward the Minotaur. "Hot dog?"

Half a dozen weenies bob beneath the water's surface, here and there nosing through a scrim of congealed fat. The Minotaur takes one. "Thanks," he says. He takes a bite. It is not a tentative bite.

The Minotaur starts to leave, but Danny Tanneyhill asks for more. "Could you give me a hand?" he says, already straining into the oak. "I want to stand this son of a bitch up."

The Minotaur helps. On the third try, they stand the son of a bitch up and prop it against the bed of the truck.

"Hold tight," Danny says, and leaves the Minotaur in a balancing act.

As Danny walks up the short ramp of the Pygmalia-Blades trailer, the Minotaur sees his bare back, sees the maze of pocks and dents in the man's flesh from lying in the gravel all night.

Danny returns with a coil of fat hemp rope and begins tying a knot.

"Let me just . . . ," he says.

Danny Tanneyhill loops and knots the rope, talking all the while.

"Got to get it . . . ," he says.

Talking all the while, and eyeballing the Minotaur standing right next to the giant tree trunk. As if . . .

"A few more . . . ," he says.

"Somebody was banging on your door last night," he says.

The Minotaur pricks up his ears.

"Couldn't see who," he says. "I was stuck under this fucking tree."

The Minotaur thinks, *Hurry.*

"They pounded for a long time. I'm surprised Neti-pot didn't come out, guns a-blazin'."

The Minotaur leaves before the last knot is cinched tight.

"I owe you one!" Danny Tanneyhill calls out again.

"Unngh," the Minotaur says. He doesn't want it. He turns to tip his horns ever so slightly. And it might be the horrible potential he sees inside the towering oak trunk, the monstrosity teeming just beneath the bark, or it may be the glare, the sunlight captured and reflected from the saw blade hanging around Danny Tanneyhill's neck. Whatever the case the Minotaur walks right across Business 220 without looking.

It is hard to miss a half-man half-bull. Fortunately the driver of the vintage pristinely restored AMC Matador is paying attention. The car skids and swerves. The Minotaur jumps.

The driver hollers loud enough for all to hear, "Watch where you're going, asshole!"

The Minotaur watches the man's arm and hand and middle finger wave furiously all the way down Business 220.

Even before he gets to the door of Room #3, the Minotaur sees evidence of the night's visitor. It's a little round pan covered in foil, sitting on the sidewalk directly in front of his door. If he'd been just slightly more rattled by the near-miss on the road, the Minotaur could've easily stepped right over, or more likely right into, the offering.

The Minotaur catches his breath, stoops to look. It's a pie pan. The Minotaur sniffs the air. He doesn't want to get his hopes up. He holds that breath of his until the door to Room #3 is closed and the safety chain is fully engaged. Until the gift sits safely on the narrow desktop. Then, with the care of a jeweler, of a sapper, even, in the act of defusing, the Minotaur lifts an edge of the foil.

The meringue is the most beautiful thing he's ever seen. Its swirls are perfect. Its peaks are browned perfectly. The Minotaur does not have to dig into the eggy surface to know what lies beneath. He can smell the butterscotch. He can feel Widow Fisk's fingertips in his mouth. No. Her name is Gwen. He will not make the mistake again. The Minotaur thinks her face to mind. It is called disappointment. He wonders about the gift. What if he had been at the door to accept it? What then?

Somewhere beneath the scent of butterscotch the Minotaur catches a whiff of sulfur. The paper mill's morning stink. He knows if he opens his door, if he listens carefully, he might hear Smitty's hammer ringing on the anvil. What if he just goes back to Old Scald Village anyway? Just shows up as if nothing happened? Just waltzes right back into the Gift Shoppe? He'd thank her for the pie. It's very possible, given what the Minotaur understands about humans, that he could simply step into denial, go back to work, take full part in the big weekend coming up. He could sit around the campfires where they boil up their hominy and hardtack, where the fatback burns to a crisp in the cast-iron skillets, where the flaps of the old canvas dog tents splay open to reveal the Domino's Pizza boxes gaping on top of the period-correct canvas cots, where droning fiddle tunes weave the night air. He could stay with the soldiers, the officers, the women, almost welcome, until they all break camp and go back to their accounting firms and custodial jobs, their kenneled Peekapoos and busted sump pumps. Then the Minotaur remembers the *Closed* sign on the Welcome Center's door. Remembers the scratchy intimacy between the broom maker's legs. It is also very likely that his return to the village would have other outcomes. The Minotaur knows this about humans, too. Besides, Minotaurs do not waltz.

He hears the Guptas come to life next door. The Minotaur thinks about the Judy-Lou Motor Lodge, the comforting regularity of laundry washing and folding, washing and folding, endless white sheets and pillowcases, thinks about maintenance, a plumbing job here, spackle and paint there. Every fall the gutters dredged of leaves and evergreen needles. Every spring some other necessary task. Staying here would be easy enough, thinks the Minotaur. The memories of Old Scald Village would soon be lost to the labyrinth of mind.

He picks up the butterscotch pie. It'll be his gift to the Guptas. His pledge. He won't take a single piece. Not even a bite. And though he couldn't pinpoint the reason why, the Minotaur opens the door to Room #3 cautiously. Snout first, cradling the pie, he eases back into the day.

But as soon as the Minotaur enters the office he knows something is amiss.

Rambabu Gupta rages into the telephone, his Urdu curses piling up on the floor. The Minotaur can understand nothing but the daughter's name: Bavishya! The Minotaur understands enough. Ramneek weeps, sitting stiff and upright in a lobby chair. She will not look at the Minotaur. In the back rooms the lights are off, but the regular flicker and the artificial laughter say enough.

The Minotaur sets the pie on the counter, where it is guarded by a painted lead Union soldier whose boots hold Judy-Lou business cards. The Minotaur looks in, sees Devmani in her diaper, her tiny fist clutching an empty Mickey Mouse sippy cup. He can't tell what's on television, but the girl is too rapt to notice him.

The Minotaur takes his pie and returns to Room #3. There, befuddled in the maze of doubt and uncertainty, future and past all balled up together, the Minotaur has no choice but to eat that pie.

CHAPTER THIRTEEN

NO SPOON. NO FORK. The Minotaur takes off his shirt and lets his fat tongue do the work. It's like Widow Fisk is in the room with him. Watching. The brown crust of meringue offers no resistance. But resistance comes nonetheless.

It is Tuesday, early morning, and the instant the bull buries his face deep in the butterscotch, a chainsaw roars to life across Business 220 and Danny Tanneyhill plunges his blade into the oak. When the Minotaur pauses, the chainsaw stops, too. Idles. Waits. The Minotaur licks his black lips and dives in again. And again the chainsaw revs up and bites into wood. The Minotaur cannot see Danny Tanneyhill at work, can only imagine the plumes of sawdust rooster-tailing in the morning sun and the beast that is unfurling from the oak. Nor can the overlord of Pygmalia-Blades see through the venetian blinds of Room #3, to the Minotaur and his mess. But each time one takes a bite the other makes a cut. Surely some hoodoo is under way. Some cosmic hocus-pocus. Some karmic skullduggery. What else could explain the synchronicity, and its perfectly timed disturbance?

Disturbance. Abruption. Cataclysm. Rift comes first in the form of sound. Noise. A ruckus of unusual scale, for a Tuesday morning in central Pennsylvania, along Business 220 in the shadow of Scald Mountain. The Minotaur, from inside Room #3, his gums caked with butterscotch custard and piecrust, recognizes the noise. Something mechanical has gone awry. And it's getting closer.

Closer. He opens the door cautiously. Danny Tanneyhill's chainsaw blade catches in a knot in the oak, binds, screeches to a halt. Everything stills, and from deep within the stillness, and from way down Business 220, from the direction of Homer's Gap, calamity appears. It is a minivan, white, hurtling down the road, ricocheting from side ditch to side ditch. The rattle and slap of metal torqued beyond its limits, the clank, calamitous for sure, testifying to what the Minotaur knows. A ball joint has seized in its socket.

"Unngh," the Minotaur says.

Smoke boils from the wheel well—right rear—and from the tire dragging flat over the blacktop. It is likely that the driver cannot tell why the van is out of control. They'll be lucky to get out of this alive, the Minotaur believes. He knows. He listens. The Guptas, too, all three with their heads out the office door. And Danny Tanneyhill with goggles covering his face, sawdust covering everything else, and a still-warm chainsaw dangling from one gloved hand. They all listen. They all watch the van—squealing and clattering—careen back and forth on the road. One side of Business 220 plummets through the trees toward Stink Creek; on the other side Scald Mountain stakes its claim with house-sized chunks of dolomite stone. Any route but the roadway could be deadly.

Ramneek shepherds her granddaughter back inside. She shouldn't see what may come.

Danny Tanneyhill moves closer to the action.

When it's clear that the minivan is barreling straight toward the Judy-Lou brick planter full of miniature American flags, Rambabu begins to wave his arms and insist on any other direction. "No, no!" he says in his best English. "No, no!"

And it works. The white van, a Honda Odyssey—dirty, filthy even—skids sideways, dips off the road into the motel lot, misses the brickwork by a hair's width or less (leaving the tiny flags all aflutter), whips back across Business 220, spins 360 degrees, and comes to a smoking stop half in and half out of the Chili Willie's parking lot, facing the Minotaur.

"Unngh," the Minotaur says, and drops the empty aluminum pie pan he's been clutching the entire time. Its clatter is deafening.

"Unngh," he says again.

The front end of the Odyssey juts fully into the road. Traffic is likely, inevitable, imminent.

The tractor trailer that chugs into sight, coming from the turnpike interchange, surprises no one. It blasts a warning from its air horn. The smoke and dust settle enough around the Odyssey for the Minotaur to see inside it. Through the windshield he expects to find terror, panic. The passenger, a boy, maybe a young man, flails about, waving his arms, shaking his head, making audible sounds. *Panic and terror*, the Minotaur thinks. Not the driver. No, not the driver.

She sits behind the steering wheel, gripping it tightly, a conflagration of red hair leaping, and those green eyes. How is it possible that the Minotaur can see that green?

The truck horn wails again, closer. Some things cannot be explained. The truck horn screams.

"No, no! No, no!" Rambabu Gupta says.

Those green eyes look out, look at the Minotaur, the shirtless horned half-man half-bull standing in the doorway of Room #3. It is not exactly fear he sees in those eyes. The Minotaur thinks to move, maybe to wave down the approaching semi, to push against the Odyssey, to help in some way. But before he can do so the girl, the woman, the driver, slams the gearshift into reverse and stomps the accelerator. With one rear wheel locked, the vehicle's backward trajectory is herky-jerky and loud, but move it does, in fits and starts, off the macadam and into Chile Willie's safe arms. And in the nick of time, too. The semi speeds by, its mammoth payload (a disassembled carnival ride, something spiderlike) rattles and yanks against the come-along pulleys and the webbing tie-downs that flap madly every inch of its journey. The truckdriver may have given a wolf whistle in passing.

As soon as the coast is clear, as soon as the threat of danger has passed, and even before the spray of gravel and dust settles, the woman breaks down, crying, heaving sobs. The minivan's passenger is out of his seat, out of sight in the rear of the Honda. The Minotaur sees the redhead reach back, crying still. The Minotaur wants to help. Rambabu Gupta plucks one tiny flag and crosses the road. A goggle-clad Danny Tanneyhill, chainsaw in hand, approaches the Odyssey.

"Mmmnn," the Minotaur says, and follows suit. He wants to help this woman in crisis. Wants to say the right thing. But his thick tongue, in perpetual bovoid torpor, gets left behind.

"Damn," the chainsaw artist says, wiping at the plastic shield. "Damn."

"It is a beautiful day after all," the motel proprietor says, maybe wiping tears from his eyes, and reaching out to offer the flag.

"Stay back!" the driver says like she means it. Tear-streaked face be damned, nosebleed notwithstanding, there is no frailty in her command. She's pointing something at them. The Minotaur squints, and though he tries to see it any other way he finally concludes that she is aiming the swooping neck and head of a concrete goose. Bang bang. Honk honk.

Rambabu wiggles the flag gently, a drooping gesture of peace. Danny Tanneyhill puts the chainsaw down, raises the goggles onto his forehead, and holds his palms up. There, shirtless as well, sweat and sawdust clotting his chest hairs and the glinting blade that hangs around his neck, the man looks glorious. *Like a god*, the Minotaur thinks. The Minotaur, his own bare chest and his dark seam flecked and smeared with pie, tiny crests of meringue at the rim of each deep nostril, is sure he looks less than godlike.

"Are you okay?" Danny asks.

"Mmmnn?" the Minotaur says, hoping it sounds like a question.

"Stay back," she says again from the driver's seat.

There is commotion in the van, a babbling, and an odd, irregular, and manic clinking. Something bouncing off of glass. She reaches back but is constrained by the seatbelt. The Minotaur and the others look on. Step closer. That's when the redhead gets out, puts herself between the Honda and the modest onslaught.

"I told you," she says, aiming the concrete goose head menacingly.

And though the young woman is slight and lean, standing with feet wide and rooted, tight skinny jeans, sandals, stars painted on her toenails, her tank top a soft gray and ribbed and (though the Minotaur feels a little guilty for noticing) clearly the only thing covering her small breasts, the way she wields that goose head, the muscles and tendons of her thin arm flexing just beneath the freckled flesh, the way her red hair claims space in the blue sky, the way the green fire rages in her eyes, the Minotaur and everybody else know they are in the presence of, what? Power? Change? A force of nature, no doubt.

"I'll break your goddamn . . . ," she says.

Her fist clenches the ridiculous weapon. Her whole body trembles. Everybody sees this. The redhead looks frantically back and forth between the van and her attackers.

"Took?" she says. "Are you okay?"

The van's passenger peeks up over the dashboard, his eyes flitting wildly, unable to land anywhere for long. He bobs, pistonlike, up and down. Into sight, out of sight.

"You are bleeding, missus," Rambabu says, touching his own upper lip.

"Can we help?" Danny Tanneyhill asks, scratching at and fiddling with his saw-blade necklace.

"Unngh," the Minotaur says, trying to be very still.

It is true enough. The trickle of blood traces a thin red trajectory from her nostrils, circumnavigates her parted lips, splits her chin down the middle—her throat, too, and sternum—and gets caught by the low neckline of her tank top. There the saturated fabric is darker, a tiny half-moon tipped on its side. The woman touches her lip, then her chin, licks her fingertip, looks more and more unsure.

That's when Ramneek steps up with a small bowl of warm water and a soft cloth. "This . . . ," Ramneek says, and her gentle touch is accepted.

Accepted by all except the boy in the van. As soon as the Indian woman touches the redhead, dabbing gently at her chin, the van door slams open, and from within a wild animal charges. A beast enraged. Growling. Snapping its teeth. Flailing its arms.

"Tooky," the redhead says. "No."

Wild eyed. Like a feral dog just loosed. And bleeding from a deep gouge in his forehead.

"Tooky," she says, reaching out.

No. Not blood. A scar. The wound is much older. It is a deep purple scar. An off-kilter triangle of ridged flesh. A mislaid third eye on his forehead.

"No, Took."

But he will not be deterred in coming to the redhead's defense. Ramneek Gupta looks afraid. Rambabu steps close.

"Fuckedy fuck fucks!" the boy says.

"Sissyyyyyyy," the boy says.

"Fuckerrrrrrrrrrs!"

"No, Took," the redhead says. "It's okay."

But the boy's fury is in full throttle. He runs, arms outstretched, the blaze on his forehead verily pulsing, runs raging straight into Danny Tanneyhill. The boy ricochets, bounces off of the half-naked and sawdust-encrusted man and into the Minotaur, who stands shirtless, his thick snout smeared with meringue and butterscotch pie filling. The boy, thwarted, falls to the macadam, looks up into the strange faces of the Minotaur and the woodcarver as if seeing them finally, fully. The anger in his face gives way to terror.

"Arrahhh!"

The boy cries. The boy tries to get away. The boy crabwalks backward, his utterance unfettered by words, a hymn to fear.

"Tookus!" the redhead says, rushing to comfort. "It's okay."

Crabwalks, the boy, right under the Pygmalia-Blades canopy and bumps full force into the biggest totem pole there. A crouching bear holds up the head of a buffalo, atop which is perched a spread-winged eagle with a giant fish in its giant talons. The pole wobbles. The pole rocks. The pole, several hundred pounds of wooden monster, begins its topple, and the boy is beneath, right in the landing zone.

Time stands still. No one moves. No one except the Minotaur.

"Unngh," he says when the totem pole hits his bullish shoulder, the rough wood digging into gray flesh. Gravity chocked for the moment.

"Unngh," he says, widening his stance to bear the load.

"Unngh," he says as the redhead helps her brother move clear.

"Damn," Danny Tanneyhill says, stepping up. "That was close. You all right?"

He's asking the redhead.

She sits on the ground with the boy leaning into her. She strokes his head and coos, "Shhh, shhh."

"Gaarrrrgh," the boy says. "Fuckerssssss."

He seems to be calming.

"Unngh," the Minotaur says, struggling to manhandle the totem pole safely to the asphalt.

"Hey," the redhead says to the woodcarver, "help the guy out."

Danny Tanneyhill does as he is told.

The redhead sits, rubbing at the boy's temples, cooing into his ear. His scar pulses. She looks at the Minotaur, his scar. No. She sees the odd pattern on his gray flesh, where the bark pressed hard into his shoulder. The oak imposing on the beast.

"Thank you," the redhead says. "Thank you, thank you, thank you."

"Mmmnn," the Minotaur says, feeling suddenly very exposed.

"My name's Holly," she says.

"This is Tookus," she says, patting the young man sweetly, as if he were a new puppy. She hums almost inaudibly, the tiniest of sounds.

The Guptas fade into the background. The Minotaur leans in, wanting to hear more. Tookus calms. Tookus looks at the Minotaur. Reaches toward him. The Minotaur thinks the boy wants to touch his scar (they do from time to time, certain people), but no. Tookus plucks something from the furrow of steel gray hairs between the Minotaur's pectorals. The Minotaur and Holly watch the boy sniff it. Piecrust, or meringue, with a fleck of butterscotch filling. Tookus eats it. The Minotaur suddenly feels the entirety of his semi-naked, part-human, messy self. Holly just chuckles.

"Buuuuttttterrrrr," the boy says. "Scotch scotch scotch."

"This is my little brother, Tookus," she repeats. "And we are very grateful. Though it looks like we caught you in the middle of something." Holly is grinning, mischief in her eyes, and looking at the Minotaur's pie-flecked snout.

"Hey, there," the woodcarver says, jutting his sawdust-covered arm into the space. "I'm Danny."

Holly pauses long enough for it to be a thing, then shakes Danny's hand. "Stop looking at my tits," Holly says, pointing at the carver.

Danny Tanneyhill turns away, smirking.

"Titties," the boy says. "Tittie tittie tittie."

"Shhh," Holly says. "Be quiet, Tookus."

But it's too much to ask. Something has tipped inside her damaged younger brother. All the fear of the accident giving way. Funny bone. Funny.

"Titties," he says, giggling so hard he can barely get the word out. "Tittie tittie tittie."

Tookus turns his head, tries to bite his sister's breast. Holly squirms out of reach. Tookus makes a grab and finds his mark.

"Titties," he says.

Eventually Holly calms her brother down.

"I don't know what happened," she says, turning toward the Odyssey.

"Um, ball joint," the Minotaur says, finally, thankfully, able to help. He knows without doubt what went wrong.

Danny Tanneyhill jockeys for position. "It sounded to me like—"

"Ball joint!" the Minotaur says again, louder. "Ball joint seized."

Holly stands and helps Tookus to his feet. She's been holding the concrete goose head the whole time, and when she tucks it into her back pocket, when the denim draws tight over her round behind, the spell (old and tired but no less potent) is cast. The Minotaur's eye twitches. Danny Tanneyhill clears his throat. They both move a little closer, and each is fully aware of where the other stands.

"Come on," she says, probably to her brother, but they all follow.

•　•　•

Crises averted, though the landscape has been altered in many ways, some more perceptible than others. Time becomes a little less persnickety.

The Minotaur goes back to Room #3, cleans himself up. Tuesday morning slips into Tuesday afternoon, and somewhere along the way the redhead, Holly, kicks at the Odyssey's still-hot rear wheel and curses. Tookus, her brother, sits in the van's open side door. The young man's arms fling hither and yon with no discernable rhythm or reason; too, his scarred head jerks and twitches this way and that, after nothing whatsoever. He sits there dropping the loose change that spilled during the earlier hullabaloo along Business 220 back into the five-gallon glass carboy nearly full with nickels, dimes, and quarters, sits there almost smiling, speaking his mind (as if he has a choice). Though there is some discernment at work.

Whenever Danny Tanneyhill, the woodcarver, comes near, Tookus speaks one way: "Dick dick dooo-dooo head. Shit licker, booger eater. Fuckerrrr."

When the Minotaur passes, Tookus sings a different song: "Butter-scotch piieeeeeee. Punkin' piieeeeeeee. Apple piieeeeeeee."

Holly comes over once or twice to comfort him, to quiet him, and only then does the boy quiet. But still he pushes.

"Titties," he says, and tries to grab a handful.

"Shhh, Tookus. Settle down." She removes his hand, kisses it.

All the while, the rest mill about. The Guptas huddle up and talk; Ramneek cradles the little bowl full of blood-tinted water like an offering; Rambabu strokes his thick black mustache. Danny Tanneyhill tries to talk about his work, but nobody listens; he offers the pot of cold hot dogs but finds no takers.

Turns out the brother and sister are traveling with all their worldly possessions: the Honda Odyssey and its contents—a couple suitcases, a few books, a concrete goose statue (the neck snapped off when the van spun in the road) belonging to their dead grandmother (Tookus insisted it come along), and a big jug of pocket change Holly saved from year after greasy year of waiting tables at Snarky's Six Packs & Subs. Turns out that's about all they have.

There are negotiations that the Minotaur isn't privy to. The Guptas open their hearts. The Guptas lead Holly by the hand to the door of Room

#7, with its new pillows and billowy curtains, the cleansing cloud of incense. The Guptas offer the stranded travelers, the wanderers—Rambabu says the word *yatri*, and Ramneek clucks approval—deep discounts at the Judy-Lou Motor Lodge. "Clean bathrooms. Comfortable beds. Free Wi-Fi." Only the Minotaur knows what their offering means.

Way up on the mountain the turnpike roars its indifference. Old Scald Village is still just down the road, but the Minotaur can't see it. He can't see anything but the undercarriage of the Honda Odyssey. No. He sees purpose. It looks better, even, than his battlefield deaths.

Late afternoon finds the van perched catawampus on a jack and three wheels, finds a toolbox open on a thick blanket, the sockets and wrenches polished and gleaming, finds the Minotaur on that same blanket sprawled underneath the vehicle. All anyone can see of him is legs. *Purpose*, he thinks. *Purpose*.

Devmani, the granddaughter, watches the whole scene unfold, sitting cross-legged on the sidewalk right by the office door. During that time she retrieves the Minotaur's (mostly) empty aluminum pie pan, drags her skinny brown fingers across its bottom until it is clean, then licks. She finds an old room key and pokes two eyeholes, pretends it's a mask. Then, for a long while, she wears it as a hat. Lords over all like a tinfoil *baba*, like an aluminous rani. But the pie pan keeps falling off, no matter how she bends and crimps it. Eventually Devmani gives up.

• • •

Up. The Minotaur looks up, his nose nearly pressed against the Odyssey's grimy muffler. He's had the wheel and the damaged parts disassembled for a while, has named them all: the crosstie, the knuckle, the toe control arm, the strut and shock absorber, etc. As long as he's there, on his back, under the Honda, breathing in the smells of miles traveled, the Minotaur may as well inspect the exhaust system. Rattle and clank.

It is a world view that he knows well, feels good in. On his back beneath the vehicle, all that is seeable is contained in the squashed rectangle of space between the undercarriage and the ground, and he sees it bottom up, head over heels, topsy-turvy, arsy-varsy.

When the door closes across Business 220 the Minotaur tweaks his head to look, to watch her come from Room #7. It is Holly, no doubt, the red hair, and now a red dress that she moves fluidly within. The Minotaur stills himself. She could be going anywhere, about to do anything. She crosses the road into the Chili Willie's lot. Less and less of her is visible as she approaches. Gone, her face. Gone, her chest, her waist, her thighs. The Minotaur picks up a wrench, any old wrench, searches urgently for a nut.

"Hey," Holly says, nudging the Minotaur's calf with her sandaled toe. The stars there, painted on blue-polished nails, make perfect sense in this world. Arsy-varsy. Topsy-turvy. If the Odyssey weren't above him, the mass of nothingness overhead would come down and crush the Minotaur where he lies.

He emerges from under the Honda slowly, so as not to snag his horns. And just as slowly finds more and more of Holly there. Her legs, her torso, that face, those eyes.

"Is it bad?" she asks.

"Unngh," he says. It is. "Mmmnn, not so."

He stands, dusts himself off. The Minotaur wants to explain the ball-joint apparatus to Holly. He wishes he had more tools, a better tongue. The Minotaur wants something to occupy his hands, so he picks up the brake calipers. They fit well in his grip.

"Thanks again," Holly says. She looks intently, unflinchingly, at the Minotaur.

"Mmmnn?" he says.

"For saving Tookus's ass," she says. "I swear, that boy . . . " She doesn't finish the sentence.

Holly squats and peers beneath the van. The Minotaur tries not to look at the way her backside fills out the thin cotton dress. When she comes back from her squat, Holly points at the Minotaur's shoulder, covered now in his soldier's jacket.

"Are you okay?" she asks. "That stupid pole . . . "

Then Danny Tanneyhill appears. "Yo, yo, cyborg," he says, pointing at the brake mechanism dangling from the Minotaur's hand. "We come in peace."

"Unngh," the Minotaur says, dropping his handful to the blanket.

"You look different," Danny says to Holly. The tone has intention.

"And you're still looking at my tits," Holly says. But even the Minotaur can tell that she's looking at Danny's chest, at the saw blade and the deep scar beneath it. He's brushed the sawdust from his face and body.

Danny Tanneyhill laughs, gets on his knees, and looks at the Honda's wheel well. "You're doing a great job," he says. "Keep it up."

"Unngh," the Minotaur says. He wants to talk about the Odyssey.

"Where's, um, your brother?" Danny asks.

"Tookus is asleep," Holly says. "I had to give him a double dose of medicine, after what happened. Not that it's any of your business."

Holly tucks a strand of red hair over one ear, dabs at the sweat on her upper lip. The Minotaur wishes she'd left both alone. He starts putting the sockets back into their red plastic tray, in order of size.

"Come over when he wakes up," Danny Tanneyhill says. "I'm cooking mountain pies. We'll have a good feed."

Holly kneels, picks up a wrench, and hands it to the Minotaur. She's not answering on purpose.

"Of course," Danny says, "you could feast on M&Ms and Cheetos from the vending machine. I hear they're top shelf."

"Mountain pies?" Holly says. She slips a small box-end wrench on her index finger and spins it round and round. "What the hell is a mountain pie?"

"There's only one way to find out," Danny Tanneyhill says.

"Hmmm," Holly answers, and looks back and forth between the woodcarver and the man-bull.

"You, too, big boy," Danny says to the Minotaur. "Come one, come all."

"Mmmnn."

• • •

It is Tuesday at Old Scald Village. Everyone is preparing for the up-coming Encampment Weekend. The Minotaur does not have to be there to know that Biddle is sitting in his Cooper's Shack on a low stool, sitting by the bucket of wet staves, trying to stay awake. Knows, the Minotaur, even in his absence, that the handful of interns from Allegheny Community College are probably getting high in the Old Round Schoolhouse, and that afterward they'll go either to Sojourner's Tavern for fresh cider and donuts or to the hayloft in Riggle's Barn, where they'll do things that young people like to do to each other. The Minotaur knows Smitty. Knows the fires are stoked, that the bellows heaves madly, the hammer pounds and pounds. Smitty, on Tuesday, makes nails. The Minotaur feels sure that Destiny, the broom maker, is on her stave horse. The Minotaur smells her there. As for Widow Fisk, the Minotaur can only hope.

• • •

It is Tuesday, near dusk. Night creeps in and strips colors from the scene. Everything is purplish. There have been many Tuesdays in the Minotaur's life. He wonders how this one will end. The Minotaur stands in the cramped bathroom and scrubs the grease from beneath his nails. He goes to the window and looks across Business 220, sees Danny Tanneyhill stack several logs into a pyramid inside of a fire pit made out of a cut-down metal drum. The minivan is still on its jack. Its owners are nowhere to be seen. The Minotaur returns to the sink, his scrub brush. It is Tuesday. Room #3 at the Judy-Lou Motor Lodge is smaller than it was the day before.

Soon enough there is commotion down the row of rooms. The Minotaur hears Tookus first.

"Dark. Ddddark. Black ass. Moony moon."

The Minotaur parts the blinds to watch Holly and her brother scurry across the road. She leads him by one hand. His other swings about madly. The Minotaur takes a dab of toothpaste and polishes the buttons on his soldier's jacket. By the time he crosses over to Pygmalia-Blades the fire rages in its pit. The Minotaur smells the gasoline residue.

"Pull up a chair, hotshot," Danny says. "Make yourself at home."

"Peeecan piieeeeeee," Tookus says.

The Minotaur is adaptable, above all else. But sometimes the process is slow, glacial in its movement. There are no chairs around the Pygmalia-Blades fire. Just stumps and benches made of logs, dragged into a semicircle.

Tookus stands at the canopy's edge, running a finger over the swells and muscles of the Hulk carving. All of them.

"Green. Green fucker. Fucking green fuck. Dick green ass green. Green asshole."

Holly sits on a low stump close to her brother, the yellowish incandescence from the droplights pooling in the red dress that is pooling between her thighs. She sits looking doubtfully at Danny Tanneyhill, who is opening his four mountain-pie makers on a card table just inside the trailer. The Minotaur sits opposite; he doesn't want to crowd anyone. If asked the Minotaur might say that he thinks gravity pulls harder at night. That the whole earth, on its wobbly axis, whips quicker through a sunless sky. It sure feels that way. But nobody is going to ask. The Minotaur is grateful for the pop and crackle of the fire and the low buzz from the hanging lamps. Things rustle all over the darkening mountain. Crepuscular things venturing out of their dens, while the diurnal creatures tuck in for the night. The Minotaur envies both. Time to eat, time to sleep, time to rut. No time for nonsense. The neon *Vacancy* sign in the Judy-Lou office window flickers on and begins its syrupy pulse. Even Business 220 seems to be nodding off.

Danny Tanneyhill steps into the middle of their circle with two bottles of beer clenched between the fingers of his left hand. He offers first to Holly, who grunts softly, twists off the cap, and chugs the bottle empty.

"Damn, I needed that," she says, and reaches for the other beer.

The carver whistles his approval and lets Holly take the second bottle.

"How about you, big boy?" he asks the Minotaur.

"Mmmnn, no," the Minotaur says. "Water."

"Help yourself," Danny says, returning to the pies. "In the cooler."

Mountain pies are not complicated. In fact much of the appeal is rooted in their (nostalgia-oozing) back-to-nature simplicity. The pie makers are two heavy metal rods hinged at one end (wooden handles at the other), and near the hinge a pair of cast-iron wells that close together to form a compartment just the right size for two slices of bread and the filling of your choice. Butter the bread, layer or spoon in your filler, close up tight, and put the business end into the fire for half a dozen minutes, give or take.

The Minotaur has had his fair share of mountain pies. Or maybe not. He watches Danny Tanneyhill spray each cast-iron well with a can of PAM, lay in slices of Wonder Classic White, two pieces of yellow American cheese, some kind of thick tomato product from a can, then one hot dog per, halved, then quartered, on a dirty cutting board. Everything smells of sawdust and motor oil. The Minotaur isn't convinced that this should be Holly's first time with mountain pies.

Across the road the office door opens. Devmani laughs her little-girl laugh. Her grandfather makes silly faces and nonsense sounds. Devmani laughs even louder.

Danny Tanneyhill sticks all four pie irons into the fire pit. "Prepare yourselves," he says, "for the shock and awe."

"Whatever you say," Holly answers.

Tookus pokes the wooden backside of a giant carved rooster and repeats the word *chickenshit* over and over.

"Mmmnn," the Minotaur says. The pies, as they sizzle and steam in their cast-iron prisons, don't smell as bad as he expected.

"Tooky,'" Holly says, "it's time to eat. Come sit by me."

The boy sits, if you can call it sitting, on a twin-trunked stump with a plank bench. The boy (or young man) moves unceasingly (arms and head in motion, legs treadling nonstop), so it is hard to get a read on his age. Then there is the scar, the deep gouge in his forehead.

Danny Tanneyhill taps the golden brown pies one at a time onto paper plates.

"Goat. Ga-ga-ga-goat fuckerrrrrrr," Tookus says, and makes a face at the woodcarver.

"Shhh," Holly says.

"Shhhhhhh," Tookus says.

"The Honda's fucked, isn't it?" she asks, looking right at the Minotaur.

"No," the Minotaur says. "Not so—"

"Here you go," the woodcarver says, thrusting plates and pies between the Minotaur and Holly. "Might be the best thing you ever put in your mouth," he says to the redhead.

"Not likely," Holly says with both sass and defiance.

Tookus bites first, and rakes the roof of his mouth with his tongue. "Hot hot hooooot," he says, much of the crumbly pie spilling to the pavement.

Holly dabs at his chin with a napkin. "Blow on it first," she says. Takes her own first bite slowly.

"What did I tell you?" Danny Tanneyhill says. "Better than sex, right?"

The Minotaur can see it clearly. Holly is grateful for the food. Just enough.

"Best thing I ever put in my mouth," she says.

The Minotaur watches her lick tomato sauce from her lips.

"So what do you think?" Holly asks again, looking at the Minotaur.

He wants to tell her what he knows about gravity. He wants to agree with her about the mountain pies. What he does, though, is struggle through the description of what happened to the Odyssey's right rear wheel, and what it will take to fix it.

"Goddamn it," Holly mumbles, and gives Tookus a swig from her beer.

"Don't worry," Danny says. "We'll get you fixed up in no time. You can stay here for as long as you want. We'll take good care of you." The chainsaw artist means most of what he says.

"No," Holly says. "I can't . . . we can't stay. We can't . . . "

She doesn't finish. It's like the statement is too big. For the moment. For her mouth. For their lives. Neither Danny Tanneyhill nor the Minotaur presses.

The Minotaur does, however, rise from his stump and head through the lot toward the motel.

"Hey," Holly says. "Where're you going?"

"B-b-b-back in a minute," the Minotaur says.

He knows that they're watching him walk into the Judy-Lou office, and they're looking even closer when he returns with two Tupperware containers. The Minotaur sets them on the table by the empty pie makers. Holly and Danny step up to see. Tookus goes to the outer ring of the statuary and begins to thump the nose of an Indian chief.

The Minotaur opens the lid of one container. "*Saag paneer*," he says. And the words fit so well in his mouth, slip so easily off his thick tongue, he says them again. "*Saag paneer*. Spinach with cheese curd."

"Hmmm," Danny says.

"Oh, my," Holly says.

The Minotaur opens the second container. "*Aloo gobi. Aloo gobi.*" He wishes he'd brought some naan, sure that the buttery flatbread would make fine pies.

Danny Tanneyhill bristles. "Let's see what you've got," he says, throwing down his modest culinary gauntlet.

Wonder Bread notwithstanding, the Minotaur makes his version of mountain pies, and the redhead verily swoons with the first bite.

"Tookus," she says, "come get some of this."

Danny Tanneyhill takes a big bite. His face concedes defeat. "Look at you go," he says to the Minotaur. "Saving the day again."

"Mmmnn," the Minotaur says.

They all eat silently for a while, because the pies are that good. Way up Scald Mountain an air horn bellows on the turnpike. Higher still the constellations stage their monotonous dramas in the moonless night. Back on earth conversation meanders around the fire. Danny Tanneyhill tells a joke about a pig farmer. Holly groans, and the Minotaur simply doesn't get it. Holly tells a dead baby joke. Danny laughs. The Minotaur is outgunned, even by the least of them, at the business of speech. He finds himself preoccupied, searching for beasts and creatures amid the constellations of freckles on the redhead's pale arms. As for the stars painted on her toenails, they're too bright for the Minotaur to look at.

The Minotaur makes another round of pies. Tookus eats his on the move, walking from statute to statue, pausing in front of each, human or otherwise. At every stop the boy takes a nibble of pie, crosses himself, says, "Body of Christ, bodddyyy of Christ," then presses the pie to wooden lips. When the boy completes his round the Minotaur is there, next in line to receive the sacrament. But when Tookus steps up, his pie is gone. The boy has eaten it all. Tookus licks his lips and lowers his head. The wooden beings make the Minotaur anxious. Tookus doesn't. Even still, the moment has an edge.

Holly seems about to speak. But Tookus acts. Acts. With both hands, two fingers up and slightly crooked, Tookus makes horn shapes at his temples. He moos. Softly.

"Mooooooo," Tookus says. "Moooooo."

"Mmmnn," the Minotaur says.

"Mooooooo," Tookus says. "Moooooo."

The boy reaches out and takes the Minotaur's horns, pulls their foreheads together.

"Mmmooooooo. Mmmooooooo."

"Mmmnn," the Minotaur says, held tight in that grip.

The boy rocks his scarred head against the bony expanse between the Minotaur's horns. Finds comfort there. Scald Mountain unfolds into the night sky.

"Mmmnn, good. Goooood. Goooood boy," Tookus says, laughing the sweetest laugh, releasing the horns, and giving the Minotaur's snout a playful tap.

The Minotaur makes a sound that almost passes for laughter.

"Hmmm," Holly says. "Who'da thunk it?"

Danny Tanneyhill clucks his tongue and goes into the trailer and comes out with a small fabric pouch holding a little glass pipe and a baggie of weed.

"Shall we go a bit deeper into this lovely evening?" he asks.

Holly looks at her brother, who has already moved on, and shrugs. The carver is already loading the pipe anyway.

"Why not?" she says.

Danny passes the lit pipe along. The Minotaur scrounges up some more wood for the fire. Tookus is pinching away at the cedar nipples of the only mermaid for miles around.

"Boobies. Boooooobieeeees."

"Took," Holly says. "Come here."

The boy settles, sort of, on the stump beside his sister. She takes a deep hit and blows the smoke gently into his face.

"You sure about that?" Danny Tanneyhill asks.

"I'm not sure about much of anything, but I know this won't hurt him."

Tookus squeezes his eyes shut tight, then squeezes both of Holly's breasts.

"Boobies. Sissy boobies."

"Damn it, Took! Stop it."

He sulks away, and she loosens the cotton dress from her chest. Offers the pipe to the Minotaur.

"Mmmnn, no," he says.

"You've got yourself a handful," Danny Tanneyhill says "With the boy, I mean."

"I guess I do," Holly says. She brings her pouting brother back into the circle of light, gets him to sit on the asphalt in front of her. Holly takes a cell phone from a pocket, and some earbuds. She wiggles them into Tookus's ears and thumbs at the phone until music plays. "My little perseverator."

"How come . . . ?" Danny starts. "I mean, are you . . . was he always . . . ?" Danny doesn't know how to finish. Doesn't need to.

"This guy?" she says. "No. This guy, this dude, this lovable little pervert was the treasurer of the debate team in high school. This guy was a monster on the alto sax. Made all-state band every year since eighth grade. This guy brought home the gold in cross-country track." Holly kisses her brother on top of his head, then traces one fingertip along his mean scar. "But this guy," she says, "was in way too big a hurry to get laid."

The Minotaur sits down, listening, trying not to bump anything with his horns. Danny Tanneyhill toes at the base of his unfinished trunk, waiting.

"Aren't we all?" Danny says.

"It's unclear exactly what the plan was," Holly says, "but Tookus and his buddy, equally dorkish in every way, tried to steal this huge metal condom machine from the wall of the men's room of Enlow's Foot-longs. They had a crowbar and a hammer."

Tookus can't hear them. He bobs his head and starts humming loudly.

"Shhh," Holly says. She reaches for the pipe. "Anyway, the thing fell on his head. Right there."

She touches the spot. They all look.

"And the rest is history."

"Damn," Danny Tanneyhill says.

"Praise Jesus," Holly answers.

Tookus jumps up and begins doing the peepee dance, pigeon toed, knees together, clutching his crotch. Oddly enough he doesn't say a word.

"Me, too," Holly says. She stands and takes her brother's hand.

"I've got keys to Chili Willie's," Danny says, jingling his claim.

"Nah. We'll go back here," Holly says, rounding the Pygmalia-Blades trailer.

Danny laughs. "Want me to check for spiders?" he asks.

"I want you to sit on your hands and keep your eyes closed."

Danny Tanneyhill squirms on his stump. The Minotaur picks a bit of dried *saag* from his brass button. Danny Tanneyhill cocks his ear and sniffs at the wind. The Minotaur hears the hiss of urine, smells the curry in it. Danny Tanneyhill reaches a finger beneath his shirt to tug at the saw-blade necklace. The Minotaur tilts his big head back and nudges an uncut cedar trunk with the tip of one horn.

Neither speaks.

"Fucking bats," Holly says, hurrying back into sight, laughing, wiggling her underwear up beneath the red dress. She bumps into the big totem pole, nearly knocks it over. "This place is a deathtrap," Holly says. "One of these days . . . "

"Art's hard," Danny says, and it's unclear whether he's joking or not. "Art is, ought to be, dangerous."

Holly laughs, puts her finger on the fat pine tear of a weeping eagle. "Dangerous, huh?" she says. "Tell me, Pygmalion, do you actually sell these things?"

"I get by," the carver says, and means it. "I don't lack for much. Though I do get a hankering, from time to time, for a companion that doesn't give me splinters."

Tookus pokes around inside the trailer. He's naming things, but too quietly to be heard.

"Commissions," Danny whispers, like he's telling a secret.

"What?" Holly asks.

"Commissions," Danny says again. "I get by on commissions."

"What do you mean?" Holly asks.

The Minotaur is intrigued but would rather not show it. He begins gathering up the paper plates and wiping out the pie makers. Danny opens a locked toolbox in the trailer and brings out a photo album. He lays it in Holly's lap.

"People know my work," he says. "I get special orders."

Holly begins to laugh as soon as she opens the album. "It's a big dick!" she says.

"Eight foot long and nearly six foot around," Danny Tanneyhill says. "Was a wedding gift."

Holly flips the page.

"That one was for a motorcycle club, a very particular motorcycle club."

Holly flips the page. The Minotaur watches her eyes widen each time. He wants to see, too. There is enough man in him. The Minotaur sidles up behind Holly and the chainsaw artist.

"I can't even figure out how you did that with trees," Holly says.

Danny laughs. "I was blessed," he says. He turns the next page for her. "See this one? That's the man who bought it. That's his wife. And that's—"

"No!" Holly says. "No way!"

"Yup," Danny says.

Tookus knocks over something in the trailer. No harm done.

"How?" Holly asks. "Do you advertise?"

"Word of mouth. One leads to another."

A pine knot pops in the fire pit. The Minotaur snorts, more heavily than he intends to. Holly's red hair ruffles. She swats at him playfully.

"Careful, big boy," she says. "Don't start something you can't finish."

Holly turns to the last page in the photo album, and Danny Tanneyhill tries to close it up.

"What's this?" she asks. "Is that you?"

"Yep," he says.

"Whoa, what happened?"

The Minotaur has to look. He's seen bodies enough. Keeps hoping to be surprised. And the photographs of Danny Tanneyhill injured and recovering get close. Two full pages are devoted to the accident. Danny on a bloody stretcher with his chest gaping, the jagged wound reaching from his clavicle down the sternum. Danny on life support in the blue light of the hospital room. Danny's stitches. And more.

"I was a badass," Danny Tanneyhill says. "A badass with a chainsaw."

He begins to finger the scar. "I ran a crew on one of the biggest tree services in the country. Wintertime, we prayed for ice storms, hurricanes and tornadoes the rest of the year. I mean prayed for them. A whole army of orange trucks would hit the road. Disaster meant dollars."

"Go, capitalism, go," Holly says.

The Minotaur has seen enough of the pictures, and though the story is tiresome he has nothing else to do but listen. Tookus is playfully grinding against the rough thighs of a life-sized Wonder Woman whose head is missing. No. Not missing. It sits upright, looking out from beneath the trailer's bumper, rolled or kicked there by the self-proclaimed god of the lot.

"I didn't care about the people or their houses or cars. I was there to clear the damage, and when there was no damage I had nothing to do."

The chainsaw carver seems sincere in his reflective moment, but the Minotaur has heard it all before, from one mouth or another. Danny Tanneyhill tells about the last time he was out with his crew, the night of the accident. A tornado, glorious in its rage, had danced out of the dark heavens and laid waste to most of a small mill town in one of the Carolinas. Danny tells the story well, touching his scar the whole time. The Minotaur watches as Holly falls prey to the narrative.

"I died," Danny Tanneyhill says. "I died. I was dead. I was dead for five solid minutes."

"Fuck," Holly whispers.

"Unngh," the Minotaur says, not impressed.

"I was cutting like a madman, in the wind and the driving rain. Ripping the limbs from a massive poplar that was blocking the road. And there, in the branches, a little pink Barbie Jeep—you know, kid sized, battery operated. And the girl. Just . . . just there."

Holly sucks air through her teeth.

"I let go of my saw," Danny Tanneyhill says, "and the blade kicked back." He makes a quick jerking gesture, re-creating the cut with his fingertips and a hiss. "And I died. And I was reborn. And here I am." The overlord of Pygmalia-Blades opens his arms.

"Fuck," Holly says. Again.

"Unngh," the Minotaur says. Again.

There is probably more to the story. Danny Tanneyhill has most likely rehearsed the denouement. But Tookus upstages the moment when he emerges from the trailer pointing a lit Roman candle.

"Look who found my stash," Danny Tanneyhill says.

Holly is less than amused. She jumps into action, but not before one fiery red star whistles up over the roof of the Judy-Lou and explodes. The boy squeals, or maybe it's a scream. Holly yanks the firework from his hands. The second projectile, blue, bounces down Business 220. Whistles. Explodes. She stabs the lit end deep into a thick mound of sawdust at the base of an uncut tree trunk and holds tight until the candle is spent.

Danny Tanneyhill shrugs, baffled by Holly's reaction.

"Don't ask," she says.

The Minotaur sees Tookus, back in the trailer, slip something into his pants.

"Tooky! Come sit with us."

Her brother resists, but Holly goes after him. Takes the boy by the hand and sings softly as she leads him back to her stump. Sings. Stump. Sings. Doesn't matter that the Minotaur can't make out the words. Sings. The song, a tithing of breath on an altar of sound. The throat a chapel. No. Cathedral. The glottis, the folds, the tongue. Hymn book.

Holly sits and turns back in the picture album. "And just how much do you get for these nasty things?" she asks.

Danny may or may not answer. Where did that song go? The momentum has shifted, though.

Holly closes the book. She reaches out and lays a palm on the huge unfinished trunk, Danny's newest acquisition. "What's this going to be?"

The Minotaur is standing right there, his horn practically touching one of the outstretched limbs. Shoed feet are taking shape at the base of the trunk, and legs (human enough) rise up its length. Beyond that, beyond the implied waistline, shape and form are nebulous. Undetermined.

"Haven't decided," Danny says.

But the way he looks from the tree trunk to the Minotaur and back, no one believes him. The Minotaur is not surprised that the carver doesn't mention nearly being killed by the very same tree mere hours ago, or that the Minotaur was the one to rescue him.

"Mmmnn," the Minotaur says.

Danny Tanneyhill lines his pie makers up on the table.

"So," Holly says, shifting everybody's focus to the Minotaur, "how come a guy like you knows about making *aloo gobi* mountain pies?"

Tookus perseverates. "*Aloooooo alooooooo aloooooooo gobi.*"

They've talked about the other scars. It is, for better or worse, time to talk about his scar. His seam. His division. The Minotaur wants to say something meaningful. He could say things about dying. He wants to tell Holly something important. But what? Can he tell her about dying on the Old Scald Village battlefield, of lying so still there he can feel the earth's staggering orbit? Can he tell her of pressing his back to the stone foundations at Joy Furnace, of the heat from the ancient fires perpetually warming his spine? Maybe the Minotaur can talk to Holly about the smells of fresh thyme and the sizzle of butter in a hot pan. Or he can reach all the way back and tell of other stone walls. Of how he was feared. Of the mounds of crushed bones, the vats of virgins' blood. The Minotaur readies his tongue.

"Mmmnn, baaaa . . . ball joint," he says.

Holly looks perplexed, then smiles. Danny Tanneyhill laughs outright.

"Hey, G.I. Joe," the carver says, "why don't you tell her about your girlfriend? The one who brings you pies."

It takes the Minotaur a minute to understand that Danny is talking about Widow Fisk, about Gwen. Then memory, as it is wont to do, horns in, and a haphazard montage flashes through the Minotaur's mind. Here, Biddle choking in the muck, and the fat plaster trout. There, the shave horse and ice chips and all that black musky hair. Now, the face of Widow Fisk. The face of betrayal.

"Mmmnn, no," the Minotaur says. In his heyday, in his glory days, the Minotaur would have trampled, then eaten such a human as Danny Tanneyhill. These are not those days.

"Girlfriend, huh?" Holly says, putting her thumb on the center button of the Minotaur's Confederate soldier's jacket. She is about to do more when Tookus walks into the middle of Business 220.

"Get out of the road, Tooky," Holly says. But it's so late, so quiet, there's no urgency in her request.

The boy stands still, then points down the road into the darkness.

"Tookus! Get your ass over here," Holly says.

It is very late. The witching hour. Maybe past. The laws of physics, the rules of law, perceptions of all sorts, get a little fuzzy around the edges. Tookus is first, and it would be hard to say who hears it, who feels it, next.

"What the hell?" Danny Tanneyhill says.

"Unngh," the Minotaur says.

Holly goes to the middle of the road to get her brother. She gets stuck there, looking with him into the distance. Distance. It suggests something measurable, but whatever it is coming up Business 220 from Homer's Gap way surely will not be bound by yardsticks or quantifiers. The earth quakes before anything is seen. The tiny American flags jitter nervously beneath the Judy-Lou marquee. The whole of the Pygmalia-Blades bestiary fidgets and twitters. Then the flashing lights come into view.

"What the fuck?" Danny Tanneyhill asks.

"Are we being invaded?" Holly asks.

Tookus shoulders an imaginary rifle. "Bang bang bang bang bang bang," he says.

It comes onward, impervious to his defense, but comes incredibly slowly, and gets louder with each gained inch. Louder and louder. Brighter and brighter. As if hell itself is being dragged up the road and is fighting every increment. Tookus starts to cry. Holly takes him over to the safety of the Judy-Lou Motor Lodge. Holds the boy. The Minotaur sees her singing into his ear. Danny Tanneyhill can't figure out which statue to rescue first. The Minotaur lowers his bullish head and surveys the scene. He will not be moved.

And though the approaching beast is horrible, is horrifying—its girth spanning the two-lane road from side ditch to side ditch, its ugly head rearing nearly above the tree line (they're not imagining this; the monster is well lit), its growl throaty and methodical, hissing, stinking of dust and, sure enough, hydraulic fluid—the trio finds it hard to sustain their terror.

"Why is the son of a bitch moving so goddamn slow?" Holly yells.

So they wait. And watch. And what is eventually born out of the black hole of unknowing is a little disappointing. The mystery revealed is a thing equal parts annoyance and nightmare. It's a building. A whole building, in transit, on a trailer. A lead car heralds the news with flashing yellow lights on its roof and a *Wide Load* warning lashed to its bumper. The insipid beams break and shatter in the dense trees by the roadside. Behind the lead car, a big rig, an eighteen-wheeler with lighted outriggers spread wide, strains and labors against its burden. The clatter of the diesel engine is deafening. The trailer it pulls straddles the middle of Business 220, and on that flatbed, a church. An old white clapboard church. Steeple and all. Shored up. Strapped tight. The whole thing.

Dingus Historic Hauls is emblazoned on the semi's doors.

"Mmmnn, okay," the Minotaur says.

He understands what's happening. The load is too big to transport in any but the leanest hours. Too delicate for haste. The old boards creak and squeal, pulling at their glued joints, straining against their pegs. And up on top the shutters flap against the squat belfry. Higher still, the priapic spire waggles toward the heavens, as if. There is no cross, only its splintered remnant. The Minotaur imagines the steeplejacks (he knows their breed) champing at the bit, rattling their scaffolds, ready to get at it, the work of restoration. The Dingus truck slogs along the macadam. The Minotaur looks into the mawing windows, imagines there the pews tumbling willy-nilly. The Minotaur imagines the hymnals, dumb and flightless birds flapping their red wings across the plank floor. Their mute squawks. The Minotaur does not imagine the driver of the truck. He watches the man pick his nose as he passes, digging deep, and looking at a cell phone. Not looking at the Minotaur or at anything that isn't on the straight and narrow path ahead. Picking his nose, tapping at the cell phone with the very same finger, and paying no attention to the sedan that's trying to get around the wide load, swerving back and forth, looking for an opportunity to pass (and likely has been for miles and miles). The driver of the car, whose path is blocked by the church, curses and swerves and honks, then repeats it all again. The parking lot of the closed Chili Willie's would be perfect if not for the Odyssey perched on its jack. The sedan skids in, barely misses the van, skids out. Danny Tanneyhill throws a chunk of wood, barely missing the sedan. And when the car whips around the wide load's other side, as if there may actually be enough room between the brick Judy-Lou planter and (either) the semi's trailer or the motel office, Holly gasps loud enough for all to hear. The Minotaur readies himself for catastrophe. None comes. The car glides to a quiet and respectable stop in the check-in lane. And while the old white church lumbers and chugs out of sight, if not out of mind, the Minotaur, the redhead and her brother, and the woodcarver watch the driver of the now-parked sedan fumble and fuss with his seatbelt.

Danny Tanneyhill crosses Business 220, holding another chunk of wood, ready. He joins Holly and Tookus, then the Minotaur.

"Is he drunk?" Danny asks.

"Mmmnn," the Minotaur says, concerned more with the Guptas now, feeling protective.

It takes the driver an inordinately long time, but when he finally emerges from the sedan, it's clear why the struggle. He is immense. Not merely rotund. Obese. A behemoth of a man in a business suit who, once standing (and nearly as wide as he is tall), defies belief that he ever fit in the car in the first place. They hear him grunt. Hear the wheeze of his breath.

"Is he drunk?" Danny asks again. But that's not the real question on their lips.

"Are those . . . ?" Holly starts. "Are they . . . ?"

She wants to know if they're real, the donkey ears atop the fat man's head. Donkey ears. Long and furred, soft points at the high tips, curling inward along the edges like leaves. Donkey ears.

"Are they real?" she asks, and looks to the Minotaur for his answer. As if he would know. Scald Mountain bites its rocky black tongue. Says nothing.

The Minotaur wants to talk about his scar. It was his turn, by the fire. Things are unresolved. Inconclusive. The Minotaur feels it. There is much more to be said. But it is late. The church has passed on its slow truck, and the fat man checks into the Judy-Lou Motor Lodge without incident.

Tookus brays loudly. "Hee-haw! Hee-haw!"

"I gotta go to bed," Holly says.

Wait. There is more to tell. More to show. The Minotaur wants to tell her things. To show her things.

Want to see how I die? he thinks to say. *This is what it feels like to . . .*

But it's hard to stop momentum. A thing in motion (even an idea or a state of mind) likes to stay that way. Danny Tanneyhill sees it. He takes his pine log back across the road. Holly may or may not have mumbled a good-night to the Minotaur.

"Wait," the Minotaur says. "Wait."

But he's the only one left in the parking lot.

Wait.

CHAPTER FOURTEEN

WAIT. THE MINOTAUR WANTS ANOTHER MOMENT. Silly, that, and knowing so he moseys back into Room #3. His mind reeling. The Minotaur decides to polish his musket. For no better reason than he needs the distraction. Though being prepared for whatever happens next is important to him. The Minotaur hears the chainsaw roar to life across Business 220. The Minotaur douses a swab of cloth with acrid solvent, tucks it into the bore, and rams it home. He'll stave off the puckish night. Top to bottom. He'll stand his ground. Stand guard. Against whom? The donkey? The man? Against butterscotch and broom straw. Sawdust. Starlight. The Minotaur pledges allegiance. He'll take it on the chin. He'll take it in stride. Take it as it comes. Come one, come all. Come the ticky-tacky night and its petty demands. Hostage taker par excellence. Tick tock, tick tock. The Minotaur's devotion will not be ransomed. The Minotaur considers the stave. Considers bottled breath and the squeaky prosthesis. The Minotaur considers his options. Considers first the hammer. The ball-peen, maybe. Not the sledge. No, certainly not the sledge. There is the beetle and the claw hammer. The cross-peen and the maul. Too, the mallet has a stake in the claim. The Minotaur considers, briefly, the scutch. The rip, the pile, the tilt. Comes back again and again to the ball-peen. Peen. What it means is this: to draw, to bend, to flatten. Knock knock. Who's there? Night draws. Night bends. Night flattens into still more night. And the goddamn knocking won't stop.

 *CHAPTER FIFTEEN*

KNOCK KNOCK.

Knock knock.

"Unngh," the Minotaur grunts, and knocks the musket over. His big head jerks, hooks the lampshade.

Knock knock.

The clock reads one two three. He's been asleep. And the goddamn knocking won't stop. The goddamn knocking has hammered him right out of his Minotaur dream. Busted his thick skull wide. And now pounds away on the door to Room #3.

"Unngh," the Minotaur says, and hurries to the door with the scents of butterscotch and smoke in his nostrils. Both. Both. He hurries to the door with stars in his eyes, and hurries to the door with his bullish heart pounding hopefully.

It's the fat man. His suit is rumpled.

"You got a screwdriver?" he asks. The donkey ears bob and sway gently.

"Mmmnn, no," the Minotaur says, rubbing his eyes.

Up close the man is all jowls. The Minotaur can't find his eyes.

"You got a pipe wrench?" he asks.

"Mmmnn, no," the Minotaur says.

The man's teeth are big. Yellow as the moon.

"You got a . . . ? Oh, never mind," the fat man says. "What good are ya?"

The fat man waddles back down the sidewalk and closes the door to his room. In other circumstances the Minotaur would have worked harder to help. Endeavored to be of use. Other circumstances.

The clock still reads one two three. The clock is broken. The Minotaur remembers it now. The night sky will unhinge itself soon enough. The Minotaur stands in the doorway clutching his musket by the barrel. He looks out across the road. Danny Tanneyhill's pickup truck is gone. He looks up and down the span of the Judy-Lou Motor Lodge. On the sidewalk, right in front of the redhead's door, stands a knee-high carving of a man-in-the-moon crescent, his smooth arc and the cuts of his fat lips and wide eyes fresh and glaring. The Minotaur shoulders his gun, takes aim. Thinks to say *Bang*, but it's not a sound that works well in his mouth.

Holly opens her door. Steps into the line of fire.

"Whoa!" she says.

The Minotaur drops his weapon, searches his brain for an explanation. But immediately it's clear that Holly is responding to the man in the moon. She walks right into it.

"Fuck! Fuck! Fuck!" she says, trying for quiet, biting her bottom lip, that mussed hair a red conflagration, holding the bare toes of one slender foot, sort of jumping up and down on the other (slender foot), the pale blue boxer shorts laying loose claim to her behind and her legs (white as apple flesh), leaning her shoulder against the doorjamb, reaching for (grappling at, really) the black-frame glasses that hang from the neckline of her T-shirt (a loose, ocher-colored thing with a faded Mighty Mouse printed on the front), that bounce every time she jumps, right between her small (but unencumbered) breasts. "Fuck! Fuck! Fuck!" she says, then sits on the stoop.

The Minotaur is sorry Holly got hurt. But he is more grateful still for the sight of her there. The Minotaur tries to nudge his musket out of sight, then goes to help.

"Ouch," Holly says, poking the glasses into place on the bridge of her nose.

"Hey," she says, seeing first the kicked moon, then the Minotaur.

"What the hell?" she says about the statue. Or maybe about him. The Minotaur can't tell. Her eyes are red, puffy, her nose snotty. It's clear to the Minotaur that Holly was crying long before kicking the man in the moon. She is stunning in her misery.

"Unngh," the Minotaur says, moving the heavy carving out of the doorway. He offers his hand.

"Thanks," Holly says, pulling herself up, almost grabbing his horn for balance. Almost. She closes the door gently. "Tooky is still asleep."

The Minotaur fumbles with the brass buttons on his jacket. He can't think of anything else to do. No reason to stay there with her. Near her.

Holly steps off the sidewalk, pinches one nostril shut with a fingertip, blows a glob of yellowy mucus onto the asphalt, repeats on the other side, wipes a glistening streak down her forearm, then smiles at the Minotaur.

"Did you ever see such a sexy sight in your life?" Holly asks.

The Minotaur has an answer for the question.

"Sorry," she says. "It's been a hard night. For years . . . "

The Minotaur notices the thick gauze of morning fog. Everything up the mountain has gone missing. The absence is beautiful. "Look," he says. Gestures with his horns.

Holly rubs her eyes. She likes what she sees. "Mmm, nice." she says. "Listen, can we talk about the van?"

"Mmmnn," the Minotaur says.

"I mean . . . ," she says, and clearly wants to say more. "Me and Tooky . . . we are . . . I have to . . . "

"Mmmnn," the Minotaur says.

"I'm taking him . . . We only have a few days."

"Tools," the Minotaur says, and is surprised when Holly follows him back to Room #3. Follows him all the way inside.

"Please don't say anything to . . . ," Holly says, and hooks her thumb in the direction of Pygmalia-Blades.

"Okay," the Minotaur says.

Then something catches Holly's eye. "Whoa, what's this?"

Holly picks up the musket like she's handled guns before. Room #3 constricts. The austerity of his present moment squeezes tight. The Minotaur is hemmed in by the past and its mountain of bones and by

numbing eternity. The very walls press in on the Minotaur and his unex-
pected guest.

"Unngh, tools," he repeats, kneeling to reach under the bed for his
toolbox, to change the subject.

His snout burrows into the bedspread, and the smell of industrial-
strength detergent chokes him. Holly steps closer, weapon in hand, just as
the Minotaur turns his head and coughs. Turns his big cumbersome head
and coughs. Turns, and the tip of his horn slips beneath the hem of her
shorts, traces in its slow rise the shallow furrow made by her thigh muscle.

"Unngh," he says. "Sorry. Sorry. Sorry."

He doesn't mean it, this accidental exposure, this swath of pale flesh,
and in trying to right his wrong the Minotaur pulls away. But the half-
man half-bull is in too deep. His burrowed horn tugs at the fabric, tugs
at the redhead, who topples onto the bed. The gun clatters to the floor.

What next? The Minotaur prepares himself for the worst.

Holly's laugh is the thing he's least prepared for.

"I hope that thing's not loaded," she says, standing, in no big hurry.

"I'm such a klutz," she says, wriggling in the blue boxer shorts to make
sure enough of her body is contained.

"Are you okay?" she says, picking a piece of blue thread from the horn
tip of the kneeling Minotaur.

"Sorry," he says.

"My fault," she says, then reaches for his gun again. "Do you collect
these things or something?"

"Mmmnn, no," he says, picking a piece of lint from his horn.

"Are you some kind of time-traveling secret agent, maybe?"

The Minotaur thinks long and hard about this one, wishing he could
say yes.

"I mean . . . ," she says, pinching at the hem of her shorts. "I mean
you're obviously not from around here."

She looks so beautiful sitting at the edge of his bed in Room #3, the
musket on her lap. The Minotaur has to turn away.

"Yes," he says. "No."

The Minotaur is not one to get frantic, but his mind races in this moment. There is no easy answer. He opens the drawer of the squat nightstand. There, between the Bhagavad Gita and the yellow pages, is a tattered piece of paper.

"Old Scald Village," Holly reads. "Oh, I get it. You're some kind of reenactor, or whatever they're called."

"Mmmnn, yes," the Minotaur says. Whatever they're called.

"Encampment Weekend," she says with exaggeration. "Annual Spring Civil War Festival."

It's a copy of the first draft of the flier. Widow Fisk, Gwen, was working out some kinks.

"You work here?" Holly asks. "Where is this place?"

"Just down," the Minotaur says, and points with his thumb.

Holly sniffles and keeps reading. "Battles twice daily. Full cavalry. Union and Confederate camp walk-throughs. You really do this stuff?"

"Unngh," the Minotaur says. He leans his musket in the corner.

"Hey!" Holly says, poking hard at the Minotaur's brass buttons. "This is perfect!"

Again the old bull wishes he could say yes. Yes, this is perfect.

"You know who would love this?" she asks.

Yes. No.

"Tooky," she says. "Tookus would really like all this."

"Unngh," the Minotaur says again, meaning so much.

The boy, Tookus, her damaged brother, would love Old Scald Village. So would the redhead. The Minotaur imagines the scene. Him leading the way. The bells from the church spire will announce their arrival. They'll visit the Tin Punch Cottage and the candle maker. Holly will pose in the pillory. The Minotaur will take them to the Old Jail, might even let Tookus close the cell door on him. The Minotaur sees it all in his wandering mind. Sees more than he intends. The Broom Shack and the fat ass of the broom maker spoiling everything. Sees the blacksmith's forge and Smitty and the branding iron.

"Tssss," is all the Minotaur can manage.

"Will you take us?" Holly asks. "Can we watch? Can we see you fight?"

The redhead standing in Room #3 of the Judy-Lou Motor Lodge sees something in the flier that the Minotaur can't. It's as if the crumpled page holds a secret. Or a solution. Or maybe just reprieve. The Minotaur sees none of this. Sees only the woman in her moment of need. Sees the need, and the way her heartbeat pulses through the Mighty Mouse T-shirt, right there on the grinning rodent's curled bicep, right there by the tiny peak of her nipple.

"Yes," the Minotaur says. Of course he'll take Tookus and Holly to Old Scald Village to watch him fight and die. He can't look Holly in the eye. Can't look any longer at the rise and fall of her breasts. Can look only to the floor, and in passing he sees the tiny drop of blood trickling down her white thigh.

"Oh," the Minotaur says. "Are you, umm, all right?"

His fingertip is close. He could easily catch the bright red droplet on his nail. In the distance Scald Mountain's camisole of fog is lifting.

"Hmmm," Holly says. She turns away, pulls the hem of her shorts high. "Just a scratch," she says. "I'll get a Band-Aid later."

She looks at the smear of blood on her finger. She's about to do something with it when they both hear the office door slam open. Holly is closer; she looks first. The Minotaur leans out from behind her.

"This is an outrage!"

It's the fat man with donkey ears.

"I strongly condemn your actions!" he says, his fat finger stabbing the sky.

"And you haven't seen the last of me!" he says, that same fat finger pointed inside the Judy-Lou Motor Lodge office.

Holly's finger, the bloody one, points toward the earth. The Minotaur's horns reach skyward. Nobody is ready for Tookus when he runs from his motel room clutching the carboy full of change. Runs full steam into the angry fat man coming down the sidewalk.

The man and his rage are immovable. "Move, boy!"

Tookus moves. Tookus bounces, unhurt but terrified. The glass jug shatters on the cement, five gallons of tip money scattering hither and yon.

"Goddamn it, Tookus!" Holly says.

It's not his fault. He cowers anyway.

"Why? Why do you always . . . ? Why does it always . . . ?"

Glass crunches under the fat man's shoes. He chucks a suitcase into the backseat of his sedan and peels out of the parking lot, back in the direction he came from in the night.

Tookus sits against the wall, shaking his hands, rocking back and forth, crying. "Fatty. Fatty fat fat. Dick titty fat fucker," he says.

"I can't do this anymore, Took," Holly says, arms raised, palms up. "I can't."

When Holly starts to cry, too, her brother gets to his knees and begins raking the money into a pile. Scooping the quarters and dimes. The nickels and pennies. And the shards of glass.

"No, no, Tooky! Stop!"

Holly rushes to her brother, but Tookus is too strong. He will not stop. Won't stop dragging his cupped hands over the rough cement, through the glass and coins. The Minotaur goes to help, but Ramneek Gupta gets there first.

"*So jaa*," she sings, kneeling in front of the boy. "*So jaa raajkumaari so jaa.*"

Tookus looks up.

"*So jaa*," she sings. Ramneek takes the boy's wrists, stills him. "*Main balihaari so jaa, so jaa raajkumaari so jaa.*"

Tookus allows himself to be lifted, standing when Ramneek stands.

"*So jaa, so jaa raajkumaari so jaa.*"

Ramneek does not look at Tookus's palms. Holly can't look anywhere else. There is so much blood. The boy stands perfectly still, his eyes squeezed shut.

"Things often appear much worse than they actually are," Ramneek says. "I will take care of this." She leads Holly's brother to the motel office, into its open door, singing all the way. "*So jaa main balihaari. So jaa. So jaa raajkumaari so jaa.*"

Holly sighs deeply, squats against the wall, and starts plucking quarters. One, two, three, four, five, six. Then she stands and hurls them out onto Business 220. They ping and clink softly on the pavement.

"Why?" she says. "It's not supposed to be this way. I'm not the goddamn mother. I'm not supposed to be his fucking . . . "

The Minotaur stoops with a Judy-Lou Motor Lodge ice bucket and gathers change. He doesn't speak.

"We have to go," Holly says. She's talking to herself, mostly. "I've made the arrangements. I've . . . we have to go soon."

Holly looks around. The Minotaur thinks he knows what she means. It doesn't take long to fill the plastic bucket. The Minotaur gets another, and together, and quietly, they resume the task.

"It's not my fault," Holly says.

"Mmmnn."

"I tried," she says. "I did the best I could. I can't do it anymore."

"Mmmnn."

The morning opens (always) incrementally. It's not long before Danny Tanneyhill drives up, his truck not done rumbling and rattling to a stop by the Pygmalia-Blades trailer when he hurries over to the motel.

"Hey," he says, eyeballing Holly's bare legs, "you'll never believe what happened."

Holly, from her squat, rolls her eyes and blows at a strand of hair. "Try me," she says.

The woodcarver doesn't ask why Holly and the Minotaur are hunkered there, amid the broken glass, pitching coins into ice buckets, but he joins them anyway.

"That fucking church," he says. "The church from last night. The one on the trailer."

"I know what church you're talking about," Holly says.

"Mmmnn."

"It fell off," Danny says, grinning wide.

"What do you mean?"

"I mean the church fell off of the trailer! It's blocking the entrance to that Old Scald Village place down the road, where big boy here works. The dumbass driver tried to turn in too fast or something."

"Mmmnn, back way?" the Minotaur says. The Old Scald service road is where big deliveries come and go.

"I don't know anything about your back way," Danny says. "But that truck is on its side, half in the ditch, and what's left of the church is jammed up against an old covered bridge."

The Minotaur looks down Business 220. Drawn. Compelled. Worried.

"There are ambulances and everything," he says. "Probably squashed some of those shit-heels in their playclothes."

"Fuck," Holly says, not quite amused.

"Exactly!" Danny Tanneyhill says. "Let's go see it!"

"Mmmnn, no," the Minotaur says. Though he wants more than anything to go. "No."

It's enough. The spell is broken.

"I don't have time for that kind of bullshit," Holly says. "I have to get the van fixed. Somehow."

Everybody looks across Business 220 at the Odyssey, still canting on its jack.

"Psshh," Danny says. "We've got you covered, darlin'. Me and cowboy here will have you fixed up in no time."

"Unngh," the Minotaur says.

The smells of the Guptas' breakfast (the buttery fried bread, garlic, maybe—potatoes, too) drift down the sidewalk. The Minotaur wishes he could go in and sit at their table. Wishes he could take Holly along.

"First of all," Holly says, "I'm not your darlin'. Second of all, what do you mean? I don't have time or money to waste."

"Don't get your panties in a wad," the woodcarver says. "I just mean that between me and the master mechanic here, we can get you up and running lickety-split."

"Unngh," the Minotaur says again. It's probably true, but he wants a say in the conversation. Wants not to be roped into a responsibility by the woodcarver's desire.

Holly looks about to cry again. "I can't afford . . . "

Business 220 stretches silently out of sight. There is crisis at one end. The Minotaur tilts his horns accordingly. What if Widow Fisk is hurt? Or Biddle, even?

"Don't worry," Danny Tanneyhill says. "Everything will be okay."

That's probably true as well, but the Minotaur interjects anyway.

"Unngh."

"We'll make a plan," Danny says. "Me and cyborg, we'll have you fixed up in no time."

"Unngh."

"Better still," the woodcarver says, toying with the saw blade around his neck and working hard (and failing) not to look at Holly's chest, "Mister Wrench here can surely handle the job, and I'll take you and Spooky down to see all the stupids at the Old Scald—"

"No," the Minotaur says. "No."

"No," Holly says.

"Whatever," Danny Tanneyhill says. "We'll stay together, then."

"I need to check on Took first," Holly says. She hands a half-full ice bucket to Danny. "Take over."

He grunts but acquiesces.

The Minotaur follows her into the Judy-Lou office, and deeper still to the Guptas' apartment. Tookus sits on a couch watching cartoons with Devmani. His hands are fat and white, ghost puppets, blimps. No. Bandages. Holly gasps.

Ramneek comes quickly to her side. "Shhh," the woman says, taking Holly by the arm. "The boy is fine. His cuts are few and shallow."

Holly gestures, one hand loosely circling the other.

"The boy simply liked the tape and bandaging. So I kept going."

· · ·

The Minotaur is just supposed to go get his tools. Just. Just gather his wrenches and pliers and screwdrivers and go back across Business 220 to meet with the redhead and the woodcarver to talk about the Odyssey. The Minotaur is not supposed to scramble out the back window of Room #3, clamber down the laurel-choked slopes all the way to the bank of Mill Run. Is not, that misguided old bull, supposed to follow the stream west. Is not, but does.

Mill Run, Stink Creek, runs red and foamy.

The Minotaur makes haste.

Finds himself quickly enough at the chaotic mouth of Old Scald Village. Hides there behind a thick clump of cattails, hoping their fat brown bloom spikes will camouflage him. The Minotaur sees but does not want to be seen.

He has several options. Decisions to make. If he shows himself, if he helps in this moment of need, maybe he'll be forgiven. Pardoned. No. The Minotaur is a realist. He knows human nature. The old covered bridge, both ingress and egress, is blocked, battered by the wrecked church. The whole scene is clotted with familiar faces. Smitty pretending some authority. Biddle smirking, doing something with his cell phone. Tow trucks. Men with wenches and cables and jacks and testosterone in abundance. An ambulance is present, its rear door gaping wide. The Minotaur looks long and hard, finds no one stretchered. Doc sits dejected on a rotting railroad tie, holding a rubber forearm and hand, his ersatz knowledge useless. And Widow Fisk? The Minotaur can't find her there.

Throwing caution to the wind, he circumnavigates the small-scale calamity, rushes, top heavy in his need, through the backyards of Old Scald Village, making his way to the Welcome Center, where he thinks he sees the *Open* sign in the window, making his way to Widow Fisk, to Gwen, to make sure she's okay, to maybe even say he's sorry. He'll just march right through the Gift Shoppe and into her office, and if anybody tries to stop him the Minotaur will . . . will . . .

"Hey!"

The Minotaur looks up. Up from his studied tread. Up and into the eyes of Destiny. The broom maker. She's in her open window. He's in the backyard of the Broom Shack.

"You're not supposed to be here," she says.

She wields a weapon, a stiff cane besom broom.

The Minotaur runs. It is not a pretty sight. He makes a lopsided sort of gallop across the graveled main street of Old Scald Village, runs past the Cooper's Shack, through the stockade and its adjacent pasture, runs, wheezing by now, around the other side of the covered bridge, heads farther down and back over Business 220, sidles along the shoulder of the road, more in the ditch than out, paying so much attention to being unseen by anyone in attendance at the Old Scald Village crisis that he trips over something and falls flat on his bull face.

"Unngh," the Minotaur says.

"Muutate," comes the answer. Gravelly and harsh. More retch than language.

It's the giant plaster soldier speaking. The giant plaster soldier, knocked from its base (by the Dingus truck, no doubt), lies in pieces on its plaster belly. Much like the Minotaur.

"Ch-ch-changeling!" the solider squawks.

The Minotaur sits up and kicks the hideous beast. A crow wriggles from the gaping neck hole, hops onto the soldier's back, struts up and down, looks at the grounded Minotaur, fluffs its black self up to gargantuan size, vomits a dissonant curse, then flies away.

• • •

By the time the Minotaur returns, everybody at the Judy-Lou Motor Lodge is mad at him.

"Where the hell did you go?" Danny Tanneyhill asks.

"We knocked on your door, Mister M," Rambabu says.

Holly doesn't speak, but her look says enough.

"Unngh, sorry," the Minotaur says, squatting by the shallow maw of the Odyssey's empty wheel well.

The Minotaur shows Holly the damage. So much damage. So much need. He tells her what is needed to get the vehicle back on the road.

Holly kneels there with him. She binds her red hair tightly in a pony-tail. She wears snug jeans, not the loose boxers. And the Mighty Mouse shirt still. It rides a little high, and the swath of soft belly flesh is so pale it threatens to gobble up all of the day's light. She's doing calculations in her head, tapping out sums, or maybe counting days. Holly cries. Says she doesn't have the money. Says she doesn't have the time.

"Mmmnn," the Minotaur says. He has some bills folded in the bottom of his haversack.

"Hey," Danny Tanneyhill says, "my buddy owns a salvage yard!"

Holly doesn't know what that means. Danny Tanneyhill explains.

"You're not fucking with me, are you?" Holly asks. "You better not be fucking with me."

The woodcarver strikes a saintly pose, palms up, eyes full of forced compassion.

"I don't have time . . . We can't . . . ," Holly says.

"Have a little faith, darlin'," he says.

"I told you," Holly says, "I'm not your darlin'. Can we go? Can we go right now?"

"We'll take my truck," Danny says.

"Unngh," the Minotaur says.

"I'm gonna get Tooky," Holly says.

The man and the Minotaur watch her cross Business 220. Watch her lug the man in the moon into her room and close the door.

"Can you handle this?" Danny asks. He touches the saw-blade necklace that hangs beneath his dirty T-shirt and toes at the brake drum on the ground. He probably means the repair job.

"Unngh," the Minotaur says, touching a horn tip (the one that touched Holly's thigh) and snapping a socket on a ratchet. He means several things.

The woodcarver and the half-bull mill around, waiting for the girl to return.

"You never said where you disappeared to," Danny Tanneyhill says. "I thought maybe you . . . "

Holly emerges from the Judy-Lou office. It's enough to shut the woodcarver up.

"Took's watching *Gilligan's Island* with the little girl," she says. "He wants to stay. I hope he'll be all right."

"Mmmnn," the Minotaur says, trying to sound comforting. He gathers the necessary tools, looks at the Odyssey's damaged parts.

Danny Tanneyhill sings to himself, "Just sit right back and you'll hear a tale, a tale of a fateful trip."

Holly keeps looking back at the motel. "He'll be fine, right? She'll keep him . . . I just need a break, just a little time."

"Mmmnn, yes," the Minotaur says. "Safe."

Danny Tanneyhill sings even louder as he loads a stubby carving of a football helmet painted Pittsburgh Steelers black and gold: "The weather started getting rough, the tiny ship was tossed."

"What's that for?" Holly asks, grabbing the faceguard.

"Bargaining power," the carver says. "And you never even thanked me for the man in the moon."

"It almost killed me," she says. "Thanks for that."

Danny Tanneyhill climbs into the driver's seat and cranks the engine. Revs it. The passenger door stands wide open. Holly looks at the Minotaur, shrugs, and climbs in. She scoots close to Danny and pats the seat.

"Your turn," she says.

So the Minotaur climbs in, and right away the horns are a problem. He has to cock and angle his big head to keep from gouging the headliner or Holly. Everything smells like sawdust and sweat.

"Unngh," he says.

"You could roll down the window," Holly says.

The Minotaur thinks it over: one horn in, one horn out. Sawdust and sweat. The Minotaur wishes he could stay.

"No," he says, and gets out of the truck.

Danny gooses the throttle. Sings, "If not for the courage of the fearless crew . . ."

"Let's switch," Holly says. "You sit in the middle."

The redhead is lovely. He'd like to ride beside her. But the Minotaur has better sense.

"Back," he says, and climbs over the side into the bed of Danny Tanneyhill's pickup truck.

Holly is mumbling protest when Danny slides open the cab's rear window. The Minotaur drags the unsecured spare tire from the tailgate to the front of the bed, positions it in the center, and sits. His horns nearly span the width of the window. Unless he lowers his snout the tips rise above the truck's roof.

"It's like you're right up here with us," Danny says through the screen.

"Mmmnn," the Minotaur says.

"We don't have too far to go," Danny says. "Just on the other side of Joy. Up over Locke Mountain."

"Unngh," the Minotaur says.

Danny Tanneyhill is overly cautious and stalls the truck. The Minotaur's big head bobbles and knocks against the cab.

"You okay back there?" Holly asks.

The Minotaur's reply is trumped by the spinning tires and spray of gravel as Danny pulls onto Business 220, driving toward midday, toward Locke Mountain, driving away from Old Scald Village, the cooper, the blacksmith, the broom maker, Widow Fisk, and the Minotaur's regular deaths (and the empty promises they hold). Even before Chili Willie's is out of sight, the Minotaur smells the marijuana coming from the cab. He hears snippets of conversation bounce around the truck and filter through the window mesh.

"I had nightmares about monster cocks made of wood," she says, "chasing me down the road."

"Those weren't nightmares," he says.

Laughter.

"Thanks, anyway," she says. "For the man in the moon, and my broken toe."

The Minotaur looks skyward. Shudders. He is not afraid of the man in the moon. But he doesn't want to listen to them talk in the cab. The

Minotaur wants to reposition himself. He gets to his knees, then squats. Though he has pretty good balance on stable ground, in the bed of the moving truck, top heavy as he is, the Minotaur has to stay low. He grabs the rail and turns his bulky head into the wind. Looks ahead. Immediately the Minotaur finds himself once again in a pickle. There is nothing streamlined about a half-man half-bull. Such a creature is not meant to move swiftly through life, to take on the world at a good clip. The very instant the Minotaur comes about in the bed of the truck, the wind begins to buffet and whip his big noggin. The pickup truck, with Danny Tanneyhill at the wheel and Holly at his side, plows down Business 220 effortlessly. But the very air that roils up over the hood, the windshield, the roof, all that passing wind slams head on into the Minotaur, roars in his deep black nostrils, barricading breath, flaps his ears like little gray handkerchiefs in a tempest. The Minotaur works hard to keep his mouth shut, his lips from flapping, too. Silly, this, he thinks, then quickly turns back around and plops himself on the spare tire.

"Are you still all right back there?" she says.

The Minotaur answers, but every syllable spills over the tailgate and is lost in the weedy ditches. The Minotaur presses his shoulders against the cab of the truck. There, looking down the narrow mountain road, everything funneling into the vanishing point in retreat, looking at what passes, what is passed, the immediate future slams continuously into him from behind. Locke Mountain rises steeply ahead. But the Minotaur can't see it.

 *CHAPTER SIXTEEN*

"HEY," DANNY TANNEYHILL SAYS, through the screen. "are you holding on tight back there?"

Maybe the Minotaur misheard. Maybe it was a command, rather than a question.

"Unngh," he says, either way.

What day is it? The Minotaur isn't sure. Traffic is light. All that's passed so far in the opposite direction is a boom truck with a wrecking ball snugged tight on its bed. *Dingus Demolitions*.

In the distance, coming up fast on the last straightaway before Locke Mountain lays claim to the topography, the Minotaur sees a car. Oddly green. Locke Mountain Road meets Business 220 on the other side of Homer's Gap. The mountain will not budge, so the road must rise. Must commit to a steep pitch and switchbacks. The Minotaur is grateful for the slower speed, but the turning this way and that and the motor's strain are troublesome. He takes what little pleasure he can from the smell of the exhaust. It comforts.

The woman, the redhead, Holly, is talking a lot. The Minotaur can tell she is turning her head as she speaks, working to include him in the conversation. Less so as the miles add up. Danny Tanneyhill tells her about an upcoming lumberjack competition.

"You should do it!" she says.

"Maybe," he answers. "We'll see."

"Regret sucks," she says.

"Maybe you should come. Be my pit crew. My cheerleader," he says.

The Minotaur doesn't hear Holly's answer. The pickup truck stops short. Danny Tanneyhill almost rear-ends another traveler on the road. The Minotaur cranes his neck, but he can't quite make out the other vehicle. Danny Tanneyhill backs off, speeds up, backs off, speeds up. Makes no difference. The other car will not go any faster, and the double lines and tight curves mean there'll be no safe passing until the top. On the next switchback, the vehicles are practically parallel, and moving in opposite directions. It's a Chevy van. An Astro. One more switchback later the Minotaur sees the big blue shield painted on the door. *Skills of Central PA.* It's a van for the disabled. A van full of the disabled. Danny Tanneyhill is impatient. He tries once to go around, at a misbegotten pull-off by a gap in the guardrails. Holly curses, and the woodcarver whips back in behind the service van. The Minotaur watches an empty beer can spin madly off the road in their passing.

"Unngh," the Minotaur says.

"Hold your horses there, killer," Holly says. "Let's arrive alive."

"Sorry," Danny says, partly to the Minotaur.

The Minotaur is about to say okay, is about to forgive Danny, when a little neon green coupe roars up behind carrying two young men, dark shades propped high on their heads, in full sway of their burgeoning maleness, hoping to pit their dumb luck and their high-performance engine against all that Locke Mountain Road has to offer.

The engine whines like a banshee when the driver downshifts. The exhaust pipe pops and stutters. In other contexts the Minotaur would appreciate the mechanics of the moment. But the two boys are staring right at him like it's his fault the truck is in their way. They ride close, bumpers almost kissing. They turn up their music; the bass beat pounds everything in sight.

"Assholes," Holly says through the screen.

"Assholes!" she says again, and louder, when the boys speed past, passing both the pickup truck and the Skills van with nowhere near the road to do so, the passenger taking video all the while on a cell phone, flipping middle fingers like they're going out of style.

"Retards!" the passenger shrieks, the Doppler effect hacking off the tail of the word.

Then, near the top, the truck stalls. Jerks. Lurches. The Minotaur's head slams against the cab and window. The wooden football helmet rolls toward him.

"Unngh," he says.

"Sorry," he says. Like it's his fault.

They crest. At the summit of Locke Mountain the rooftops of Joy in the pinched valley below become visible. The courthouse clock tower with its moony face rises over all but the several church spires and steeples, bunched together in the span of a few blocks. Too, on the next ridge, a line of massive windmills, their hundred-foot blades chopping away at the entire morning sky.

"I never get tired of this," Danny says.

"The near-death experience?" Holly asks.

"No, the view."

"Same thing," the Minotaur says. Nobody hears him.

The slope is more forgiving on the downside of Locke Mountain.

"Pennsyltucky as far as the eye can see," Danny Tanneyhill says.

At the first short straightaway he stomps the accelerator to pass the Skills van, but the truck isn't built for speed, so it's a languid affair. The Minotaur looks over at all the passengers and their scared eyes in the windows. He's about to wave when Danny's truck finds some oomph. They pass at last.

At the bottom of the hill, on the outskirts of Joy, Danny skids to a halt by the gas pumps at Yoder's Amish Country Market. It takes the Minotaur (his body, anyway) a moment to believe they've actually stopped.

"Gas," Danny says. Maybe hoping one of his passengers will contribute to the cost.

"I'm going to call and check on Tookus," Holly says. "I hope he's okay."

Danny rattles the pump's nozzle into place. "I'm sure the Diphthongs will take good care of him," he says.

"Don't be a dick," Holly says. "You want anything, M?"

Danny makes his best "Who, me?" gesture.

"Mmmnn," the Minotaur says. "N-no thanks."

Holly pauses at the door, looking closely at something on a bulletin board, and as soon as she goes inside the market the Minotaur realizes that he doesn't want to be there, in the bed of the truck, under the watchful eyes of the gargantuan plaster Amish man and woman who sit gape mouthed and cockamamie in the outsized buggy by the road's edge. What is it with these people and their statues? He shivers through a quick memory of the deposed plaster soldier. The Minotaur comes from a place of monumental effigies. He understands, or at least is familiar with, the human need to outsize. But here on the Allegheny Front, in the middle of Pennsylvania, in a fresh millennium, he can't tell if these characters are supposed to be the founding Yoders or what. It would be hard to say for sure whether they're laughing or screaming in agony. Danny Tanneyhill, the woodcarver, on the other hand, drawn by genetic affinity, maybe, goes over to rub at the plaster knees and feet.

The Minotaur grunts and climbs out of the truck, almost stepping into the path of the Skills van stopping at the opposite side of the gas pumps.

The Minotaur sees through the window one of the passengers, a grown man, pick a flake of skin from his scalp, then eat it. When the man looks and sees the Minotaur, he smiles with such sincerity that the Minotaur has no choice but to try and smile back. Smiling does not come easily for the Minotaur. Danny talks to himself by the plaster Yoders. When the Minotaur looks back, all the passengers in the Skills van have their faces pressed against the windows. They smile and wave. All of them. Big smiles. Big waves.

The Minotaur meets Holly coming out of the store. She's tucking a folded piece of paper into her back pocket. Almost secretively. She pats the curve of her backside and winks.

"I got us some pickled okra," she says, holding up the quart jar for the Minotaur to see.

"Unngh. Back soon," he answers.

Soon. Very soon.

The Minotaur pauses at the bulletin board, scans the mishmash of fliers and ads and pleas, trying to figure out what Holly might have plucked from the offerings. But there is too much to take in. Cockamamie papers pinned this way and that, some typed out, some with pictures, some just scribbled. Things for sale. Missing cats, dogs, humans. Services offered or hoped for. Too much. The palpable *want* on display overwhelms him.

The inside of Yoder's Amish Country Market is also too much for the Minotaur to bear. The narrow aisles, the high and deep shelves, those neatly ordered rows and rows and rows of goods, too much. Things in jars, pickled or otherwise. Things in bags. Noodles of all sorts. And candy. So many bags of candy, so many colors. The Minotaur sees a display rack of Bag Balm. Turns away quickly. The Minotaur thinks to get something for Devmani. Doesn't. The Minotaur is a little desperate but tries not to show it. At the register he reaches for the nearest thing. A cellophane-topped box of something called Gobs, thick white goo sandwiched between, and oozing from, circles of chocolate cake so dark they're almost black.

"Unngh," he says to the plump young clerk in her starched bonnet.

"That'll be three dollars and forty-seven cents," she says. "We got pennies if you need them."

The Minotaur takes the box of Gobs and hurries from the store. He looks briefly at the bulletin board by the door, layered thickly with fliers and notices and ads and pleas of one kind or another. Holly and Danny Tanneyhill are standing by the plaster Yoders. Danny is pretending to put his hand under the plaster dress.

The Minotaur goes directly to the Skills van. The official state logo on the Astro's door is circular, and toothed like a sprocket. The small print around the circle is dirty and hard to read, but the Minotaur can make out *Social Services* and *Special Needs*. Over his lifetime the Minotaur has yet to meet a human who didn't have some sort of special need, but the occupants of the van—all of them pressed against the windows now, watching him approach—may need more than most. The Minotaur stands by the Chevrolet's door long enough to determine that no one is going to open it. He tugs. They gasp.

Eight, maybe ten people are inside the van. The Minotaur cannot with certainty determine the ages or genders of most. The Minotaur wouldn't try. It's not important. There is fear, genuine fear, in the eyes that register any kind of emotion. The Minotaur does not want to frighten.

"Gobs," he says, offering the box. *G*'s come easily to his mouth. "Gobs."

"Gobs," the person in the closest seat repeats. Bucktoothed. Rheumy eyed. And grinning big. "Gobs!"

Then they all start—"Gobs Gobs Gobs Gobs"—and somebody reaches into the box, takes a bite. Then they all do. "Gobs Gobs Gobs." Somebody slides over, makes room for the Minotaur.

Gobs! The Minotaur takes a bite. The Minotaur considers the invitation. Why not? It is a viable option; he has nothing else to do. No other real obligations. The Minotaur has left whole lives behind many times. Has abandoned much. Has been abandoned by much. He could just climb right into the Skills van and eat Gobs all the way down the road. At the moment the outcome is hard for his bullish imagination to grasp, but could it be any worse, any better, traveling with the Skills van full of compromised humans than where he's headed now? Gobs!

They gesture. They beckon. The Minotaur considers the invitation seriously. Would he be more welcome? More useful? More or less monstrous? He thinks about Holly and her damaged brother. The Minotaur wishes he'd brought some napkins.

"Hey, M," Holly says, peering around the van. "What's up?"

"Gobs," the Minotaur says, and because the word works so well on his tongue, repeats it. "Gobs."

She smiles. It's soft. And sad. And beautiful. "You've got a little . . ." Holly makes a wipe at something imaginary on her own chin.

The Minotaur touches himself but misses the mark. Holly licks her thumb tip and dabs off a blot of white Gob cream from the corner of his mouth.

"Unngh, thanks."

"Want to trade places?" Holly asks.

It takes the Minotaur too long to realize that she's talking about seats in the truck. Bed or cab. Danny comes to the rescue. He raps on the truck bed three times.

"Climb in, cowboy. We don't have far to go."

"That's what they all say," Holly answers.

The Minotaur watches Danny Tanneyhill look over at the Skills van, then shudder. The man at least has the good common sense not to say anything.

"Rain," the woodcarver says.

They all look skyward. True enough. On the far ridge the wind turbines churn up a turgid gray cloud bank.

"My mama used to say, 'It's comin' up a cloud,'" Holly says.

True enough.

The Minotaur settles onto his spare-tire seat against the cab of the truck. If he didn't know any better he'd swear that the oversized eyeballs of both plaster Yoders stare straight at him all the way down Locke Mountain Road.

The Minotaur hears Holly spin the lid of the jar; he smells vinegar instantly. It's a timeless aroma, and always welcome.

"What's that?" Danny Tanneyhill asks.

"Okra," Holly says. "Pickled okra."

Even without looking the Minotaur knows she's offering the jar to the driver. The Minotaur hopes against all hope that the woodcarver hates what he tastes. The Minotaur wants to share the jar, the experience, with the redhead.

"Not bad," Danny says.

It takes some wiggling, but Holly slides the window screen open enough to stick her hand through, a glistening and pale green okra pod in her fingers. She doesn't speak. The Minotaur takes it directly between his teeth, onto his tongue.

"Mmmnn."

Holly talks and parses out the quart jar of pickled okra one pod at a time. She seems to be telling a story. The Minotaur hears only about half the story, but he gets his fair share of okra.

They pass through farmland, steep and stony pastures delineated by sagging barbed wire. They pass the derelict Deer Masters: Expert Meat Processing ("From Dead to Sausage in No Time"). The yellow trailer marquee, surrounded by weeds, reads *Fuck You* on one side and *Fuck Me* on the other. They pass another sign, messy black letters brushed onto a sheet of plywood: *Clean fill wanted.*

A mile or so later they arrive at Jolly Roger's U-Pull-It, so stated by the colossal pirate ship mounted on two poles and looming over the gate and the *Enter Here* shack. The vessel—a porous hodgepodge of car parts (fenders and doors and hoods and roofs) welded together to form something that is, if not exactly seaworthy, at least maritime in attitude—sways atop its moors in the wind of the coming storm. *Jolly Roger's U-Pull-It* is stenciled on both starboard and port. It's hard to guess how many acres of junked cars are hidden, surrounded by the high wooden fence. Hubcaps, hundreds of hubcaps, hang on the entire road side of the fence line.

"You live in a weird fucking place," Holly says.

"We all do," Danny Tanneyhill says. "One big world, baby."

"True enough," Holly says.

She offers the Minotaur her hand as he climbs out of the truck. He declines. He distributes the tools among his pants pockets. He wishes he'd brought the toolbox.

CHAPTER SEVENTEEN

"WHAT THE HELL?" HOLLY SAYS. "What the hell is that god-awful noise?"

God-awful. The Minotaur has known much god-awful in the long span of his horned life. Fact is, the bull-man was conceived in and born out of the god-awful. Like a lot of folks. But this noise, though not pretty, not soothing, not melodious, not even particularly or fully controlled by the creature that makes it—of this noise, the Minotaur would disagree with Holly's word choice. He knows well the full spectrum of god-awful.

The sound comes from inside the squat shack.

"That is not an indigenous animal," Danny says.

"Something killing or being killed," Holly says.

The Minotaur grunts as he lifts the wooden football helmet over the side of the truck bed.

Maybe it's the sky rumbling.

"Mmmnn, tuba," he says, cradling the statue in one arm and tugging at the door with the other. But neither Holly nor Danny acknowledges him.

"A duck fucking a chicken with a jackhammer," the woodcarver offers.

Enter, the door commands, so they do. They enter together, to an off-key but emphatic blatt. An avalanche of imprecise notes, blown wholeheartedly. The tuba player sits on a high stool behind a counter.

"Tuba," the Minotaur says again.

Tuba. He knew it. Already the Minotaur likes this place. He is hopeful. Almost optimistic. He knows his way around junkyards. Maybe he can teach Danny Tanneyhill a thing or two. Maybe show Holly what's what.

The office of Jolly Roger's U-Pull-It, where the tuba beast sits bellowing at them, is a utilitarian room. Austere. Ascetic. (Except for the goddamn earsplitting racket.) A room, a place, where woe comes easily and ecstasy, though possible, takes much more work. It's little more than a rectangular box with one door in and one door out. No windows. Nothing on the walls. Two long rows of fluorescent lights on the low ceiling. It is an unforgiving light. They stand there, warts and all. Everything is ridiculously clean. The only things in the room are a waist-high counter with a computer monitor at one end and two stools—an empty one on their side and a high stool behind the counter, upon which sits a tuba man. A man half flesh and half brass. No. The Minotaur looks closer. It's a sousaphone. And a man. A skinny man. His skin almost the color of the tarnished instrument encircling his body. He wears it well.

The man puts his lips to the mouthpiece and blatts for all he's worth, up and down a tortured scale, then winks.

"You smell like pickle," the salvage man says. He seems to be talking to all of them, but his eyes never leave the Minotaur.

Danny Tanneyhill belches loudly. "You're playing a tuba," he says.

"What?" the salvage man asks. He tugs at a thin yellow strand, pulls out a pair of earplugs that drape over and dangle from the serpentine valve tubes.

"I didn't know you play tuba," Danny says.

"I don't," the man answers. "And it's a sousaphone."

They stand, Danny in the middle, and look at the man with the sousaphone on the stool. The Minotaur cannot suppress his small awe at the man's ability to get the complicated loops of brass over his head. Nothing fits over the Minotaur's head.

What's that noise? the Minotaur wonders.

"Who's your friend?" the salvage man asks, still looking right at the Minotaur.

"Brothers and sisters, before you sits, in all his tubaphonic glory, the legendary Jolly Roger himself. Sultan of salvage. Imbiber of renown. And erstwhile shantyman."

Roger smiles. At the Minotaur. Roger perches on his stool between the door they came in and the door into the junkyard, at his back. Sits there like the gatekeeper of either heaven or hell. Sits, an indifferent Saint Peter, a benign Cerberus. His guests await judgment.

The Minotaur hears the nonsense spill out of the man's head and pool on the counter.

"Roger, this is Sergeant Major Big Boy, chief mechanic and bottle washer."

"Is that a wrench in your pocket?" Roger asks.

"Unngh," the Minotaur says.

"And this lovely lady—," Danny says, eyeing Holly up and down.

Roger interrupts. "Do you remember those Amish kids who got shot a few years ago?"

The Minotaur shudders. He looks back to see if the plaster Yoders are looking over his shoulder.

"All girls," Roger says.

What's that small small noise? the Minotaur wonders.

"Fucker came into their school and shot ten little girls, killed five of them, then shot himself in the head."

"What the hell are you talking about, Rog?" the woodcarver asks.

Roger taps at a cell phone lying on the lower shelf. The small noise stops.

"It's a documentary," he says. "On A&E. Do you know what the son of a bitch did for a living?"

"What?" Danny Tanneyhill asks.

"Unngh," the Minotaur says. Earbuds, not earplugs. The noise he'd been hearing was the tiniest of voices. Spokesmen for the atrocity. Mongers of malfeasance.

"Drove a milk truck," Roger says. He pokes at the cell phone again, unpauses the tragedy, rendered in a few measurable pixels on a three-by-five-inch screen. "Sorry," Roger says, stopping the action again. "Do you know what the community did? The mothers and fathers and neighbors of those dead and injured little Amish girls?"

"What?" Danny asks.

"Guess," Rogers says. Demands, really. "Guess."

"Raised a barn?" Danny says. "Opened a roadside Pickled Dead Guy stand? What?"

"They paid for his funeral expenses," Roger says. "They paid for the burial of the monster who murdered their children."

Danny whistles with too much sincerity and takes the open stool.

"What's this world coming to?" he says.

"Wonders never cease," he says.

"If they're not stopped," he says, "them Amish are liable to start a regular epidemic of love."

"What's a shantyman?" Holly asks.

"I've seen you before," Roger says to the Minotaur. "Lots of times."

"Unngh," the Minotaur says.

"I've seen you lots of times," Roger repeats. "Playing army man at Old Scald Village."

"Mmmnn," the Minotaur says.

"What's a shantyman?" Holly asks again.

The Minotaur wants to get into the junkyard, where he belongs. It's hard to breathe in this office, this holding pen, this purgatory. Plus, he can feel the urgency welling up in Holly. The Minotaur heaves the giant wooden football helmet up onto the countertop, where it lands with a thud.

"Damn, dude," Roger says. "You do know how to get a boy's attention."

Danny Tanneyhill sits on one stool, Roger on the other. When the salvage man leans forward to touch the carving, the woodcarver slips his balled fist in and out of the horn's gaping brass bell, grunting all the while.

"Yo, man," Roger says. "Get out of my horn hole. You don't know me like that."

"Where'd you get this thing, anyway?" Danny asks.

"Dude brought it in the other day," Roger says. "I traded him a whole

Chevy Vega for it." Roger gives a slobbery little blow into the mouthpiece. "Or maybe it was a Ford Taurus," he says, winking at the Minotaur. "I don't remember."

"Please," Holly says, "can we just . . . ?"

Roger looks at Holly, at her shirt, and sings the Mighty Mouse ditty: "Here I come to save the day!"

Holly gestures her frustration. Shrugs, palms up.

"Sorry," Roger says. "Sometimes I forget my manners. What can I do for you?"

"H-H-Honda," the Minotaur says. He wants a stake in the claim. "Odyssey."

Roger squirms inside the sousaphone, situates himself at the computer. "What do you need?"

The Minotaur tells him. He utters the few necessary words, and Roger taps away at the keyboard.

"I've got three," he says. "Right quadrant, Row 11." Roger looks at the exit door, then back. "I've seen you before," he says.

The first thunderclap startles them all. In the windowless room the Minotaur had forgotten the approaching storm. The Minotaur's flinch is barely perceptible, but Holly jumps and leans fully into him for the briefest moment. Rain pelts the roof in unseen fury.

"Damn," Danny Tanneyhill says.

"Guess you'll be riding the storm out with me," Roger says. "You can help me rehearse. We've got a gig this weekend."

"No," Holly mumbles.

"Ladies and gentlemen," Danny says in his best emcee voice. "Please put your hands together for Jolly Roger and The Allegheny Bilge Rats Shantyyyyy Choirrrrrrrrrrrr."

"Do you sing?" Roger asks the Minotaur. "Or play sousaphone? I bet you sing."

"No," the Minotaur says, the room seeming more airless by the minute.

"We'll hook you up with an eye patch and a tambourine," Roger says. "You'll be our guest star."

"I don't have time for this," Holly says. She means both the storm and the conversation.

"I'm not going out in that rain," Danny Tanneyhill says, wiggling into the stool.

"I'm not asking you to go anywhere," Holly says. She chews her bottom lip. There is rage in her green eyes.

The Minotaur sees it. Sees worry, too.

"I'll go," he says, moving toward the rear door.

"Wait," Roger says, contorting on the stool, inside the horn, to reach under the counter. He comes up with a big umbrella.

"Me and the lovely lady will stay here and work out the terms," Danny says.

"I'm coming with you," Holly says to the Minotaur.

Danny Tanneyhill is still voicing his protest when the door closes behind them. Even in the deluge the Minotaur smells the rust and cracking plastic and decaying rubber and fluids seeping into bare earth. He sucks it all in. The Minotaur snorts his approval, and the rain lets up. It might be coincidence, or it might not. Holly opens the umbrella anyway. Two of its wire spines dangle uselessly.

"Just in case," she says.

The Minotaur looks out over Jolly Roger's U-Pull-It, looks at the lay of the land. Sometimes the taxonomy of a salvage yard is impossible to figure. Sometimes the junked and wrecked autos are dumped by nothing more planned than proximity. Sometimes, without rhyme or reason, the cars and trucks, partial or whole, are merely laid to rest where there's space. Anybody looking for anything specific needs some luck.

The Minotaur leads the way.

Jolly Roger's U-Pull-It is not that sort of salvage yard. The organization is clear—make and model, genus and species. The rows are neat and orderly. Almost too much so. Location numbers are posted on high poles. The Minotaur cannot help respecting the sousaphone player. But no, the Minotaur does not sing.

"That dude really wants to blow your horn," Holly says.

The Minotaur likes being under the umbrella with her, though she can't seem to get both of his horns and her own head covered.

"Unngh," the Minotaur says.

He takes the tools out one by one, gathering them in his hand. Right quadrant, Row 11 is easy enough to find, but the Minotaur takes the long way around.

"Sorry," Holly says the next time she hooks his horn tip in the umbrella's ribbing.

"Mmmnn, my fault," he says, then leads the redhead through the densely packed rows of Dodges and Mercurys. Around the Nissan corner. Past three destroyed convertibles.

"Close," he mumbles.

The Minotaur is thinking the words *déjà vu*, but there's no way he can mouth them to her.

"This place gives me the creeps," she says.

The Minotaur wants to explain to Holly the potential for the magical to happen in the junkyard. He knows it. He's experienced it. *Look*, he'd say if he could. *See how the cracked glass looks like a spider web. The hulking still bodies like giant crustaceans. Hear how the rain pings and plunks a different song everywhere you turn.* He'd say, *Listen. In the silence you can hear the rust creeping along. Hear the sun and moon and all their desperate shining.* If the Minotaur could, if he knew how, he'd take Holly into this car, into that car. *Sit here. Take the wheel. Close your eyes.*

"You know some of these people died," Holly says. "You just know it."

"Mmmnn," the Minotaur says. What he means is that not everything here comes from tragedy. Some things simply wear out, and there is beauty in that. Too, sometimes death is not unwelcomed.

They find the Odysseys side by side, as promised. The minivan in the middle has no rear door. The Minotaur sees an empty bucket inside, upturns it for Holly to sit on.

"Thanks," she says.

"Do you think this will take long?" she asks.

"Do you think this will cost much?" she asks.

"No," he says, laying his tools on the damp ground by the rear wheel well. "No."

"I hope not," she says.

"No," the Minotaur says again.

"The pirate dude likes a trade, but I've got nothing to give. I'd give him a tit flash, but—"

"Mmmnn, no," the Minotaur says, shaking his big head.

"Well, he's more interested in your horns than my hooters anyway," Holly says, laughing and tapping both of the Minotaur's horn tips with her fingertips.

"Mmmnn, yes," the Minotaur says.

He goes to work right away. He knows exactly what to do, what he needs.

Holly shields them from the sporadic rain and talks.

"So, is it weird?" she asks. "Is it weird doing the reenactment thing as a . . . you being . . . you know?"

The Minotaur knows what he needs. He feels for the ⅝-inch socket.

"Not so much," he says.

"I think Took would really like it. The battle stuff, the costumes."

"Uniforms," the Minotaur says. He's surprised at the ease with which words fall out of his mouth in her presence. The Minotaur is on his back beneath the Odyssey, his snout nearly rubbing the undercarriage. His bottom half, his human self, Holly keeps dry.

"Thank you so much for doing this," she says. "I don't know what I'd have done without you and dumbass in there."

The Minotaur hears bemusement in her voice. They both hear thunder rolling over the distant mountain. If he cocks his head just right he can see her legs, the wet hems of her jeans.

"This trip," she says. "This trip with Tookus is . . . It's a hard one."

The Minotaur turns the ratchet just to hear it click.

"He doesn't really know where we're going," she says. "I promised him, I promised myself I'd give him one last adventure."

The Minotaur pulls the strut free from its bracket. He thinks about the places he's seen and been during his time in Pennsylvania. Pigeon World. Peachy's Miniature America. Squaw Caverns. Somewhere there's a coal-mine fire that's been burning underground for two decades. The Minotaur doesn't remember the abandoned town's name.

"Mmmnn," the Minotaur says.

"Pittsburgh," she says. "We're headed to Pittsburgh. I found a place . . . "

"Mmmnn," the Minotaur says, his utterance bouncing off the undercarriage.

"I can't," she says. "I mean, I don't always make the best decision, the right choice. Who does? But I can't do it anymore by myself. I have to get on with my own life."

He reaches out and places the part by Holly's bucket.

"And now all this mechanical nonsense," Holly says.

"No," the Minotaur says. Not nonsense.

"Why do you think he told us?" Holly says. "That Roger dude, I mean. Why'd he tell us about all them dead kids?"

"Unngh," the Minotaur grunts from beneath the junked van. His senses, his horns, all of him trapped happily there. It is futile to question almost anybody's motivation for almost any action. But he's willing to imagine some fraction of goodness into the junkman's equation.

"Fucking weirdo," Holly says.

"Fucking dead Amish kids," Holly says.

"Fucking killer, and fucking mothers and fathers and their fucking Amish forgiveness," Holly says.

The Minotaur breathes deeply.

"Truth be told," she says, "Tooky probably won't know the difference. They'll take good care of him. He won't remember. He'll forget me in a week."

There is always potential for magic in a salvage yard. Always. The pig stampede is right around the corner. Always.

"He doesn't remember our mom or dad. We have to be there on Monday. And the money in the jug, well . . . They'll take good care of him.

Won't they?"

"Unngh," the Minotaur says.

"I promised him," she says. "One last adventure. And now . . . "

"Unngh, soo . . . sorry," the Minotaur says, or tries to.

Holly mishears. "Hey!" she says. "You're right! That's it!"

"Mmmnn?" the Minotaur says, but inflection is difficult for him. His old tongue swallows up nuance.

"Old Scald," she says. She puts her hand on his leg as she talks. Squeezes his calf. "You can take us! We'll watch you fight. Maybe Took can wear a costu . . . a uniform!"

In the salvage yard there is always the potential for magic. The Minotaur opens his mouth, and the clouds burst overhead. Hunkers down, since it's time for the truth. The Minotaur opens his mouth again, and the rain retreats. The Minotaur searches for his tongue inside the moment. He should confess. He should tell Holly the truth about what happened at Old Scald Village, and why he can't take them there. About his horns and what they do. About his shame.

"Unngh, yes," he says.

"Okay," he says.

"Tomorrow," he says.

"Mmm," she says. Nothing more. There's been enough talking.

Holly starts to sing. Softly. The Minotaur doesn't recognize the song. No matter. The Minotaur lied. He has sung before, in a different life, in another salvage yard. The Minotaur finished his task awhile ago but wants to stay in the presence of her song. Each note a raindrop in the endless desert of his eternity. The Minotaur wants to drown in those notes. No. Each note a white-hot pinprick in the abject black of his always. The blind Minotaur takes his time. Wallows in it. Sweet time. Sweet time.

"What do you like most?" Holly asks.

"Mmmnn?"

"About the reenacting business. What do you like most?"

"Mmmnn, the dying," the Minotaur says.

"Oh," Holly says.

"Okay," he says at last. "Done."

The Minotaur pulls himself from beneath the Odyssey, gets to his knees. Holly stands. The umbrella, lively in a sudden gust, almost pulls her off balance. The Minotaur almost reaches for her. Holly grabs hold of the Minotaur.

"I like these horns," she says.

"It's too bad . . . ," she says, and leaves the statement incomplete.

Just as they're about to go back into the office Holly asks the Minotaur not to tell Danny about Tookus about the finality of the trip.

"I'm making the best decision, aren't I?" she asks. "The right choice?"

"Mmmnn," he says.

"Thanks."

Holly opens the door in the middle of Danny's story.

"Her daddy was a state trooper," Danny says. "I was thirteen. She was fifteen."

"Hey, there," Roger says, eyeing the Minotaur's handful of auto parts. The sousaphone hasn't moved. "Find everything all right?"

Danny drums his fingers on the countertop. The room smells like pot smoke.

"The very first time we ever got hot and heavy was in the front seat of her daddy's patrol car. I stuck my finger inside, and she started kicking. Kicked on the blue lights, kicked on the siren. I was still inside her when he busted out the window with his gun."

"Unngh," the Minotaur says.

"Hey," Roger says, gesturing at the woodcarver. "I was telling dick-for-brains here that my shanty choir has a gig at Ag-Fest this coming weekend. You should come!"

"What's an Ag-Fest?" Holly asks. "Sounds rancid."

"We celebrate our glorious agrarian culture," Roger says. "There's all kinds of funky music and food and stuff. We'll be spreading the shanty love at noon. Come see us. Hell's bells, come sing with us! Our motto is, 'All you have to be is loud.'"

"Unngh."

"I don't do loud," Holly says. "Right now, anyway. How much do I owe you?" She looks back and forth between Roger and the Minotaur.

"You're all set," Roger says, giving the football helmet a solid thump.

"You are the prince of pirates, Roger," the woodcarver says.

They head for the door. Jolly Roger licks his lips and fingers the valves.

"So, when are you going to give up that sexy necklace?" Roger asks.

"This thing?" Danny Tanneyhill asks, pulling the saw blade from inside his shirt.

It glints even in the fluorescent light. The Minotaur sees it reflected in Holly's eyes.

"This little old thing, you'll never get your hands on, brother. It's the source of all my secret powers."

Roger is blowing long and hard on the sousaphone when they exit.

"We'll take the turnpike," Danny says. "Be home in no time."

CHAPTER EIGHTEEN

THE PENNSYLVANIA TURNPIKE is three hundred and sixty miles long, beginning to end.

But who would do such a thing? The Minotaur would. Beginning to end. End.

The pickup truck hurtling through this midday, this midweek, midstorm, holds an odd trinity.

But who would do such a thing? The Minotaur hunkers in the bed. There is no other way.

Just sit right back and you'll hear a tale.

An obbligato of rain and roaring traffic attends the journey.

The Allegheny Front is one hundred and eighty miles long. Roughly. This valley is drenched. The Minotaur is drenched.

There were seven tunnels on the turnpike. Now there are four. Where do old tunnels go?

There is the migratory bird flyway. Thermals—lift and loft. The sun's ransom.

A tale of a fateful trip. The ecclesiastic earth. Grounded gods.

"I like these horns," she said. The Minotaur will not kowtow to hope.

The internal combustion engine is easy to understand. The carburetor sucks fuel, fires the plugs. Too, there are five lug nuts per wheel. The truck and gravity are one. Orbit this. Orbit that.

There is a moon (lug nut) up there, behind the storm clouds, more or less, two hundred thirty-eight thousand nine hundred miles away. The sun, farther flung. The rest of the celestial menagerie, too.

The Minotaur sits with exactly two horns in the back of the truck. Soaked. Sopping. Head down, gyres of rainwater spiraling from his horn tips. Okay.

The Minotaur has a thick snout. The Minotaur has two eyes, two lungs, one heart.

The Minotaur is at the mercy of gravity, too. Believe it or not. Makes no difference.

Holly has a heart.

It is not made of pine.

Of Holly's heart, this much can be said: "I like these horns."

"The dying," he said.

"I like these horns."

The veins and vessels that carry her blood might just measure seventy-five thousand miles. If you laid them out end to end. But who'd do such a thing? In the face of desire it is all meaningless. A drop in the bucket of want.

 CHAPTER NINETEEN

THE MINOTAUR LIFTS HIS WATERLOGGED noggin when the truck slows in the long sweeping curve before the tollbooth. He wipes his eyes, but it does little good. He is rain drenched. Saturated.

The truck swerves when Danny reaches into his pockets for money.

"Be careful," Holly says. The Minotaur hears it clearly.

Looking backward, he sees the four lanes of turnpike traffic (two each eastbound and westbound) flare too quickly into and out of the wide bank of tollbooths. *Cash Only. E-ZPass.* Watches the drivers in the opposite lanes fight for position as they funnel down into one unforgiving pair of lanes. Watches, too, the swell of vehicles slowing and piling up behind him. Them.

"You still back there?" Holly asks.

The Minotaur shudders. It is not the hiss of air brakes on the semis rattling up on either side that disturbs him, despite the gritty spray of rainwater from the massive wheels. Nor the innocuous couple in the innocuous sedan just to his right, the woman pretending to sleep on the man's lap. It's not even the rust-pocked camo-painted compact SUV riding up on the truck's rear bumper, revving and revving its piteous little four-cylinder engine, the driver clearly glaring at the Minotaur as if the bottleneck of traffic is somehow his fault. No. None of this perturbs the soggy Minotaur. What bothers him, hunched there in the back of the truck in the April rain, what gripes his craw is the easy laughter he hears from the cab of the truck.

"You still back there?"

The truck lurches forward. The Minotaur doesn't answer.

The SUV nearly rear-ends the truck. It skids, stalls, the engine sputtering to an uncertain stop. Rain steams away on the hot hood. The Minotaur sees the feathered arrow shaft jammed into the hole where a radio antenna ought to be. Danny Tanneyhill inches ahead, unaware. The driver of the SUV gets out, in his Walmart security guard uniform, and opens his hood, whacks hard at something with a screwdriver. The Minotaur could be of some help here. If asked. The driver goes back, turns the ignition, and after several weak gyrations the engine catches and spits back to life. He does not need the Minotaur's help. Does not want it. Would not accept it. The driver comes back to slam the hood, turns to the Minotaur with one hand at the ready on the pepper spray at his belt, aims the other hand, middle finger up high, then pointed pistol-like.

"Bang," the man says.

Someone behind him blows a horn.

There is more than hatred in his eyes. No. Eye. One good eye. The other is covered by a milky blue caul. It's like a tiny planet is orbiting in his eye socket. But the good eye rages.

"Bang bang."

"How are you holding up?" Holly asks through the screen. Breaking the spell.

The exchange at the booth is quick enough, but as they pull away the Minotaur catches a glimpse of himself reflected—refracted, maybe—in the pair of bi-fold glass windows hissing shut. For one infernal instant his big head is bifurcated and multiplied, erupting from and spreading out on both sides of the toll collector's massive afro.

"Unngh," the Minotaur says. The Guptas have warned him more than once about Ravana, the demon king.

The Minotaur tucks his snout and waits. He's in a pickle. A pickle of his own making. Tomorrow he's agreed to take the redhead and her brother to Old Scald Village. To watch him fight and die.

Tomorrow is too far away to worry about. Soon enough they're back on Business 220, coming from the far side of Joy. The SUV and its angry driver are on their tail briefly, roaring around them. Good riddance, the Minotaur thinks. But the driver whips off the road without signaling and skids to a stop on a steep dirt path into dark woods. Danny has to slam the brakes hard.

The Minotaur sees them on the rear of the SUV, three bumper stickers:

There's a Place for All God's Creatures, Right Next to the Potatoes & Gravy
Gun Control Activists Taste Like Chicken
Poach This, Bitch!

Good riddance.

CHAPTER TWENTY

THE JUDY-LOU MOTOR LODGE looks good in the rain.

The concrete goose, headless still, sits dressed in a yellow rain slicker by the office door. Gifted there by Tookus, most likely.

"What shall we do with a drunken sailor, early in the morning!" Danny Tanneyhill sings at the top of his lungs, and not half bad.

"What?" Holly says, getting out of the truck.

"Shave his belly with a rusty razor!"

"You're scaring me," Holly jokes.

"Put him in the scuppers with a hose pipe on him!"

The Minotaur doesn't want to hear Danny sing anymore. He rattles the Odyssey parts more than necessary over the tailgate. Rambabu Gupta comes out of the office, his black eyes full of welcome, and beckons them inside. Holly and the Minotaur. They watch Danny go to the Pygmalia-Blades trailer, open the rolling door, and enter. Singing all the way.

"Put him in bed with the captain's daughter!"

The soft chittering of the office door bells soothes the Minotaur, though Holly seems a little startled.

"*Gooooooooo laaaaaaaaab,*" Tookus says from the back room. He says it again, and more excitedly, when he sees Holly. "*Gooooooooo laaaaaaaab jaaaaaaa muuuuuuuun.*"

Devmani Gupta jumps down from the couch with one of the honey-soaked dumplings raised high. The syrup trickles down her little-girl fingers and pools in her palm before she sticks the cake into the Minotaur's mouth.

"*Gulab jamun*," she says with pride, then licks at her hand.

Tookus seems content. Well cared for, if a bit sticky. He sits, as much as he is capable of sitting, watching cartoons. Devmani is amused by his spastic motions. Her presence, calming. The bandages are gone from his hands, a few Band-Aids in their place. On the counter in the office, Rambabu has lined up five ice buckets. Each one is filled with coins in tight paper rolls. Gratitude overwhelms. Holly cries but tries to hide it. They let her.

"Guess what, Tooky," she says. She sidles up to her little brother and whispers in his ear.

Tookus grins, giggles, tries to grab her breast, then sticks his tongue out at the Minotaur. Devmani copies him.

"Tomorrow," Holly says to Tookus.

It is late afternoon. The rain has plans for the rest of the day. The Minotaur and Holly stand on the sidewalk and look across Business 220. The Minotaur tells Holly he'll fix the Odyssey tomorrow. After? Before? He wonders what Holly will do until then. Wonders what he has to offer. Danny Tanneyhill has several chainsaws lined up. He lubes the blades. Everything smells like honey and sawdust and oil.

"It'll be dark soon," Holly says. "I'm going to get Tooky cleaned up and give him his medicine."

"Mmmnn," the Minotaur says. He feels rainwater dripping down his spine.

Holly takes something from her back pocket. The thing from the Yoder's bulletin board. It's soggy, and the ink has smeared.

"Fuck," she mutters. Holly crumples the paper and tosses it to the ground.

The Minotaur forgives her trespass. He'll pick up the litter eventually.

"So," Holly says, "tomorrow, first thing?"

She's talking about the Honda, right?

"Unngh."

Danny is still singing. The rain is still falling. The highway steams.

"I wonder if he sleeps in that thing," Holly says.

She collects Tookus, thanks the Guptas again and again.

In passing, the boy takes hold of the Minotaur. "Hornsssssss," Tookus says. "Horny horn horn."

Holly smiles, loosens her brother's grip.

In passing, the redhead takes hold of the Minotaur. No. She only speaks. "I know, Took," she says. "I like them, too. I reckon we all do."

The Minotaur stands alone on the sidewalk, looking across Business 220, looking up the steep side of Scald Mountain to where it disappears in the soupy gray cloud. Trucks roar by on the invisible turnpike. He picks up the scrap of paper, thinking maybe he'll decipher it later and bring the news to Holly.

The Minotaur goes into Room #3, closes the door, closes the curtain. He flattens the wet paper on the dresser. He thumbs at the thermostat, and the heater fires to life. The Minotaur is rain soaked to his core. He hasn't been this wet in a long time. He turns the light off. He strips down. Naked. He lies on the narrow bed atop the rough blanket. Everything smells like sawdust and motor oil and honey. The Minotaur settles his horns into the lumpy pillows and waits for things to dry. He'll wait as long as it takes.

CHAPTER TWENTY-ONE

HERE LIES THE MINOTAUR. Horned for his entire life. Hemmed in by errant desire. His tongue fat as a mattock blade. Hear him chop at speech. Silence, then. There is gristle in the creature's teeth older than everything around him. Except maybe the Allegheny Mountains. In the plat books the world gets hacked to bits. It's the wholly human need to parse out all, to make sense of, to control. The gridded planet. Find your place. Know your place. The Minotaur knows where he falls, and falls short. Knows, too, his strong suit. It's his hands. They are capable hands. Adept with tools. Daedal, even. One time, lifetimes ago, there was a bird carved from an apple. The brilliant white flesh and the deep red peel. A girl touched his hand. Chop chop. One time the Minotaur saw an old man in purple short-short overalls and no shirt set fire to a calico cat. It was at a party. Everybody but the Minotaur was human. The Minotaur did not ask to see any of this. The Minotaur did not ask for the pitch black of his first stone prison, nor for the blinding thread that led him into eternity. He sees too much now. Time stops and starts, folds and unfolds, loops and undulates. The Minotaur believes in no gods. But he is sustained nonetheless.

The Minotaur is not one to get his hopes up. Not one to count chickens, cross bridges, etc. Not often, anyway. When the moon finally broadaxes its way through the night's cloud cover, the Minotaur hears a door open and close. Goes, then, to his own door, waits. If it is Holly. If she knocks. If he answers, naked. If she enters. If and if and if.

Maybe he'll fess up. Maybe he'll tell the truth. Maybe. Anything she wants.

Parts the blinds, just enough. It is Holly, there in the muted gaze of April moonlight. There by the *Judy-Lou Motor Lodge* sign. Standing still. Thinking, maybe. She plucks a little American flag from the planter, waves it at the selfsame moon halfheartedly, the moonlight trying as hard as it can to out-pale, out-beauty the white flesh of her bare legs. Loses, the moon. The Minotaur sees it all. The moonlight, the T-shirt, the flag, the wave, the legs, the pause. What is she waiting for? The Minotaur eases the door's chain bolt from its slot ever so quietly, just in case.

Holly, in motion, goes back to her own Judy-Lou door. Does not enter but listens, one ear pressed just below the brass room number. Stays until something (or more likely nothing) satisfies her, then heads down the sidewalk. Holly has made a decision. Holly has made a choice.

The Minotaur's heart is as capable as any other. Century after century of pumping the mixed blood has taken its toll on the old organ, but still it beats harder when Holly approaches. Keeps beating hard when she walks right past Room #3 and on across Business 220.

"Mmmnn," the Minotaur says. Parts the blinds still more. Watches Holly tap at the Pygmalia-Blades trailer door. Watches it gobble her whole in one bite.

The Minotaur snorts. Grunts. Everything stinks of honey and moonlight and sawdust. There is nothing he can do about it. The Minotaur bears witness. Has for centuries. Millennia. Forever he is conscripted to watch the actions of humans. And a thing once seen cannot be unseen. He steps outside, good sense be damned. Stands dead center of the parking space allocated for Room #3.

"Unngh," he says in the direction of Pygmalia-Blades.

It's been a long time since the Minotaur was naked in the open air. The trailer door closed behind her. Holly is inside. He saw it happen. A car approaches from way down Business 220, the splay of its headlights swelling. The Minotaur will not be moved. But he covers himself. Lays a very human hand over his very average cock, as if that's what passersby would notice. The car speeds by without slowing. The Minotaur ventures closer. And closer still. Maybe she was drugged. Maybe hypnotized. Some black magic at work. The Minotaur has never trusted the woodcarver's dark arts. That tongue of his, the woodcarver's, a chisel, an adze, a rasp.

The Minotaur stands naked in the middle of Business 220, looks up and down the road. His bull half and his man half cast one shadow. Faint. A little of the moonlight gets caught in his horns. The Minotaur tips his head, lets go of the light. Maybe they're just talking in the trailer. Just.

He approaches. The Minotaur is not stealthy. There's no way around that fact. But he makes it unscathed through the wooden beasts of Danny Tanneyhill's menagerie. Just. He hears them breathing. The statues. No. The humans in the trailer. Throaty. Scald Mountain breathes, too. A cold wind, an accusing wind, unfurls down its slopes, chills the naked Minotaur.

He could yank the trailer door open. Could see. Could save Holly from the woodcarver's clutches. It's within the realm of possibility for the Minotaur to do so. Possible but not probable.

The Minotaur circles the trailer, listening. Maybe they're just praying. Maybe they're conjuring up a god or two, for the betterment of all. Maybe. An opossum, conjured out of the underbrush, shuffles by, lollygags, and in godlike fashion pays no mind to any of the shenanigans taking place in the Chili Willie's parking lot. Maybe they're singing in the trailer, though the possibility stings the Minotaur deeply. Maybe, in his upset, the Minotaur sits himself down on a rough stump, leans against the half-cut trunk he'd saved the woodcarver from earlier, and sitting there naked in the April night, the bark digging into his flesh, maybe he realizes that those carved legs and feet and the half-formed body hacked out of the trunk are meant to be him. Sees the nascent horns taking shape.

The realization sears. The Minotaur grunts. Or maybe it's them grunting. And maybe the grunting is too much. Something about a straw and a camel's back. Maybe the Minotaur stands up too quickly, his horn tip piercing the canopy. Maybe he recoils, stumbles, nearly falls.

Maybe that's why he doesn't hear Tookus approach.

"Ffffuckerrrrr. Ffuuuucking fucker. Fuckinggggggggg fuckerrrr. Sissy!"

The Minotaur sees the boy, arms in constant motion, conducting an unseen orchestra, a symphony of anguish. The boy doesn't see the Minotaur.

The Minotaur scuttles around the side of the trailer. And what with all the singing and praying inside the trailer, Holly and Danny Tanneyhill don't hear the boy weep. The Minotaur hears it. Tookus cries on the other side of the Pygmalia-Blades trailer. Cries and cries. Wordless, finally, or pure babel towering, then toppling. Syllables scatter lifeless on the ground.

The Minotaur wishes he could help somehow. The singing and the praying reach a fevered pitch, boxed up as they are between the naked Minotaur and the weeping boy. The boy. Numbskull. Lamebrain. Bedlamite. Retard. Moonstruck. Dum-dum. Slaphappy. Touched. Brother.

Tookus quits his vigil and goes back to his room at the Judy-Lou, leaving the door ajar. The Minotaur follows, sort of. His bullish heart is conflicted. What to do? He hesitates, and in the moment of indecision everybody hears the explosion.

The explosion.

The explosion blows the door open wide. The flash strips away the night for the briefest instant. Sound, too. Everything rings. Tookus staggers out of the motel room shaking his head, holding his ears, blinking his eyes, mouth agape.

A firecracker, the Minotaur thinks. *An M80*. He knows these things.

Tookus, staggering still, hurt, maybe, or maybe not, but shell shocked, circles in the parking lot. The Judy-Lou office door is flung open and Rambabu Gupta steps into the night. His knee-length silk kurta, iridescent gold, seems alive. The man's eyes are wide and searching.

That's when the Minotaur remembers his nakedness. He scurries, crouched, big head all a-wobble, behind the only other car in the Judy-Lou lot. Peers through the windows to watch Danny Tanneyhill yank up the trailer door and stand, not quite covered by his boxer shorts (red ones, with a fortune-cookies-and-chopsticks pattern), looking far too defiant. The saw-blade necklace keens in the moonlight. Holly rushes out past him, tugging up her own underwear.

"Move," the Minotaur hears her say.

"Aw, come on!" Danny says, hands up. "We're not done."

The Minotaur watches Holly pause ever so briefly, pick up a stick, clench her jaw. Sees her release the urge, drop the stick, shuck off the bond of anger, and go toward Tookus.

Ramneek Gupta comes to the door. "Be careful, *pati*," she says.

"Tooky," Holly says, opening her arms, "are you okay? You should be sleeping. You were supposed to—"

"Unnnnngggggg," Tookus says, squeezing his head tightly with both hands. "Fuckkkk. Pussy pussy tit lickerrrrr."

"Shhh."

Rambabu Gupta goes into the open room.

"What happened?" Holly asks.

Ramneek is the only one clearly present. She doesn't answer.

The Minotaur squats naked behind a car at the far end of the lot. The doorknob of the nearest room jiggles, and the half-bull half-man scrambles. The Minotaur, haunches up, head down, trots on all fours around the building. There is no time for shame. He's been here before. At the rear of the motel the Minotaur stands, tilts his head away from the brick wall, and hurries along the skinny patch of earth down to his own bathroom window, where, after some graceless and likely obscene contortions, he climbs through, dresses quickly, and goes, flustered, out the front door of Room #3.

• • •

The resolution is swift. Tookus had dropped a lit M80, stolen from Danny Tanneyhill, into the toilet of the Judy-Lou room. The ceramic bowl shattered, the tank cracked and fell apart, water gushed onto the tile floor, piss yellow and clotted with fecal matter. Humans at their most animal.

"This is very bad business, Mr. M," Rambabu Gupta says. "Very bad. I do not understand what happened."

The Minotaur steps in to close the valve. He will not be deterred by the human filth.

"Unngh," the Minotaur says. No more.

Tookus sits on the edge of the bed fidgeting, confounded by his still-ringing ears. Holly kneels with a towel to mop up the water. The white towel tints pinkish where she touches. Holly looks at her hands. The Minotaur and Rambabu look at her hands and see there the lines of tiny crisscross cuts on each of her palms. The Minotaur helps Holly stand, leads her to the bed. He will clean the mess. Danny Tanneyhill stands in the trailer door, sweaty, indignant, strangely beautiful in his apathy. The Minotaur hears the trailer door slam shut. Or maybe it's the chittering of the saw-blade necklace.

"I do not understand, Mr. M," Rambabu says. "These people and their bloody hands."

"I thought he was sleeping," Holly says. "I gave him his medicine."

Holly will not look at the Minotaur.

Ramneek comes into the room. The room that was to be Bavishya's. Becky's. It is ruined. Tookus is not bleeding. Not wounded visibly.

Holly, up off the bed, wrings the sopping towel into the sink. Kneels again. "I'll pay for the damages," Holly says. "We'll sleep in the van."

The Guptas converse quietly in their native tongue.

"I'm sorry," Holly says.

"I'm sorry," Holly says. "I'm sorry."

Ramneek Gupta lays a hand on Holly's shoulder. Opens her other hand, in which lies a key to another Judy-Lou room.

"Go," Ramneek says. "Sleep. In the morning I will make for you the scramble egg and the bacons."

• • •

Of sleep, the Minotaur gets none, excited as he is by what the coming day promises. This incident, this small-scale destruction, is a gift. A saving grace. It means the trip to Old Scald Village will be delayed, put off, maybe even forgotten. The Minotaur is content to lie in the narrow bed and wait for sunlight to meander down Scald Mountain. When it does, as soon as he can see clearly the lay of the land, he gets to work. The toilet has to be replaced, the plumbing reconnected, the Odyssey's universal joint and brakes installed. Useful. The Minotaur will be useful all day long.

By midmorning he's made the trip to Scald Plumbing Supply and has the shiny new American Standard toilet in place on its red wax seal. Rambabu nods in gratitude when the water begins trickling into the tank. Before noon the Minotaur is across Business 220, kneeling on a flattened cardboard box by the side of the jacked-up Odyssey. His hands are slick with axle grease.

Danny Tanneyhill putters around beneath the Pygmalia-Blades awning as if nothing happened. The woodcarver pauses from time to time and stares across the road. Just before noon he sells a carving of an angel to a woman in a convertible VW Bug. She flies away happily.

Just after noon a car pulls up to the Judy-Lou. Two bedraggled parents and half a dozen kids, the whole brood wearing and wielding a mishmash of Old Scald Village Gift Shoppe purchases, pile out of the vehicle. They check in and unload at the far end of the motel. Within minutes Devmani Gupta has joined the gaggle of children running back and forth between the cars and the brick planter, shooting at each other with rubber-tipped arrows and cap guns, squealing and dying giddily all over the place.

The fracas wakes Holly. Holly enters the day. The Minotaur watches as closely as he can without seeming to watch. Tookus follows his sister from the motel room. The kids shoot at each other and laugh and run, and when Tookus tries to join in—"Bang bang bang bang bang," he says—it scares them. All but Devmani.

"Get in here now!" the sallow-faced mother hollers from their room, and they flock to her call.

The shirtless father steps in the doorway, puffs up his chest, glowering at Tookus. Devmani takes Tookus's hand and pulls him into the office. Holly goes, too.

Before long the Minotaur smells bacon. And just as he is tightening the final lug nut Holly crosses Business 220 bearing a plate covered in foil. An offering plate. A tithe of sorts. The Minotaur half-expects her to veer left, toward Pygmalia-Blades, but no, she walks right up to the Odyssey.

"Hey," Holly says. Sheepish. Like she's been found out. Caught at something. The reflection of her red hair partially eclipses the shiny foil. Holly uncovers a small mountain of bacon and pale yellow egg. "Hungry?"

"Unngh," the Minotaur answers.

The question is both ridiculously simple and impossibly complicated. He shows the redhead his filthy hands. Holly thinks. Holly reaches and with two fingers wiggles a strip of bacon from the pile. It would be easy enough for her to feed the Minotaur. She holds the bacon up. Given the wide expanse of his bony forehead and the long snout, the Minotaur has to cock his head to see the piece of meat. *Tithe pig.* It's an old phrase. Easy enough for him to be fed.

"Unngh," he says. Easy enough to just open his mouth.

"Hey, there!" Danny Tanneyhill says way too loudly as he approaches.

Holly sighs and eats the piece of bacon.

"Everybody sleep okay?" the woodcarver asks.

Nobody answers. Holly crimps the foil back along the edge of the plate. She's nervous. Twitchy.

"Listen," Danny says. "I'm sorry about—"

"I slept just fine," Holly interrupts. "Why wouldn't I?"

Holly almost drops the covered plate. She will not look at the Minotaur. She glares at the woodcarver.

"Why wouldn't I?" she repeats.

Neither Holly nor Danny Tanneyhill knows what the Minotaur saw.

"All I meant . . . ," the woodcarver says.

Holly hands him the plate of food.

The Minotaur sticks the bladed end of the lug wrench into the jack's nut and begins cranking; the Odyssey rocks gently in lowering.

"Look at you go," Danny Tanneyhill says to the Minotaur, then scoops up a finger full of scrambled egg.

"Done," the Minotaur says to Holly.

"Thank you so much. I don't know how I'll repay—"

"Dude's a regular wizard with a wrench," Danny says with egg in his teeth.

"You've got egg in your teeth," Holly says.

Danny goes to work with his tongue. "Anyway," he says, "I had a great idea."

"Here you go," Holly says, offering the Minotaur a napkin.

"You and T-boy have had a hard couple of days," the woodcarver says.

"Couple of days, huh?" Holly says.

"At least," Danny Tanneyhill says. "And I want to treat you to something. To show you something. You and your brother."

The Minotaur snaps the jack into place in the compartment at the rear of the van and slams the door. Of course Holly will say no to whatever it is Danny is offering.

"What?" Holly asks. "What do you want to show me? I'm not sure I want to see anything you've got."

"It's a place," Danny says. "A special place. A secret place. Besides, you owe me one."

"What?" Holly says.

"Unngh," the Minotaur says.

"I mean, I owe you one," Danny says, grinning.

Holly looks at the Odyssey, looks (briefly) at the Minotaur, looks up and down Business 220, looks finally at the sun hurtling overhead.

"You sound like a ten-year-old boy," Holly says.

"Come on! We can take the van. Everybody's invited, even big boy here."

Holly backs up against the Odyssey, winces, and touches her rump.

"It's right over the hill," Danny says. "We'll be back by dark."

Holly sighs.

Holly has a choice to make. Decisions to reach.

"Let me talk to Took," she says.

"Okey-dokey," Danny Tanneyhill says.

When Holly gathers herself to cross back over Business 220, the woodcarver starts to follow.

"Alone," Holly says.

CHAPTER TWENTY-TWO

THE MINOTAUR SITS IN THE REAR of the Odyssey. In the way-back. He had to climb in slowly, navigating the seatbelts and grab bars before plopping into the dead center of the last seat. The tips of his horns brush against the pocked and stained headliner. The Minotaur keeps his head low. Tookus has the middle-row bench seat all to himself, and consumes it fully with his nonstop twitching and flailing and jabbering. Holly drives. Her red hair burns against the high bucket seat's black fabric. The woodcarver rides shotgun. A cloud of sawdust swirls around him. Maybe not.

"It's not far," Danny Tanneyhill says. "Just over Dumb Hundred Road."

And off they go, the motley cargo of the Odyssey, like a bargain basement ark, understaffed, half baked, harebrained. Forty days and forty nights, or a mere handful of miles. No difference. The Minotaur looks for Holly's eyes in the mirror. He's cleaned himself up. He's tried one final time to decipher the rain-smeared paper from Holly's pocket. Crumpled it. It's clear enough; there are some things one never gets to know.

"Blaaaaa-bla-bla-bla-bla-bla-bla," Tookus says.

"Shhh," Holly says. "Settle down, Took."

Tookus is pilloried, held prisoner by his own stroke of misfortune. The brother begins drumming the backs of his hands against the minivan's roof. The Minotaur wonders if the boy remembers the promised trip to Old Scald Village. Wonders if his sister had to lie, or if the boy's brain simply let the promise go unnoticed. Tookus begins to box the van's headliner with both fists.

"Nnnnnothing!" he says. "Nnnnnnnothing. I seeeeeee nooooothing. Nooothing!"

"Okay, okay," Holly says, and pokes a button on the dashboard. A small video screen drops open from an overhead console.

"Nnnnothing! I seeeeeeeeee nothhhhhhhing," Tookus says, practically giddy with anticipation.

The screen flickers to life; the Odyssey fills with soundtrack. Peppy. Military through and through. Hup, hup. Left, right, left. Snare drums and brass and those godforsaken piccolos.

"Is that *Hogan's Heroes*?" the woodcarver asks, laughing. "You know they're all Jews, right? Even the bad guys."

"So?" Holly says.

"They're Jews playing German officers, in a concentration-camp sitcom."

"We all have to play something," Holly says.

"Do you remember the one where the fake Hitler—"

"I've never watched it," Holly interrupts. "Tooky, put your earbuds in, please."

Tookus wiggles the little plastic orbs into his ears, plugs the cord into place, grins madly, and turns his head from side to side in slow arcs.

"It keeps him quiet," Holly says.

They drive by Old Scald Village. Holly stares, unflinching, straight ahead. The Minotaur has to close his eyes.

"Yo, cowboy," Danny Tanneyhill calls back. "I saw the poster for your blood fest."

"Unngh?"

"The shoot-'em-up at Old Scald this weekend. You ready to get your dead on?"

"Shhh!" Holly says.

The Minotaur opens his eyes, sees Holly in the mirror, quickly averts her look.

"Why do you have to talk so goddamn much?" Holly says to the woodcarver.

"There go them wadded panties again," Danny Tanneyhill says. "I was just trying to—"

"Yes," the Minotaur manages to stammer. "Dead."

He notices something dangling from the thin crevice at the bottom of Tookus's seat back. He reaches for it. The Minotaur knows the thing between his fingers is fabric, but that's all he knows. He tugs once, twice, and on the third time the crumby stuffed mermaid doll is birthed.

"Unngh," he grunts.

The Minotaur begins picking bits of food and detritus from the doll. Butterscotch and gunpowder. The scents fill the Minotaur's big snout. He can't separate them. There is a tear in the mermaid's tail. The Minotaur doesn't mean to pull so much stuffing out.

"I didn't bring any money," Holly says.

"This better be good," Holly says.

"This better be free," Holly says.

The Minotaur knows that all her coins sit in their tight paper rolls in the motel room.

The Odyssey's windows are tinted, and the Minotaur looks out at the muted world as it passes. The sign says that the Scald Mt. Rod & Gun Club has adopted the highway, but the Minotaur knows an orphan when he sees it.

"How much farther?" Holly asks.

"Unngh," the Minotaur says, too quietly for anyone to hear.

Tookus giggles loudly and suddenly and hits the van's roof with both fists. Danny Tanneyhill jumps in his seat, turns as if he's going to speak. As if.

There is more that the Minotaur wants to say.

"Turn right," Danny says, and just before they leave Business 220 an ambulance passes, lights whipping the day into froth, siren at full roar. Holly begins touching the front of her shirt, looks as if she's about to reach over to Danny, but instead turns and plants her thumb in the center of her brother's shirt.

"What in God's name are you doing?" Danny asks.

"Looking for a button," she says. "If you don't touch a button when you see an ambulance, you'll be the next person to ride in one."

Danny Tanneyhill laughs. Danny Tanneyhill talks a blue streak. Talks about his chainsaw. Talks about its splintery outcomes.

"Tell me a secret about yourself," Danny says to Holly.

"No."

"Come on," he says. "Don't be such a pussy."

"Stop looking at my tits," Holly says.

"I'm not looking at your tits," Danny lies. "Tell me one little secret."

Even the Minotaur can tell he's looking at Holly's breasts. The Minotaur is certain Holly will not take the woodcarver's bait. Certain.

"When I was little," Holly says, "I used to eat scabs."

"Yum," Danny says, then jumps right back into his own narrative. "One time my folks took us to this backwoods retarded zoo. I was a little little kid. We pulled up a long bumpy driveway. Dirt. I spilled a cup of Cheerios in my lap."

The Minotaur wishes he had earbuds like Tookus. Though they probably wouldn't stay in his ears. The Minotaur wishes he had different ears.

Danny Tanneyhill continues. "There was a barn with a huge monster pigeon head painted on the side. I was looking the pigeon in the eye. I wasn't watching out the other window. My mama shrieked, 'Look at that! I never saw a pigeon like that before!' It wasn't a pigeon. It was an ostrich, or an emu, some huge motherfucker. My mama laughed when it stuck its nasty head in the window. Laughed when it started pecking the Cheerios out of my crotch. I was trapped in the car seat, and I was wearing shorts. It pecked and pecked, and she laughed and laughed, until I was bleeding. I was too scared to make a sound."

"Yum," Holly says.

"Whose?" Danny asks. "Whose scabs did you eat?"

"Mine," Holly says. "Mostly. Mostly mine."

"Nnnnothing! I seeeeeeeeee nothhhhhhhing," Tookus says, and smacks himself on the forehead until Holly stops the van and makes him quit. Someone has posted No Trespassing signs every few yards on the left side of the road.

"You never did tell me where you're headed," Danny says.

"I didn't?" Holly says with feigned surprise. "Gosh! How inconsiderate of me."

"Some sort of top-secret mission?" Danny asks. "You'd have to kill me after telling?"

"I might kill you anyway," Holly says, then looks in the rearview. "How're you doing back there?"

"Mmmnn," the Minotaur says.

Danny Tanneyhill has his arm out of the window. He bangs a steady rhythm on the door with his thumb.

"The convent," the redhead says. "I'm joining God's army."

"Are ya, now?"

"Yep. This time next week I'll be on the battlefield for my Lord."

"Huh," Danny says, and pokes his thumb toward the backseat. "What about . . . ?"

"Tooky's going to be an altar boy, a career man."

"Right," Danny says.

"Go right at the fork," Danny says.

"That's Dumb Hundred Road," Danny says.

The Odyssey's engine stutters, catches, and the van lurches ahead. The Minotaur reaches out both hands, steadies himself.

"I'm serious," Danny Tanneyhill says. "Where're you headed? What's the hurry?"

Holly ponders her answer. "School," she says finally.

This might be true. The Minotaur pricks up his ears.

"Culinary school. Classes start Monday."

"What about . . . ?" Danny searches for the best words. "What about Mister Giggles?" He gestures with his head and thumb at Tookus.

Holly sucks her teeth. "Tooky . . . Took's going home. Sort of."

"Like a group home? Or a hosp—"

Holly stomps the brakes briefly, but it's enough to shut the wood-carver up. The Minotaur is braced enough. Tookus surges against his seatbelt. Begins to perseverate.

"Titty titty titty titty pinnnnnnnnch!"

There is rage in Holly's eyes. She pulls the van to the shoulder by a boggy swath of land at the road's edge. Dozens of dead trees jut straight up out of tannin-black water. She turns to soothe her brother.

"Sorry," Danny Tanneyhill says. "I didn't mean to . . . "

"It's okay," Holly says. "I overreacted."

"I got to pee," the woodcarver says, hopping out of the Odyssey. "Be right back."

Tookus calms quickly, goes back into the world of *Hogan's Heroes*.

"Can we talk?" Holly asks the Minotaur quietly.

The Minotaur has many answers. Has much to say. But his old tongue won't play ball. And Danny is back quickly.

"You could stay around these parts awhile," Danny says. "You could start school next term."

The Minotaur grunts. Holly sucks her teeth more vehemently.

"How much farther?" Holly asks.

"Mmmnn," the Minotaur says.

The woodcarver clucks his tongue. Holly winces again, uncomfortable in her seat. The Minotaur remembers the scratch from his horn. Thinks infection. Hopes not.

"Look," Holly says, pointing out the window at the bog, all those limbless trunks bleached white as bone. Rank and file. Morass and mire. Like an army marching out of death.

"Look," she says to the woodcarver. "They're coming after you."

• • •

"Can we talk?" she said.

What will he say? How will he explain?

Here the Minotaur backslides. Lapses into fantasy. He is not above this sort of dalliance. Here the old bull gives in. And Holly. The redhead. In this version of the future the Minotaur swings wide the door of Sojourner's Tavern. The church bells and their mad clappers fill the blue blue sky with glorious noise. Herds and gaggles of schoolkids dash hither and yon, dipping candle wicks at the Dumpert House, pecking out butterfly and heart shapes in the Tin Punch Cottage. Scald Mountain, the namesake of the village, whistles a piney tune high overhead. The Minotaur swings wide the door, hears the happy pop of muskets, gunfire on the distant battlefield. The Minotaur is not there, dead or about to die. The Minotaur is in Sojourner's Tavern. Open for business. The scabbard and cartridge box swapped for an apron and a pair of kitchen tongs. The church bells beat the silence to a bloody pulp. On the porch opposite the tavern, Doc wields a rubber femur. Waves it, grinning, at the Minotaur. The air is dry as husk, as broom straw. Or maybe it's not church bells. Maybe it is the anvil, hammered. The Minotaur shudders, dismisses the thought, goes into the tavern, into the kitchen, to his helpmeet. A redhead stands at the wood stove. She's checking a batch of hand pies, ground lamb and a vegetarian option. She wears a gingham dress. A white apron. They fit her well. Maybe it is the anvil and the hot stinking eye of the forge. There's powder on her nose. The Minotaur leans close, blows gently. She nuzzles his thick neck. The piecrusts are perfect. The church bells. If only the church bells would still their goddamn clappers. Ding dong ding dong ding dong.

• • •

"Ding dong," says Tookus, then again and again. "Ding dong ding dong ding dong."

The Minotaur comes back to the moment, back to his seat in the Odyssey.

Holly gets out of the driver's seat. She's left the key in the ignition. The warning bell insists on it. Ding dong. Ding dong. Holly opens the sliding door. Daylight floods the space. A flat white April daylight. The Minotaur squints, follows Tookus out of the Odyssey. They all stand in a line, looking at the high fence and the tattered banner draped across the weathered signs.

"*Closed for the Season*," Holly says. "This is it? This is your special place? And it's closed for the season?"

The woodcarver had hoped for more enthusiasm. Much more. He'd hoped that Ghoul's Farm, with its ten-acre corn maze, bungee pumpkin launch, petting zoo, and zombie barn would, even closed, woo the redhead, in a roundabout sort of way.

"I thought the boy would like it," Danny says.

"You're a regular Einstein, aren't you?" Holly says. "That brain of yours just won't quit."

Holly takes her brother by the hand and walks to the locked gate.

"What do you think, M?" she calls over her shoulder.

The Minotaur steps up to the *Ghoul's Farm* plywood sign. The weathered board is the same flaky gray as his bull skin. The Minotaur looks into the cartoon zombie faces, the rotting wounds, lips and gums peeled back to reveal bits of gnawed gore in the chipped and missing teeth, looks at the eyes, into their wormy sockets. The Minotaur looks closely. What does he think? These are not the dead that one should fear. But there's no way his fat tongue can voice this thought.

"Unngh," he says.

The woodcarver grabs hold of the padlock and chain at the gate. Rattles them. The lock pops opens easily. Danny Tanneyhill holds the chain aloft, touting his dubious victory. He kicks the gate. The gate swings wide. Tookus takes off running full bore, disappears into the corn maze.

"Goddamn it!" Holly says, mostly at Danny. "Do something!"

"What am I supposed to do?" he asks.

Holly runs after her brother.

The woodcarver shrugs his shoulders at the Minotaur. "Women," he says. "Can't live without 'em, can't kill 'em."

The Minotaur refuses to take part.

She runs after her brother. Danny, giving in, follows, taking his handful of chain along, tripping on his way past the now-gutless scarecrow tied to the stile and the several outstretched mannequin arms reaching from among the bales of stacked hay forming the entry walls.

"Mmmnn," the Minotaur says.

The Minotaur wants to help.

The Minotaur wants to help. He does.

The dirt path turns just inside the hay bales. Left and right. A high screen of dry and yellow cornstalks latticed with chicken wire and posts blocks the way. The entire maze is constructed thus. Ten acres of criss-crossing bare earth walkways hemmed by cornstalk fencing, dead ends galore, one entrance and one exit. Through maze walls that are rife with breaches, ruptures, gaps—kicked in by rowdy teens or surrendering to rot—Tookus disappears immediately. He could be anywhere. The Minotaur wants to help.

The Minotaur stands at the mouth of the maze. The mouth of the maze whispers. Both secrets and lies. Tells stories. Makes lists. Everything the Minotaur has ever done, right or wrong. In the name of love. The Minotaur hears the redhead calling for her brother. Hears, too, the boy whooping and shrieking. It might be terror. It might not. The Minotaur wants to help. The humans, the fully humans, are deep in the maze. The Minotaur can forgive them their exclusion. They know not what they do. Bullshit. The Minotaur is not without insight, his own blunt wisdom. He has little to offer the girl. He understands the woodcarver's appeal—the fire in his eyes, that saw blade around his neck, that scar. The Minotaur knows about scar tissue. He slips a fingertip inside his shirt, scratches mindlessly at his own. More seam, really, than scar. There was no transplant. No aberrant puzzle making. No. The graft that made the Minotaur took place at the core of desire, where the very cells are gargantuan. Desire. Take heed, the whip. Desire is not the heart's mollycoddler. Desire rides a wrecking ball, leaves havoc in its wake. Take heed.

Desire, both wrecking ball and prison. Of prisons the Minotaur knows much, having dragged his own stone labyrinth behind him forever. Stacking and restacking. O mortar! O brickbat! Sometimes the slog is so arduous that the yoke of his history bears down on his haunches, shreds the ligaments, plucks a discordant hymn on the tendons, grinds into the shoulders, the clavicles crackling under the strain. Sometimes, though, it's back there hurtling and buoyant. Sometimes the Minotaur forgets, for whole eons, that the labyrinth is nipping at his heels. Then, sometimes—say, late April in the Allegheny Mountains, at the cusp of an already weary millennium—the Minotaur stops short, too short, and the stone walls topple toward him. Move.

The Minotaur wants to help. The mouth of the maze beckons, chides. He wants to help. To enter. The span of his horns, the anatomy of all that is bullish about him, heaves into the desire. The Minotaur steps up to the gateway, crosses the threshold into the maze, into the labyrinth, and five thousand years squash him flat.

CHAPTER TWENTY-THREE

DREAMS THE MINOTAUR OF CONSTELLATION and curse. Word. Word.

Of milk money. Of pig iron and steam engine.

Dreams the flock of grackles. The field of narcissus.

The apple's flesh and the swan, redeemed.

The Minotaur dreams the chambered pit. The planks and bones. Reflection, that uppity gasbag.

Dreams perfect attendance, the ritual bath, some kind of trophy with the head broken off.

Blessed be the Cub Scouts and the leaky oak gall.

First aid and second aid and third aid and fourth aid and fifth aid and sixth aid.

On the seventh day they rested. The Minotaur dreams of bloodlines.

The moment of cramped ecstasy. One longs for hooves. One hoofs for length.

Dreams the Minotaur of blueprints. Bluebells. Blue balls.

Of bunk and flapdoodle. Hocus-pocus and prattle.

Butter churn and backslider. The evangelical twat.

Dreams the Minotaur of refraction, that babbling whore.

Everybody says so.

The Minotaur dreams a chicken-scratch manifesto and amendments out the yin-yang.

The solipsistic acre and Mercator's comforting hacksaw.

The yolk stalk and roasting ear.

Dreams the proclamatory titmouse and a congregation of dither fish.

Dreams the precursor to loft and drag. As abominations go it is first-rate. Blessed be the bloody stumps that built the bunkhouse. Blessed the balm and the broomstick.

Dreams, too, the dervish in us all. Whirligig and geegaw.

And now let us praise the crow. Prince of the glottal stop. Stop.

Praise the crow, his chortle, his chutzpah.

Praise the crow. The begetting crow who lies with cloven hooves.

Who lies quiet among clacking looms.

Who begat the whole black shebang. Who?

 *CHAPTER TWENTY-FOUR*

"HEY."

The Minotaur falls dead to the Pennsylvania ground. Belly up. Rots.

"Hey, are you okay?"

What? No. Not dead. Not rotting. The Minotaur opens his eyes.

"Are you all right?"

He is not. He is not on the Old Scald Village battlefield. It is no longer dying season for him. He lies, back to earth, looking up at the boy, Tookus, who stands between his horns dropping corn kernels one at a time onto the Minotaur's wide and bony forehead.

"Stop it, Tookus," Holly says. She's kneeling at the Minotaur's side. Cornstalks rise halolike over her head. Beauty. "Are you okay? Are you all right?"

She speaks so quietly. The wind, though slight, rustling in all that goddamn dead corn makes it almost impossible to hear anything.

"What happened?" she asks.

The Minotaur doesn't hear how he answers her questions.

"Bully bully bully bully bullyyyyyyy," Tookus says.

The Minotaur stands, wobbles, and takes the boy's arm.

Holly grabs on to the Minotaur. "Let's get you to the van," she says.

No. Not all right. Not dead. Never. There at the mouth of the maze the Minotaur stumbled over his eternity. The full bore of his forever crashing down on his horned head. He speaks. No. He bleeds. No. He sits against a fence post.

"Hey," Danny Tanneyhill says, emerging from the Ghoul's Farm zombie barn. "I found the pumpkin launcher!"

Tookus, the boy with the deep pock in his forehead, kneels in front of the Minotaur. Tookus, the damaged boy, weaves his head back and forth slowly, looks directly into the half-bull's bullish eyes.

"Shhh," Tookus says. "Shhh. Everything is going to be all right."

The boy is present for that instant. The Minotaur sees him.

Holly sits down beside the Minotaur; Tookus sits on his other side and tries to tickle the bull-man's ear with a piece of corn shuck.

"What happened?" Holly asks.

"N-Nothing," the Minotaur says. It's more true than she could ever understand. "Nothing."

The woodcarver stirs up the dust around them. "Let's go launch some pumpkins," he says.

"Shut up, Danny," the redhead says. "Can't you see we're . . . " She doesn't finish the sentence.

The woodcarver drags a hay bale over and sits close. "Yo, chop steak," he says to the Minotaur. "I met a friend of yours yesterday."

The Minotaur isn't interested. He leans against the post, collecting himself.

"I think his name was Smitty or something. Said he knew you from Old Scald Village."

Danny Tanneyhill is drawing out his tale. The Minotaur thinks of trampling the man to death but decides against it.

"I had a nice long talk with him. Seemed like a nice guy."

The old bull tries to get to his feet, but it's too soon.

"Steady, M," Holly says. "Just stay here awhile."

Holly isn't particularly interested in Danny's story.

The woodcarver picks his teeth with a piece of straw. "You'll never believe what he told me," Danny Tanneyhill says. "He said you ran that horn of yours up the skirt of one of the girls—the broom girl, I think it was. He said you got fired."

"Unngh," the Minotaur says, standing unsteadily on his human feet.

Danny, laughing a little too loud, runs into the corn maze and out of sight.

Tookus, guileless above all else, thinks it's funny and runs after the woodcarver.

The redhead looks torn. Looks confused. Looks confounded by the story and what it implies, and by her brother's departure.

"What the fuck?" she says to the whole world.

Holly follows her brother yet again into the corn maze.

The Minotaur comes to his senses.

What was he thinking? He ought to know better.

The Minotaur gets to his feet.

The Minotaur does well enough, with his cumbersome head, on flat earth, in a right frame of mind. Not here. Not now. Not on the rocky path of human desire. O labyrinthine moment! Move, old bull! The Minotaur looks around. Gets his bearings. Walks toward home.

CHAPTER TWENTY-FIVE

MOVE, MINOTAUR.

The Minotaur heeds the warning, stomps the life into his (booted and human) feet. The Minotaur knows where he is. Knows the toothy ridge of the mountaintop. Knows the valley just beyond will lead him home. The bullish heart, the chamberous heart, pounds. The quartered heart. Climbs, the Minotaur. There is no other recourse. The Minotaur has stamina. The Minotaur needs nothing from the mountain. The mountain itself is ancient, eroded by time to a rounded and well-treed peak within view. Conquerable. Up. The bull-man leans into the hill.

He knows little. Knows, though, that he doesn't need these three humans or their nasty bags of human tricks. Knows that he, the old half-bull half-man, will endure with or without them. Knows little but that he is capable of trudging up and over the worn-out mountain.

The crow, however, has a different idea. The bird comes barreling right out of the sun, scorched black and cawing to beat the band. Dives at the Minotaur's head. The Minotaur swats, but he's way too slow. The crow lands somewhere behind him and begins to chatter. The Minotaur knows better than to look back. The Minotaur knows it's best, safest, to keep his eyes straight ahead, looking only where he steps, paying attention to the rising earth, the crow be damned. Looking back means trouble. Looking back, down the slope, from on high, the Minotaur knows he'll see the whole lay of the land, knows the perspective will be broad and deep. Knows he'll see the big picture, and knows it's easy to be deceived by a big picture. Or even that the truth will be unbearable. The crow caws. The Minotaur will not turn. Will not. The crow retches, or maybe it's a giggle.

"Unngh," the Minotaur says to the crow.

The crow guffaws at the top of its black lungs, then goes on about its black day.

"Unngh," the Minotaur says. Stupid crow. Stupid maze. Stupid horns. Stupid summit of a stupid mountain. The Minotaur scrambles down the slope. He will endure.

The Minotaur stays off the roads. He'll walk the necessary miles through the fields and woods. He knows where he is. He knows where he's going. More or less. No, he doesn't. It doesn't matter. Off kilter. Out of balance. The Minotaur stomps his way through Pennsylvania. The Minotaur trudges unfamiliar ground, through the forest. There are no tracks before him. And behind, his steps, his boot prints, could easily be mistaken as human.

The fickle beast of change that is fast on his heels leaves no tracks. But the Minotaur feels it, that hot breath of transmogrification on his neck. He remembers the little unicorn girl from the battlefield, remembers thinking her a harbinger. Remembers the damaged soldier from Joy Furnace, a wheezing portent in his own way. Maybe the Minotaur should go back to Joy Furnace, should stoke the smelter to life and burn everything.

The Minotaur walks and walks, walks into his despair, pitching his arguments to the gibbous moon. Looks up, waits for an answer. But the moon is stoic. Cat's got its tongue. Then comes fortune. Occasionally fate is kind, even to monsters. The Minotaur recognizes a peak in the distance. Knows he is one wide valley away from familiar turf. Hurry, Minotaur. Or not.

He crosses an unknown road to a bare field. The field leads to a tree line, a copse of evergreens and stark white birches. Beyond the tree line, who knows? He walks. Five thousand years drag behind. No. Five thousand years push at him. Either or. The Minotaur treks across the rutted field. Each step is tenuous. The Minotaur walks and walks. The Minotaur has endurance. He has walked for centuries. No small walk will defeat him.

Past the trees, through the cedar boughs, is yet another field. Vast. And empty but for corn stubble. Farmland. Agrarian lives. The afternoon sun wanes, a luminous cataract low on the field's horizon. The Minotaur trudges ahead. And coming to the end of the cultivated patch of earth, the Minotaur finds a river that crooks through the trees. Beyond the water a steep bank rises high. The Minotaur stands at the river's edge, looks up and down the stretch of water searching for a log, for steppingstones. Clotted here and there with branches and roots and debris, the river isn't particularly deep, but it is wide. To cross or not are the options.

The Minotaur looks and thinks. Thinks and looks. Both quiet endeavors. Then he hears the noise. It spooks him. The Minotaur is rarely spooked by the natural world, but the sound he hears this day bores into his spine, scuttles along his nerves. There is no wind. There are no birds. Only the noise. It pulses, now softly, now louder. It comes from a throat, a mouth, maybe more than one. It is close. There is nothing but empty field behind the Minotaur.

He scours the bank across the river. There. It is there, on a skinny sand bar, hidden by brambles, rustling those branches. He sees the source of the noise. Hears more clearly the distress in its cry. The sound is more sob than anything else the Minotaur has ever heard. An otherworldly weeping. It is a beast in trouble. This is the Minotaur's first thought.

He rushes into the river with cautious urgency. Cold water fills his boots. The wool of his uniform wicks at the frigid river. The Minotaur will not be deterred. Cold is nothing more than the absence of heat. But as he approaches the scene the Minotaur slows. Maybe he is misinterpreting. Maybe what is happening at this river's edge is something private. Not meant to be witnessed. Then the cry again. A struggle, a tussle in the sticks. The Minotaur half-squats at the bank. Creeps. Sneaks. Wants to back away. To run. But the cry beckons him onward. And when he gets close enough to see, the spectacle takes the Minotaur's breath. There, partly lying, partly crouching, is a half-man half-beast unlike any the Minotaur has seen in a long long time. Horned and booted. Furred and clothed. Hoofed but with human hands. Affinity. Kinship. An undeniable hope. The Minotaur wants to, needs to, help this creature. He moves closer, but slowly. There is wisdom in caution.

Deflation comes suddenly. Disillusionment. The Minotaur has been duped again. Gulled again. Hoodwinked by his own mind, his own kind. What lies weeping in the cold muck and debris is no hybrid, no crossbreed, no mongrel. It is a hunter in camouflage. And it is a full-grown buck. Both. There was a time when these were two creatures. Man and buck. Now they lie as one being. Being.

The Minotaur draws nigh, sees the man on his back, propped against a thicket. Sees the sweeping neck of the buck bent low, and the gory wound. The horn burrowed deep in the man's belly. Sees, in the gut-shot buck's gaping flesh, the lung's struggle. They are both breathing. But it is messy. The Minotaur looks around. Sees hoof prints and boot tracks come together. They are both breathing. Blood pools around them, inches toward the river. The man has one free hand, and with it he pushes feebly against the animal's forehead. The buck, with its only good hind leg, paws at the ground, trying to run or to drive the horn deeper. And the sounds—moaning, gurgling, belchlike croaks—are almost slapstick in their excess.

The Minotaur could simply leave. He has that option. Nobody would know. Nobody would care. He steps closer. The man is trying to speak. Or maybe he is just trying to keep the breath coming and going. The Minotaur kneels. He looks into the man's face. He recognizes the man. The man has one good eye. The other is covered with a milky caul and rolls willy-nilly in its socket. It is the Walmart security guard from the encounter at the tollbooth. His rifle is trapped between his body and the buck's. The Minotaur looks at the animal, too. There is recognition in its eyes. The buck's legs tremble and twitch. The Minotaur has no need to try and figure out what happened. It is enough to know, to see, that it did. There is utterance, bloody utterance, from the lips of both creatures. There is fear in their eyes.

The Minotaur is able to step into the thicket, to get close. To squat there on his haunches. To cradle, in his small way, the moment, the man, the buck. He rests one hand on the wounded man's chest near the heart, makes small delicate circles with his fingertip. The Minotaur gently strokes the buck's neck with the other. The man weeps softly. The deer chortles softly. The Minotaur lows with them, laments with them. Waiting. The sun rolls on along, without regard.

CHAPTER TWENTY-SIX

GOOD.

The Minotaur feels he has done some good.

Buoyed as he is by his deed, the Minotaur walks Business 220 with a spring in his step. He'll go back to the Judy-Lou. He'll forget all about the redhead and her damaged brother. Put them all behind him. He'll clean up his musket. He'll report for duty this coming weekend at Old Scald Village like nothing ever happened. He'll nod at Smitty, right at him. He'll die on the battlefield, twice on Saturday, once on Sunday. He'll wash the uniform and polish the gun. He'll die well. He's good at it. The Minotaur knows who he is. Where he is. Business 220 is right beneath his feet.

Business 220. It is dark. The Judy-Lou is just around the bend. The Minotaur is almost home. The hunter is dead. The buck, too. The Minotaur is satisfied enough with his role in their passing. It is dark, and in the dark, down the road, the pale lights in the motel parking lot shine on the Odyssey. The Minotaur prepares himself for the worst. Business 220 is his road; the Minotaur will not be cowed. Hearing his boot heels striking the macadam the Minotaur walks, with a good head on his shoulders, all the way back to Room #3, where he bolts and chains the door.

The woodcarver's truck is gone. The Odyssey is parked, but that means nothing. The Minotaur sits on the bed with the musket in his lap. He hears laughter. No. It is not laughter. It's the Guptas talking. Devmani is watching cartoons. The Minotaur sighs, leans his horns into the wall, and lets the sound comfort him. Soothe him. Until the knock comes. The options are limited. The Minotaur is ready. For anything. And though the knock is soft—sheepish, even—the Minotaur readies to fight. He props the musket against the nightstand. No, not fight. He opens the door without looking through the peephole.

"Oh, my God!" Holly says.

It's Holly. She says, "Oh, my God! What happened? Are you hurt?"

She was prepared to say something else. Something accusatory, maybe. But the blood on his coat threw her off course. It's Holly. The redhead. She's alone. The Minotaur looks over her shoulder to be sure. She reaches out to touch his jacket. He remembers the blood. The hunter's blood. The buck's blood.

"Blood," he says.

The redhead's eyes widen. "I'm calling for help," she says, and comes inside, reaches for the phone.

The Minotaur lays his finger on the button. "No," he says.

"You're bleeding."

"No," the Minotaur says. "Not mine. Not my blood."

"Is everything . . . ?" the redhead begins to ask, begins to reach out and touch the bloody coat. She does neither. She looks at the Minotaur, then looks toward the road and the woodcarver's domain.

"Yes," he says.

"I saw your light," she says.

"I was watching," she says.

"I was," she says, "worried."

Room #3 is a small paneled box, poorly lit. It contains a double bed, the lumpy mattress, loftless pillows, stiff sheets, and a blanket good enough. It contains battered utilitarian furniture. There is a metal trash can beside a low mostly useless desk. The outdated telephone and bulbous lamp take nearly all the space on the nightstand. The Minotaur has no idea what's in the drawer.

The room contains Holly. Fully. She stands so close to the chrome hanger bars that she has to bend her head. She stands with her hands behind her back. The Minotaur can tell that she's fidgeting her fingers. She is wearing jeans. They are blue and tight. The Minotaur doesn't notice. Yes, he does. Notices, too, how the T-shirt clings. The Minotaur pulls out the chair, gestures his offer for her to sit. Holly shakes her head.

The room is cramped. The room smells of bodies, dying and otherwise engaged.

"You left," she says.

"What happened?" she asks.

The Minotaur wants to tell her about his long walk. The Minotaur wants to tell her about the blood, where it came from, who spilled it. He wants to tell her how he carefully covered the man and the animal with branches, twigs, and leaves. Wants to tell her how he helped. How he held them both in their passing. The Minotaur wants to ask her questions, too. The Minotaur looks out of the motel room door, up and down the sidewalk, then across at Pygmalia-Blades.

"Unngh," the Minotaur says.

The room contains silence. So much silence. The Minotaur and Holly stand at opposite ends of the cramped space. The room contains the Minotaur's horns and dried blood. Contains, too, something of the chisel and rasp and hammer, and all that stone dust. The Minotaur needs to change his clothes. He has another uniform. A chef's jacket and checkered pants. From another lifetime.

Holly watches him retrieve these from a box beneath the bed. She doesn't question. The Minotaur carries it all—the uniform of his past, his impossibly wide horns—into the impossibly small bathroom. He closes the door. He strips down. He begins to wash himself in the sink. He doesn't know if she will stay.

She does.

The Minotaur puts his soiled Confederate uniform in the tub and turns the spigot on. The Minotaur hears Holly move about his room. Hears her approach the door. Hears her lean against it. Breath and heartbeat.

"Is it true?" she asks through the thin wood panel. "What asshole said? What he heard?"

"Unngh," the Minotaur says. "Sort of."

And he bumbles (through the thin wood panel) through something like an explanation. He's sure, at the end, she'll just leave. Almost hopes she does. It would make things simpler.

The Minotaur opens the bathroom door. Holly stands right there.

"I'm sorry," she says. "Sometimes we all make bad choices."

"Mmmnn," the Minotaur says. He knows.

"You're misbuttoned," she says, reaching to fix his coat.

Holly backs away. Moves into the room.

"Took's getting edgier by the minute," she says. "It's like he knows something is about to happen. Something is changing."

"Mmmnn," the Minotaur says. He shrugs and wriggles inside the new coat.

"Just a few more days to kill," Holly says. "I just have to keep Tooky occupied until Monday. To find some way to pass the time."

"Mmmnn," the Minotaur says, wishing he had something to offer.

"I just wish I could know for sure," she says. "Sometimes I don't make the best . . . "

"Mmmnn," he says.

"I'm trying not to think about what happens after I drop Tooky off," she says. "To him or me."

Release. The Minotaur wishes he could say the word.

Holly tucks a strand of red hair behind her ear and moves another inch or so. The Minotaur moves, too, but he's not so surefooted. The Minotaur kicks the musket. The musket clatters to the floor, its useless barrel aimed right at Holly, who jumps out of the way, thinking maybe it's loaded, having no reason to believe otherwise.

Holly sucks her breath and stumbles backward into the doorknob.

Holly grimaces. Her face contorts.

"Owwwww-waa!"

Holly lays a hand on her backside. Room #3 contains Holly and all of her pain.

So much hurt for just a bump against the doorknob, the Minotaur thinks. "Okay?" he asks.

"Listen," she says. "I need a favor. I think . . . I think I need your help."

Anything. The Minotaur is ready. His readiness surges through the very marrow of his bones. And when the Minotaur leans close to the cloth-and-wire lampshade, that readiness pops, arcs in a minuscule blue bolt from his fingertip. No. It is just static electricity. The light flickers.

"Mmmnn?"

Holly looks at the Minotaur. Looks like she's unsure of how to proceed. It is late April, inside and outside Room #3. May is in the wings. In the offing. Just over Scald Mountain, maybe. Primping. Preening. Stropping its beak and whetting its claws. Spring's wild rumpus has already commenced. The lunatic moon champs at its bit. A car speeds by out on Business 220; all the tiny American flags in the Judy-Lou Motor Lodge's brick planter flutter on their tiny wooden skewers. *Anything*, he thinks.

"A splinter," the redhead says, and commits fully to her confession.

"I think I have a splinter," she says, unbuttoning those tight blue jeans.

"I think I have a splinter," she says. "In my . . . "

Holly turns sideways to the Minotaur. She eases the jeans down over one haunch. It hurts her to do so.

"I don't know how I got it," she says, cocking her hip.

Holly lays a hand on the television set, steadies herself, hooks a thumb in the waistband of her underwear, reconsiders, slips a finger under the thin strip of lace around the leg hole, pauses.

The Minotaur falls into the abyss. Almost.

"We need some light," Holly says, then hops the short patch of carpet to the bathroom. Flips the switch. Pulls up the fabric of her underwear ever so slightly, but nothing in the world can be seen in the pale wash of insipid fluorescent light. The Minotaur could have told her as much.

"Come here," Holly says.

"I don't know how I got it," she says again.

"Come here," she says again.

The Minotaur knows.

"It's too dark," she says.

The Minotaur could have told her as much. He knows. He knows where the splinter came from.

"Can I trust you?" Holly asks. It's a rhetorical question.

"Unngh," the Minotaur says. "Yes."

Holly brushes past the Minotaur; their two reflections briefly inhabit the lifeless television screen. Noir. Holly stands at the foot of the bed, looks at the Minotaur, takes a breath, pulls her pants halfway down, lies on her belly. The bed creaks. The Minotaur could have told her as much.

"I think it's right here," she says, and with one crooked finger folds the cotton panties in on themselves, tucking the bunched fabric into the deep, arched cleft of her ass, exposing fully one glorious white freckled mound of rump.

"Can you see anything?" she asks.

"Unngh," the Minotaur says.

He sees the birds. The birds. Delicate and impossibly small against the white of her panties. Birds in flight. Birds at rest. A cardinal, an oriole, a jay. A cardinal, an oriole, a jay. Over and over again.

"Can you see anything?" she asks again.

The Minotaur has to get closer. He has no choice. He tries not to breathe too hard, the tip of his long snout, the deep black wells of his nostrils, so close to her bared thighs. Nevertheless there is his breath, and the sudden goose flesh up and down the backs of her legs.

"I don't know how it got there," she says.

The splinter is half an inch—longer, even—and angles deeply smack dab in the middle of her cheek. A quarter-sized patch of inflamed flesh surrounds the point of entry. Its tip is too deep to see. *Cedar*, the Minotaur thinks. He thinks he smells cedar. He knows for sure he smells the black Pennsylvania mud caked in the soles of his boots. Smells, too, blood and the potent urine of a rutting buck. Smells gunpowder, maybe, and through it all Holly. All of Holly. The splinter is cedar. He'd bet money on it. There are probably thousands of such splinters on the floor of the Pygmalia-Blades trailer.

The Minotaur's hands are capable of great tenderness. He could, with the tips of his thumbnails, his knuckles resting on her behind, pressing, he could pinch and squeeze the splinter out. But his nails are so dirty, and her flesh is so white, so clean.

"Birds," the Minotaur says. "Umm . . . I mean tweezers."

Holly chuckles. The Minotaur bumbles into the bathroom, fumbles the first-aid kit; several small things clatter across the tile floor: scissors, a spool of white tape, a pencil.

"You okay in there?" Holly asks.

"Mmmnn," the Minotaur says, kneeling to retrieve the tweezers from behind the toilet.

He washes the tweezers, and washes his hands, too. The Minotaur stands at the sink looking into the mirror. He leans just enough around the doorjamb to see, to see if she is still there on her belly, on his bed. The Minotaur does this again two, three, four times, surprised each time by Holly's present and half-naked backside. A cardinal, an oriole, a jay. Holly lies, her chin resting on her clasped hands, humming. Humming. The red hair that drapes her face burns against the bedspread's looping gray pattern.

The Minotaur steps bedside. Holly looks up, smiles, picks at something on the blanket, flicks it away.

"Have to touch," he says.

"Yes," she says.

"Of course," she says.

"Go ahead," she says.

The Minotaur bends closer; he needs to see better. The Minotaur gets down on one knee. It's too close. Too something else. He pulls up the chair. Sits.

"Okay," he says.

The Minotaur cups his hands and blows into the well. Warmth. The Minotaur is capable of warmth. Holly is (almost) perfectly still.

"Touch," he says, but doesn't. The Minotaur's quandary is ancient.

Holly waits. Will wait as long as necessary. Scald Mountain turns a blind eye.

The Minotaur gets to work. At the first brush of his fingertip her muscle flexes. The white gluteus tightens involuntarily. Grows taut inside its flesh, though a fine and freckled jiggle remains. The Minotaur appreciates much this looseness, this fullness. Can't help himself. Can't stop himself (man or bull) from brushing her flesh one more time, just to watch the reflex.

"What're you doing back there?" Holly says, laughing.

"Tweezers," he says, then nudges the delicate tips against the angry red flesh where the splinter went in.

"Oww-oww-oww!" she says.

"Mmmnn, sorry."

It's too deep. The skin is too inflamed. The Minotaur knows what to do. His sewing kit is within reach. He slips a needle from its paper sleeve, needs something to sterilize it. The Minotaur remembers an Old Scald Village butane lighter in the medicine chest.

"Back in a m-minute," he says, and true to his word returns to the squeaky chair quickly, thumbing at the lighter's flint wheel. He waves the needle in and out of the sputtering flame, then waits a few seconds for it to cool.

"You know," Holly says in the wait, "I've fucked up so much. With Tooky. And I want to get him there safe and sound."

"Unngh," the Minotaur says.

What he means is that every past is littered and scarred. What he means is that the present moment is the only moment that pulses, that breathes. What he means is that he himself is capable of great tenderness but has also done great harm. The Minotaur knows that sometimes mercy requires expedience. Haste. Sometimes it can't be about how much a thing hurts.

The Minotaur lays his palm on Holly's bare ass cheek, fingers splayed on either side of the splinter, and with his other deft hand drives the needle home. Holly squirms. The Minotaur puts his forearm down on her thigh. Lickety-split, he ferrets out the splinter's gnarly end with the needle and, forgoing the tweezers, pinches the splinter between his thumbnails and plucks it out.

"It's a fucking two-by-four," Holly says, looking at the splinter lying in the Minotaur's open hand. "Thanks," she says. "You're a lifesaver."

He wants to thank her. He wants to keep that splinter. Wants, really, to push it deep into his own flesh. Anywhere. To make it his. Forever. Silly boy. Holly reaches back to touch the spot.

"Wait," the Minotaur says. There may be more splinters. He wants to look. To help. Doesn't. "Band-Aid," he says.

Holly takes his advice. She waits, and something in the waiting inspires her.

"Hey," she says, "I just had a great idea."

"Mmmnn," the Minotaur says.

He daubs a cotton ball soaked in rubbing alcohol onto the small wound. The redhead winces against the sting. The Minotaur blows gently. A rustle of wings. Sometimes Room #3 is so full that it could not hold even one more breath. Sometimes Room #3 is so empty that whole centuries get lost inside it.

"What is the name of that festival?" she asks.

"Unngh?"

"The pirate dude, at the junkyard," Holly says. "The guy who was drooling over you. He told us about a festival this coming weekend. That's where we'll go."

The Minotaur puts the needle back, puts the tweezers back, puts the other things back.

"What is it called?" Holly asks. "Fag Day? Ag-Day? No, Ag-Fest. That's it."

Everything in its place.

"We'll solve the mystery," she says. "We'll see us a real live sea shanty."

Everything.

"Come with us!" Holly says. "You! Come with us!"

The Minotaur's final gesture is to tug the panties back into place. He untucks the rolled fabric, and the flock of printed birds settles over her cheek. A cardinal, an oriole, a jay. Holly gets quiet. Holly is blushing.

"I have to get back," she says. "To Tookus. I'll see you in the morning. We'll go in the morning."

And that's it. She's up, zipped, and out the door. The Minotaur watches her go.

The Minotaur goes to the tub and in the dim light washes his filthy solder's uniform by hand. Rinses, washes, rinses again until there is no more mud, no more blood. The Minotaur wrings out the pants, the coat. Drapes them over the shower rod. Goes to bed. All night long the water drips into the tub. All night long, against the porcelain. The Minotaur dreams of anvils ringing. All night long.

 *CHAPTER TWENTY-SEVEN*

"**Horny horn horn!**" Tookus says, then tugs on the yellow shoestring he's lassoed the Minotaur's horn with.

The Minotaur feels the tug. He's glad the boy came out of the maze. Alive. The boy sits behind him, in the Odyssey's middle seat. Holly drives. The Minotaur rides shotgun. So much movement of late. The Minotaur is discombobulated but doing fine. Rejuvenated, even. He's staved off the labyrinth one more time.

Tookus removes the loop of string, twirls it, and tosses again. Catches the Minotaur again.

"Horny horn horn!"

In the night the Minotaur heard Danny Tanneyhill return, heard the chainsaw huffing and puffing, hard at work, heard the thumping and cursing of the woodcarver as he loaded something in his truck, heard the truck drive away. No matter.

In the morning the Minotaur found on his doorstep a Tupperware container full of *gulab jamun*, so sticky and dripping they held the early sun captive. A gift from Ramneek. An offering. A note as well: "Our Becky will be coming home in a few days. We will have you over as dinner guest, Mr. M. You will like her." The Minotaur knows better. But the Minotaur is moved by the undying hope.

In the morning, in the van, Tookus unlaced his sneakers and began the game. The Minotaur is patient. The boy means no harm. The Minotaur knows well the lure of a yellow thread. Knows the impossibility of not following it.

The Minotaur thinks about the previous day, the previous night, the hours just past. Change is afoot. Always afoot. Even the Minotaur has to dance sometimes. Rope-a-dope. The tub of *gulab jamun* sits open on the van's center console. Everybody's fingers are sticky. Holly checks on her brother in the rearview mirror. Then checks again. And again. The boy is in constant motion. His arms and hands will not cease. His eyes will not settle. The boy is handsome. Or near enough. His deep scar blazes. Tookus chews on something. It's the tail of the stuffed mermaid.

"Tooky," she says, "cut it out."

He doesn't. "Nnnnothing! I see nothing!" Tookus says.

"We're almost there, Took," Holly says.

He lassos the Minotaur again.

"Tooky," Holly says, "cut it out."

He doesn't.

"Mmmnn, it's okay," the Minotaur says.

Tookus pulls the string taut and traces its length with his fingertip. Back and forth. Back and forth. The Minotaur follows, each back-and-forth a different path, a different life. What if the condom machine hadn't fallen off the wall onto the boy's head? What if the blow had been just an inch to one side or the other? What if Daedalus's plank heifer had collapsed under the burden of desire? What then?

"Titty dick pussy hole," Tookus says when the Odyssey slows at Adult World and turns into the parking lot of a defunct Kmart. The lot is bustling, the vacated department store repurposed. A banner sags, tied loosely to the *K* and the *t* over the doors. It advertises the Joy Ag-Fest.

"What a weird place for a farmy thing," Holly says.

It's true. Joy proper is visible in the distance: its church spires, the courthouse clock tower with its canting weathervane pointing relentlessly groundward. The Joy Ag-Fest, however, is on the fringe, on the periphery, at the edge of Joy. This fact clearly hasn't deterred festival goers. The strip mall pushes up against a line of wooded hills; the hemlocks and maples seem to be rallying for a takeover. What was the Kmart (and is now, for the moment, the main location of the Ag-Fest) sits in the middle of the long building. Anchor. Crux.

"Move!" Holly says to the couple strolling in front of the Odyssey. But she says it quietly.

Anybody looking down from above—anybody, say, about to hurl themselves from the Joy courthouse clock tower or, say, anybody lashed to the whipping blades of the windmills lining the far ridge—anybody can see that the Ag-Fest is laid out like a cross. Adult World is at the foot of the cross. Adult World, there beyond the pale of its slapdash fencing— desire's cleave, the purdah, the mechitza, the Zion curtain—Adult World is the footrest, a sub rosa suppedaneum. And on up the cross, the stipes, the nave, a narrow path lined with vendors all the way to the transepts, the patibulum (it depends on perspective, hollow or solid), lined with still more vendors. The strip mall itself—Kmart in the middle, a Goodwill store at one end, Uncle Bubbles Pet & Hunting Supplies at the other— makes up the apse, the altar. Anybody observing from on high could see this, but down in the throng form is not so clear.

"Move!" Holly says again, and taps at the minivan's horn. She just wants to park the Odyssey.

The couple, middle aged, more or less, lollygags. They wear matching sweatshirts the color of corn. Matching sweatpants, potato brown, work hard to contain their (matching) amorphous bodies. One of them carries a greasy paper plate, balances there a mountain of gravy-soaked French fries. The other carries—clutched under an arm, and awfully stiff—a child. Boy or girl? Hard to say, but stiff as a board for sure. The Minotaur wonders if the child is okay.

"I hate those things," Holly says.

"Mmmnn?"

Before Holly can answer the couple veers right, stops by a bean-shaped sedan, and props the child against the bumper, his face hidden in folded arms.

"Mmmnn?" the Minotaur says again.

"Booger booger booooooooger," Tookus says, and wipes his fingers on the Minotaur's shoulder.

"Those stupid things," Holly says, pointing at the leaning child. "I mean, what's the point?"

Then the kid topples, stiff legged, lies still beneath the car. The couple seems unconcerned. Then the Minotaur realizes that it's not real, the child. It's a floppy hat, a little sweatshirt sewn to a little pair of jeans, sewn to a little pair of sneakers, and all stuffed just enough to look childlike.

"I mean, really," Holly says. "What's the fucking point?"

Holly parks the Odyssey.

"Are you ready to have some fun, Took?" she asks, all the while loading her shoulder bag with rolled coins.

"You stay close, Took," she says, all the while weaving the yellow shoelace back into the boy's shoe.

"I'm glad you came," she says, looking briefly at the Minotaur.

That's the point, he thinks.

The crowd, the ever-present potential for herd mentality, nibbles at his peace of mind, but Holly wears jeans, tight jeans, and a white shirt with lots of buttons. The Minotaur tries not to stare. It's a look that he likes. His train of thought is derailed by a splinter.

"Which way?" Holly asks.

From somewhere deep in the festival's belly comes a wailing. Ecstatic or woeful, animal or other. Hard to tell. Everything smells like cotton candy and things deep fried. The Minotaur is at home in these scents.

"Mmmnn," the Minotaur says, tipping his horns toward the fray.

But before they can move the trio has to wait for the bean-shaped sedan to pass. "Look," Holly says, pointing at the forgotten plate of French fries on the roof of the car, the tiny trickle of gravy creeping down the window.

It's crowded, and the crowd seems hardly agrarian. It's not so unlike the masses that flock to Old Scald Village to watch the battles. Few of them come to learn anything about the history of the events, the places. They come, it seems, to be entertained, expectant and entitled. And what passes for entertainment is terrifying.

"I think I hear a tuba," Holly says, grinning. "Or a sousaphone. Let's go find your boyfriend."

The Minotaur, Tookus, and Holly merge into the funneling herd.

Tookus yips or cackles (something happy) and rushes over to the very first vendor's table, crowded with things made of feathers (painted, glittered, or not) and glued to other things.

"Wait up, Tooky," Holly says, but she's already fishing in her purse for money.

The Minotaur cranes his veiny neck, looking up the double row of tables as far as he can see. There must be thirty, forty vendors at least on this stretch alone—Ambrosial Emporium, The Nut Lady, Wee People, and Novelty Marshmallow Shooters among them. Tookus makes the noise again. The Minotaur will follow this addle-brained boy and his red-headed sister to every single table if necessary. That's the point.

Led by Tookus, they stop next at Lovers-Not-Fighters Pitbull Rescue. The front edge of the table is lined with bulldog bobbleheads. A mug of free pencils nudges against a huge water dish ringed with baby-blue paw prints, the dish serving as the collection plate for donations. There's a wire crate under the table where half a dozen pups sleep, belly up. The rescue organization volunteer sits in a folding chair. She wears a pink smock. She looks tired. Behind her a poster stands on an easel. The pictures are horrific. She's flanked by two battle-scarred dogs on leashes. They look even more tired. Tookus bumps the table, and the bobbleheads go wild. The leashed dogs pay no attention. One pants and scratches himself. Snorts, bends to lick at his outsized balls. The Minotaur notices the missing eye, the stitched line that begins on the dog's forehead and ends somewhere under its jaw.

"Unngh," the Minotaur says.

Holly has already pulled a roll of dimes from her bag. She gives it to Tookus and points at the water dish. He points at the bobbleheads.

"Damn," Holly says.

It's the bobbleheads. They've all synchronized, tongues lolling, eyes wide, each and every one nodding at the same time ever so slightly to the left, as if looking at the Minotaur. He shrugs his big shoulders, like it happens all the time. He's about to say something when Tookus bolts across the crowded midway. He doesn't go far; the pull of Novelty Marshmallow Shooters is too great.

"Tookus," Holly says.

But the boy has already picked up one of the guns, an army green contraption made of half-inch PVC pipe, a tee, a couple of elbows, some straight pieces. Other colors (pink, camo, black, blue) are lined up on the table, other sizes, too, and some of the guns have brass nipples. Air power. A bowl of mini-marshmallows sits in the middle of the table. Mini-marshmallows litter the macadam around the booth and trail off in both directions, most of them squashed flat.

Tookus loads up, places his mouth around the blowpipe, and does in fact blow. "I shot your booooooooooob," he says to his sister.

Holly laughs. "Okay, killer," she says. "Put the weapon down."

He does as he is told, then reconsiders. Then reconsiders. Picks up, reloads, fires at a woman galumphing by. She pushes a dilapidated stroller; the toddler is singing nonsense.

"Fatty fat fat ass," Tookus says, dead on target.

The woman may or may not feel the blow. Holly doesn't wait to find out. The Minotaur watches her drag Tookus to the edge of the crowd and scold him. No. The Minotaur watches her. All of her. The boy grins sheepishly the rest of the way up the row. The Minotaur watches Holly follow.

Once again they don't get very far. Something smells familiar. Before the Minotaur can identify the scent Tookus takes him by the arm. Pulls him over to the Wee People booth. Wee People. Those little stuffed kids, faces buried in folded arms. Not real, no matter how convincing they look, leaning there in a knee-high line around the table, against the canopy's guy wires, and in and out of the small cargo trailer parked in back. Not real.

"Goddamn," Holly says. "These things creep me out. I'll be over there."

Not real. Over there. Not real. All that the little faces imply. All the, what, embarrassment? Shame? Sadness? Not real. The little dresses and little Mary Janes, the little overalls and boots, not real. There is no life inside the figures. None. Tookus kneels by the table's edge and tugs on the Minotaur's sleeve. Holly is over there. The Minotaur can't tell what she's looking at. Tookus wants the Minotaur to kneel with him. The vendor, maybe the Wee People maker, is trying to get something out of his teeth with a credit card. He's paying no attention to the boy and the bull-man. What's the point? He's seen it all anyway. Tookus pulls.

"Mmmnn," he says.

"Mmmnn," the Minotaur says, getting down on one knee.

The boy folds his arms on the table, rests his forehead there, face hidden. Real. Not real.

"Mmmnn," Tookus says, peering out just enough.

"Okay," the Minotaur says, and (as best he can) hides his big bull face. The Minotaur wonders how long he'll have to stay. He'll stay as long as it takes. That's the point.

Tookus begins to speak. Uninterrupted. "Now I lay me down to sleep I pray the Lord my soul to keep if I should die before I wake I pray the Lord my soul to take. Now I lay me down to sleep I pray the Lord my soul to keep if I should die before I wake I pray the Lord my soul to take. Now I lay me . . . "

Tookus prays. Real. Not real. The Minotaur prays, too. No. Don't be silly. There is no prayer for him.

"Mmmnn," the Minotaur says. Then his non-prayer is answered.

"I hear music," Holly says, putting a hand on each of their shoulders. "This way."

This way. Anywhere. That's the point. Something smells familiar. Other things reek of the new. Tented stages are at both ends of the crossbeam row that traverses the front of the strip mall. Vendors to the left; vendors to the right. Holly veers right, tows her brother past the tables of baubles and geegaws and tchotchkes, past the tables of good causes with their free handouts (and hefty tax on the conscience) and thematically chosen tithe plates. The Minotaur navigates the crowd deftly. Turning his horns this way and that. Following the redhead in her blue jeans and white shirt. He fits right in. No. Not really. The Minotaur steps, both seen and unseen, through it all. There is no mystery here. It's how humans behave. It's how humans have always behaved.

Holly follows the sound. It is music of sorts, to be sure, but struggling under the burden. The squawks and honks and drumbeats are just this side of rhythm. A herky-jerky siren song pulls them to one stub of the Joy Ag-Fest. But the stage is empty. Just beyond the canopy the Minotaur sees a young woman painting the Uncle Bubbles Pet & Hunting Supplies storefront window. *Angel Sale. Today Only. Buy 1, Get 1 Free.* Big looping letters.

"Unngh," the Minotaur says, confounded by the bargain. He wouldn't know what to do with even one angel. Then he sees the painted fins and the gills, the cartoonish grin and bright eyes. Angelfish, two for the price of one. Sees, too, something standing by the Uncle Bubbles front door, something not quite right, something even more disturbing than cut-rate angels.

But before the Minotaur can go investigate, Holly wrangles his attention. "Look," she says.

He does, and when the Joy Junior High marching band makes its cacophonous way out of the Ag-Fest building and down through the crowd, toward the stage, she has to pull Tookus out of the way and hold him tight. What was it she said about her brother the night of the mountain pies and the church on the road? "This guy was a monster on the alto sax." Tookus squirms. The Minotaur understands monster, but not saxophone. He does know, however, what it means to lose a part of one's self. Tookus writhes. The Minotaur can't tell if he is terrified or ready to join in. *Let him go*, the Minotaur thinks.

They are children, the entire rank and file of noisemakers, still on the cusp of humanness. Goggle eyed, gangly limbs akimbo. Embodying both galumph and scurry. So much more like ducklings, pups; like hatchlings, cubs, shoats; like whelps; like fingerlings. So much less like grown humans. And when the gawky glockenspiel player—the sweet poult, the cosset—trips over her flopping spats and nearly drops her instrument, catching the Minotaur's eye the very instant shame boils up in beautiful florets on her cheeks, the Minotaur is overcome with, what? Is it love? Love for her nascence? Love for the (eternal) brevity of her blush?

They bottleneck and bumble to a halt, all trying to get up onto the small stage at the same time, bump their mangy blue hats, the mottled white plumes, together. The band teacher—a nervous little man with an uncooperative toupee, a man who looks like he stepped right out of an animated television show—flits around wagging his impotent baton. The Minotaur watches. The Minotaur wonders. Tookus is sputtering wetly through his loose fist, trying to sound saxophone-like. The Minotaur sees a tall, skinny boy (with bad posture) raise his trombone into place, sees the look in the boy's eye (the one not covered by a sheaf of pink hair), knows that the boy wishes his instrument were a weapon, a machine gun, maybe, maybe even dreams it so, and each note he blows—raking the trombone's tarnished bell back and forth at the crowd, at the backs of his bandmates— each note is a bullet, deadly and true.

Love. The Minotaur can't be sure, but he wants something, something good, for (not from) each of these children, and for the spastic little conductor, too. They hurl themselves halfheartedly into what is probably supposed to be the national anthem, and it takes several bars before they trap the right key, the right pitch. The onlookers struggle to remove their caps and choose their right hands and locate their hearts. The Minotaur decides, then and there, that if they march off the stage he will join them. He will march, too, wherever they go.

"Let's go," Holly says, "before they find out I'm a pinko commie fag."

She pulls the Minotaur and Tookus away. Tugs them over to Uncle Bubbles to escape the patriotic moment and its inherent dangers. Not quite ready to let go, the Minotaur watches the band from the rear. A motley blue hive twitching on the papery nest of youth, the cacophony hot and untamed. The Minotaur wants to stay.

"What the fuck?" Holly says. "Is that supposed to be you?"

The Minotaur has to look. Has to pull his attention away from the floundering band.

"Unngh," he says.

"It is," Holly says. "That son of a bitch."

She reaches out and touches the carved half-bull half-man all-oak statue propped by the Uncle Bubbles front door. It stands as tall as the Minotaur himself. But its two horns are misshapen and odd sized. One points up, the other straight out. The lopsided face (more dog than bull) may be grinning or scowling, toothy and gape mouthed. The naked chest and arms are knotty and twisted, everything painted the color of mud. The Minotaur statue's legs, however, the sawn trousers, are nearly normal and rise from almost believable boots.

"What a dick," Holly says. "Can you believe it?"

"Mmmnn," the Minotaur says. He can believe almost anything. Besides, there are far more painful things than mockery.

"Bully bulllllllll bull," Tookus says, and plucks at the couple of bungee cords keeping the statue vertical.

Holly bends to read the flier stapled to the faux-Minotaur's midriff. "Pygmalia-Blades Ag-Fest Special ½ Price!"

Holly looks up and out at the crowd. She reaches for the bungee cords' hooks.

"Take Tooky over there," she says, pointing at a vendor's table full of plants.

The Minotaur does as he is told, and looks back only when he hears the thud. The redhead has unleashed the ersatz Minotaur, the old mongrel's clunky doppelganger, and all it could do was topple.

"Hurry, hurry, hurry," the redhead urges, laughing. "I think the head broke off."

Change is inevitable.

They mix into the fray (sort of) just as the applause is dying out and the Joy Junior High marching band begins to disperse. All the white plumes jiggling at snout level make the Minotaur nervous. Holly, the redhead, makes the Minotaur nervous. She's dangerous. And he'll follow her anywhere.

"Oooo," she says.

"Come over here," she says.

"Smell," she says, cupping a scarlet geranium's full bloom in her open palm. The red petals bleed through her fingers.

"Smell," she says, bringing that upturned palm to the Minotaur's unprepared snout.

"Smell," she says, and the stolen scent bleeds into the deep black wells of his nostrils.

Drown, Minotaur. This smell in the redhead's palm has come from the core of the earth. From the first garden. This redhead's smell supplants all other sense. The blind Minotaur, the deaf Minotaur, the mute Minotaur, led by the girl. Hurtling through space. Or just to the next table, where Holly pinches off a twig of fresh thyme, rolls the tiny leaves in her fingertips.

"Smell this," she says.

The Minotaur does as he is told. He knows the scent well, but the moment is foreign. The Minotaur almost takes her finger into his mouth. Almost. They crowd together at the table of potted herbs. The Minotaur and Holly.

"Mmmnn," the Minotaur says.

Tookus babbles somewhere within earshot.

More. The Minotaur wants more. There is a crowd, and they are part of it. The Minotaur wants more. That's the point.

"This?" Holly says, reaching.

"Couldn't you find a white boy?"

What?

The moment warps.

"What?" Holly says.

The Minotaur opens his eyes. Maybe they were never closed. He is here with the redhead and her damaged brother. Here. In the middle of Pennsylvania, at the edge of Joy. Toddling into another millennium. There is commerce. There is want and gratification, though the standards are low. What?

"You couldn't find a white boy to do that with?" the man asks.

It doesn't matter what he looks like.

One table over, the vendor's tent is hung all around with wind chimes. Old padlocks and skeleton keys dangle, tarnished spoons and forks with tines curled obscenely, cut glass, too, but mostly beer bottles. These things hang, still, in the parcel of windless time.

What?

There is a table of Slinky toys, humped and waiting beside their boxes. Tookus is there poking at the google eyes of a Slinky serpent with a bright pink tongue.

"Nobody wants to watch you and that thing rub all over each other."

It doesn't matter what he looks like. His companions, a woman and two children, sneer from behind his legs, over his shoulder.

"Skank," the man says. He's eyeballing Holly. Won't look at the Minotaur.

Holly is stunned. Holly shakes her head, comes back to herself. "That's what you teach your kids?" she asks.

The Minotaur watches Holly. Rage blossoms, rises up from the freckled plane of her chest, over her clavicles, up the sinewy throat. Holly opens her mouth.

"Trash," the man says.

It doesn't matter what he looks like.

The Minotaur sees the pulse in Holly's throat, a bird trapped forever there, beating its wings incessantly. Sees, too, her eyes, yellow-green coins of fire with hard black cinders at their core. Sees there the anger and the fear.

"You need a good white dick," the man says, "to set you straight."

The man stands in the middle of the passing crowd. The man stands with his companions. The man not so subtly traces a finger up and down his crotch. A good white dick.

Holly looks around. The Minotaur sees it. She looks for Tookus, or a weapon, maybe. An escape route.

Holly squares her shoulders, lifts her head, and faces the man. "Fuck you," she says.

"What?"

The question is timeless. The question vexes. Plagues. Rankles and roils. Harangues. Galls. Flummoxes and befuddles. Hounds. Bedevils. Dogs. Dogs. Dogs.

Who says it?

"What?"

Tookus says it. Clear as a bell. He stands there holding a paper plate, three plastic forks, some napkins. On the plate, a wide slice of butterscotch pie with perfect meringue. On the boy's face, in the boy's eyes, cognizance.

"What?"

Sometimes love is enough. Sometimes understanding and tolerance and compassion—sometimes these are fierce enough. Sometimes, though, a Minotaur needs to step up. The bull-man does just that. The bull-man comes between the redhead and the fool. The bull-man steps back into his history, pulls his full savage lineage into the here and now. The Minotaur rallies the ghosts of every virgin and every warrior sacrificed to him in that black stone puzzle. The Minotaur grunts once.

"Unngh."

And that is enough. The breath that billows from the Minotaur's nostrils washes over the man and his family. The man's good white dick shrivels, retreats. The man's wife farts loudly, wetly. The man's children fall to the ground, wailing. The wind chimes go mad. Clamor and clang. The Slinkys unfurl, quiver in their loose coils. Then the gods speak from on high.

"Judging for the Henceforth Joy Dairy Goat Award will begin momentarily."

CHAPTER TWENTY-EIGHT

"ALL COMPETITORS SHOULD REPORT to the judge's table in Building 3."

The gods are surprising in their message.

No. No gods, these. A speaker is mounted on a pole over the Ag-Fest banner. It is up to the living and breathing. It is up to the living. The breathing. The living.

"There," the Minotaur says, and leads Holly and Tookus to a picnic table at the other arm of the cross, by the Goodwill and another tented stage.

They sit and share the pie, taking modest bites, one forkful at a time, each grateful in the ways that they can be. The Minotaur looks around. She's here somewhere. Butterscotch and gunpowder.

They don't talk about what just happened. They don't need to. Or can't.

Up on the low stage something else is about to happen. Up there a group gathers in a disorganized clump. Thirteen, fourteen, fifteen people. Maybe more. It's hard to tell who's in charge. The people at the other picnic tables and the rest of the festival goers seem indifferent. Tookus licks at his teeth and gums. Butterscotch. Holly presses a fingertip into the bridge of her nose, squints hard.

"Unngh," the Minotaur says, wishing he could say more. He wants to be a good soldier. A good confederate, even.

"Thanks," Holly says. "For, you know . . . "

"Hippie dippie do," Tookus says, pointing at a man with a long gray ponytail setting up an easel and a poster in front of the stage: *Keystone Sacred Harp.*

"Here comes Jesus," Holly says.

They've taken a shape on the stage, organized themselves into a square. Four bodies wide on every side, two deep in most places. All facing in toward each other. No one looks out at the audience. They look inward, look nowhere, or at their own motley gaggle.

"A cult if I ever saw one," Holly says, preparing for the worst.

The Minotaur has seen worse. The group onstage is mixed. A balance, precarious or not, of men and women, youthful and not, plump, pallid, lean, wholesome, etc. A swath of central Pennsylvania.

"I think that woman is looking at you," Holly says to the Minotaur.

"Mmmnn," the Minotaur says. Meaning, *who?*

What draws this odd lot together is unclear as of yet, but drawn together they are, face to face, squared. The hollow space they define crackles with nothingness, with potential.

"What's it mean, Sacred Harp?" Holly asks. "There's no harp."

Then the Minotaur sees the books. Everybody on the stage, in the square, holds a book. Thick and too wide, with stiff carmine red covers. Maybe the group is bound to, or by, their books. It happens.

"She is," Holly says. "She's giving you the stink eye. That, or she wants to jump your bones."

Then the Minotaur sees her. Gwen. Gone, the bonnet and gingham dress and apron, her Old Scald Village garb. She looks different. She stands with her book open. She looks up from the pages. Maybe she smiles. Maybe it's some other reaction.

"Do you know her?" Holly asks.

Before the Minotaur can answer a man steps into the center of the hollow square. He is an Amish man. They all look alike. No, they don't. He is a determined man, everything about him. Beard and all. Plain folk. Plain to see.

"Jesus," Tookus says. "Jeeeeeeeeeesus."

The man raises one hand to his waist, palm up, arm crooked at the elbow. They focus. They wait. The silence is brief and eternal.

"La so laaaaaa," the man says, each note pitched higher than the next.

Each note edgy and uncompromising. The man's final *la* hangs, sustains, and the rest of the group grabs hold.

"Laaaaaa . . . "

The sound swells as each member offers up voice. A keening. A beast coming to life. An engine with heart and blood and bone. The man in the center lifts his hand, and song erupts.

"La la so mi so la, so mi la, la so mi . . . "

The empty space now saturated with sound. Overflowing.

The man's hand marks fierce time. The voices weave in and out of harmony and discord, aligning, colliding gloriously. Others, many others, mark the beat. Up and down, lift and fall.

"What the fuck is happening?" Holly asks. Perplexed. Beguiled, even.

"La so fa la so la so mi la . . . "

"I can't hear words," Holly says.

Tookus sits still as stone, his eyes wide and fiery.

The Minotaur sees Gwen's face, and like the other faces onstage hers is rapt. The body and the sound are one. *Are words necessary?* he wonders.

Holly sees the Minotaur watching the woman, watches the woman see the Minotaur.

"Which is it?" Holly teases. "Stink eye or lust?"

The words may or may not be necessary.

"La so fa la, so mi la . . . "

Throng and pulse. The audience may or may not be watching. It doesn't matter at all.

There comes a sliver of quiet, thin as a knife blade, the Amish man's hand raised high, and when it falls the silence is guillotined. Words.

"What wondrous love is this! O my soul! O my soul! What wondrous love is this, O my soul!"

There are four walls of noise, four lines of music, each row of singers voicing different notes, mouthing different sounds. The words are the same. The Minotaur gives in to the moment. He imagines this collective out of its unity. Who are they? How do they spend their days? Whom do they love? Whom do they fear? Are their scars and hurts present with them up on that low stage? It doesn't matter. They are there. Words.

Here and there a note, a single voice, maybe, pierces through all, bullets the sky. Now and then the bedrock, the bass notes, quake the very ground. The Minotaur watches, sees Tookus begin to move his arm up and down, trying to match, to catch, the timing.

"What wondrous love is this that caused the Lord of bliss to bear the dreadful curse for my soul? For my soul? To bear the dreadful curse for my soul!"

Fewer than twenty people are singing on the stage by the Goodwill that afternoon at the Joy Ag-Fest. But the voices are legion, are manifold, are countless. The sound, the song, will not be contained by the measly tent or the worn-out mountains that surround them all. It's not about the words.

Tookus leans in. Up, down, up, down.

"This is wild," Holly says. Rapt, too.

"When I was sinking down! Sinking down! Sinking down!"

"La la la," Tookus says.

"Mmmnn."

The Minotaur smells popcorn, cotton candy, manure.

"When I was sinking down, beneath God's righteous frown! Christ laid aside his crown for my soul, for my soul! Christ laid aside his crown . . . "

It's not about the words. It doesn't have to be about the words. Some sing with closed eyes. Some see everything. Others look at nothing. Gwen is gone. More or less. She is there on the stage, in the body, but the song has consumed her being.

"To God and to the Lamb . . . "

The lyric is shackled to the beat; the beat will not yield.

"La la la la!" Tookus hatchets the air. Gets louder and louder. "*La la la la la!*"

Her brother's ruckus breaks Holly's spell. She goes to the boy's side. "Shhh, Tooky," she whispers. "Not so loud. Shhh."

"*La la la la la!*"

"I will sing, I will sing! To God and to the Lamb . . . "

"*La la la la la!*"

Louder and louder the boy gets, his arm now chopping free of time and pace.

The Minotaur watches, wants to help, wants the song not to stop.

Holly takes a deep breath, encircles her brother, whispering in his ear. But the music has riled the boy. He will not be soothed.

"*La la la la la!*"

Up, down, up, down.

The Minotaur watches a balloon escape the tiny fist of a girl wearing a safety-orange onesie. The balloon orbits as it rises. The Minotaur sees enough to know. A unicorn rears there. Her father catches it in the nick of time.

Tookus pulls away from Holly and begins to swing both arms. People look. People gawk. Some aim cell-phone cameras. All is fodder. The Minotaur steps in, wraps the boy in his arms, picks him up bear-hug fashion, carries him away from the table, away from the song. The song continues. The song always continues.

"And when from death I'm free, I'll sing on! I'll sing on!"

They are a spectacle, for a moment, the three of them. But the rubbernecking populace has a short attention span. As soon as Tookus calms the cameras point elsewhere. The Minotaur carries Tookus all the way into the Ag-Fest building.

"What in God's name was that?" Holly asks, looking back over her shoulder, through the door, wanting more of the sounds, the song, but unable to say so.

Widow Fisk. Gwen. The Minotaur didn't expect her. He looks back, too, over his meaty shoulder. Will he see her again? He would like to tell her that things are changing. Things have changed.

"Mmmnn," the Minotaur says.

Tookus squirms in the Minotaur's grip. Things have changed. They're inside now. The Ag-Fest building bustles in a different way. Sort of. The parade float, its wheels perfectly chocked, is blocking the ingress, intentionally or not. The float, wreathed in garlands and bunting, is cordoned off. Atop it, on a throne made of giant Slinky boxes, sits the Joy Slinky Queen, right beneath the banner that names her so.

"What is it with these people and their Slinkys?" Holly asks. Then she reads the poster.

Tookus squirms again. The Minotaur releases the boy from his grip.

"Oh," she says. "They're made here."

Several other posters contain much Slinky history and photos of all the Slinky Queens in succession. Actual Slinkys are even on display. The Minotaur can't tell new from old.

"Took," Holly says, "do you want to go up and meet the Slinky Queen?"

Somebody answers for him. *"You've opened the gates of hell!"*

They all hear it. It's loud enough, and spoken with such raging confidence that it's hard not to believe. But nobody else seems to be paying attention.

"You've opened the gates of hell!"

Tookus smiles. Makes a face. "Bulllly bull bull," he says, then walks the few steps over to the arcade game plugged in right by the door. Why not?

"You've opened the gates of hell!"

The voice is ragged, repetitive, the speaker turbaned, wild eyed, swarthy. Somewhere out of sight goats bleat. On the game's monitor are gunfire, bomb blasts, gibberish meant to be Arabic.

"You've opened the gates of hell!"

"I don't know about hell," Holly says, "but this place gets weirder by the minute."

Tookus wants to play. The flickering terrorist on the small screen beckons, challenges.

"Bang bang bang!" Tookus says.

The goats concur.

"Not now, Took," Holly says.

The Minotaur doesn't know about hell either. "Unngh," he says.

They stand for a moment, maybe at the gates of hell, and look into the teeming festival crowd. No kitsch vendors here. Tables and bins of vegetables and fruits, cakes and pies, things brined and pickled. Farther back, smelled and heard at the moment, rather than seen, animals. The competition is stiff.

"Where to?" Holly asks.

"Bang bang," Tookus says, tugging at his sister's arm.

"Not now, Took."

A bedraggled family of four shuffles in from the parking lot. The kids, rabid post-toddlers, circle their parents' legs, demanding everything.

"Give me a quarter."

"I'm hungry."

"I have to poop."

"Juney said poop!"

"You've opened the gates of hell!"

The mother feeds quarters into the slot.

"I wanna play."

"Move!"

"It's my turn to shoot."

"Daddy, I want to kill the sand niggers."

The goats bleat again.

"G-goats," the Minotaur says, preferring any company, caprine included, to the ignorant herd that just entered. The Minotaur leads the way.

"Come on, Tookus," Holly says.

"Bang bang bang bang," Tookus says, leaning against her pull.

"Hey," she says, "I see tractors, Took. How about a tractor ride?"

That's all it takes. The Minotaur follows, the promise of tractors too sweet to resist.

The tractors are corralled at the rear and in the center of the vast building, each dealer setting up camp in a different quadrant of the make-believe farmyard, bright green Astro Turf laid out within the post-and-rail fence line. A barn-and-silo façade, overly bright and oddly scaled, rises against the back wall. Tookus, enthralled, wants to ride them all: the blue Fords, the red red Kubotas, the pea green John Deeres. But Holly promised more than she can deliver. No tractor rides are available. Only brochures and enthusiastic salesmen. Holly somehow (flirting too subtly for the Minotaur to fathom) convinces the Ford dealer to let Tookus climb up onto the big black springy seat of the largest machine on site. No more. The Minotaur watches Holly slip a business card into her back pocket. Watches the tractor dealer ogle the redhead's backside, then try to come to terms with the Minotaur's horns. All the tractors are brand spanking new, radiant and beautiful. Almost beastlike in their simple me-chanics. The Minotaur reaches into an engine housing. He doesn't care who sees it. He runs his palm over the manifolds. Intake. Exhaust. They are cool and still. Waiting. The smells of the new tires and engines are more than the Minotaur can bear. Too, the array of farming implements with their toothy blades and wheels and rakes and more. Sexier still the names: tiller, reaper, picker, planter, plow.

"Unngh," the Minotaur says, heading for no good reason to the Farm Arts & Crafts Competition tables, Holly and Tookus hot on his heels.

"Don't touch," Holly says when her brother reaches for the painted eggs.

"Those are quail," the young woman behind the table says. She sits on a three-legged stool, hunched over and so bent into her task that she speaks without looking up.

"Those are quail," she says. "The little ones are finch. Then chicken, then goose."

The eggs are painted. Two dozen perch in open paper cartons angled along the table's edge. Several nests, some real, others made of curled paper or ribbon, hold still more eggs. All sit like fat jeweled orbs lined with sharp geometries or brilliant swirls. They sit as if they possess all the weight in the world. And who's to say they don't? The Minotaur wants to feel the impossible heft.

"This single big boy here is emu," she says, leaning back with one tiny paintbrush in her hand. "And I'm gonna win first prize with it."

A droplet of gold paint is on brush's fine hairs. So small. A whole day's worth of sunlight is captured there. The emu egg, raised like magic, looks to be levitating from a jeweler's vise. It is dazzling. An azure blue laced with gold and dotted with fiery red. Little pots of paint surround her workspace. Her fingers are tipped in color.

"First prize," she says.

"Egggggggzzzzz," Tookus says. But he keeps his hands to himself.

A placard in crisp calligraphy reads, *The Perfect Gift For Any Occasion*; reads, *Fine Jewelry*; reads, *Make Great Christmas Ornaments*; reads, *Special Requests Taken*.

"Ornaments, huh?" Holly says.

She picks up a red bauble, holds it to the Minotaur's horns. "You ever decorate those things for Christmas?" she asks.

The Minotaur chuckles. Though it could be mistaken for another kind of sound. Holly picks up a delicate pair of earrings. Finch eggs painted sage green with ocher stars. She holds them to her own ears.

Horns, the Minotaur thinks.

"What do you think?" Holly asks.

Horns. They look stunning. The green and yellow against her freckled flesh and the red hair. Perfect.

She looks at the price tag and returns the eggs to the table. "Another time, maybe," she says. "Wait up, Took."

"Goats," Tookus says. He lowers his head into the crowd and aims at the *Petting Zoo* sign, beyond the corn-shucking contest.

The Minotaur pauses, thinks, acts without overthinking. He digs in the deep pocket of his Confederate gray trousers, lays some folded bills on the egg painter's table. He doesn't count. He hopes.

"These," he says, pointing to the sage and ocher finch eggs.

"Okay," she says. She doesn't count.

"Good choice," she says. She looks up and winks at the Minotaur.

"Let me get you a little box," she says.

Petting zoos are problematic for the Minotaur. His allegiances get tugged and strained. And he inevitably gets pawed and poked. Petting zoos are best avoided. But for Holly, for Tookus, the Minotaur will endure. They are already inside the gate, shuffling through the scattered yellow straw. There's a small crowd, but mercifully all the kids are clumped around some poor creature at the back of the stall. Holly proffers a quarter; Tookus thumbs the coin into the gumball machine cum food pellet dispenser. The goats and sheep, three little pigs, the single llama, all swarm the boy and begin to nudge at him with their assorted snouts. The Minotaur slows in his approach. The petting zoo's warden, the gatekeeper, is a farm wife. Pragmatic. No-nonsense. Careful in her emotional dealings. She eyeballs the Minotaur, speculating. *What if? What if?* The woman smiles, to herself mostly, and takes off her gloves. Her hands are powerful and callused. She opens the gate and tips her head at the Minotaur.

"Unngh," he says, tipping his horns at the farm wife. "No."

The Minotaur stands outside the bent-pipe corral and watches Tookus and his sister. The boy is excited. Happy. Holly is happy. The Minotaur sees it in her eyes. He'll stand there, he'll wait, as long as it takes. That's the point.

The Minotaur looks into the petting zoo compound, his back to the rest of the thronging Ag-Fest. Kids love a petting zoo. Parents welcome the distraction, the photo ops. He wonders what unfortunate beast is getting all the attention at the far end of the stall, and when the crowd shifts the Minotaur is able to see the papier-mâché horn tied to the bony forehead of a haggard dwarf donkey.

"Unngh," the Minotaur says. Yet another portent? Change is afoot.

The ersatz unicorn's horn leans to one side, the tip bent and cracked. The ends of the rope that ought to be holding the horn upright dangle from the donkey's mouth. The creature chews mindlessly. The Minotaur looks away, not wanting to make eye contact.

The Minotaur watches Holly, Tookus, and the rest tromp around in the muck. Watches the farm wife's son flit about with his little shovel and broom, barely able to keep up with all the droppings. Watches the woman in charge standing by the cages in the corner (some of them holding weary or terrified bunnies or potbellied pigs; a turtle the size of a pie pan scratches at her boot), standing there in rubber gloves, one hand perched and ready on a holstered bottle of antiseptic spray. Everything is just this side of disease outbreak. The Minotaur couldn't be more content.

Then he hears them.

"Give me another quarter."

"I'm still hungry."

"I have to poop."

"Juney said poop again!"

The Minotaur turns to gauge their distance. Catches the mother's eye. Or more accurately, gets caught in it.

"I want to pet that thing," she says way too loudly.

The Minotaur's skin crawls. All of it. Mercifully Holly comes to the rescue.

"Where to now?" she asks.

But Tookus wants to show the Minotaur what Holly bought for him. A petting zoo souvenir.

"Poooooop," he says, holding up the shellacked cow chip by its leather strand. "Uuuuunicorn poooooooooooop."

The tight swirls, the striations of light and dark matter captured in varnish, look like a tiny galaxy. Tookus hangs the cow chip proudly around his neck.

The Minotaur opens his palm; it holds the box, his gift to Holly.

She makes a sound, a soft coo (maybe speech, maybe not), and tries not to tear up after she hooks the finch eggs into her ears.

"I wish . . . ," she says, looking back and forth between Tookus and the Minotaur. "I wish we didn't have to go to Pittsburgh. To . . . I wish we could just stay here forever."

She says it plain as day. The Minotaur hears it. He thinks so, anyway. But they're on the move. Things are different. Things are changing. Through the eons of his horned life the Minotaur has come to understand that it is sometimes—often, even—the shortest distances one has to traverse that are the most treacherous. He couldn't say as much out loud. But he knows it.

Treacherous.

It should not surprise the Minotaur that Old Scald Village has a table at Ag-Days. But it does. He sees the poster advertising next weekend's Encampment. It's propped on an easel. Big happy letters advertise the scheduled battles. The Minotaur sees the photographs. Widow Fisk's bonneted face. A battle under way, the picture perfectly capturing the tongues of fire and smoke from the cannons. The Minotaur imagines himself there, belly up in the April mud, the blue blue sky the only thing holding him to the earth.

"Hey!" somebody says.

It's Biddle, at the table, with a wobbly little barrel between his feet and a ball-peen hammer clutched in his fat hand.

"M! Over here! It's Biddle."

Of course it is.

"Oh," Holly says. "Your friends are here."

And before the Minotaur can protest Holly heads to the Old Scald Village table, to Biddle, to Smitty. Biddle sits with his bucket and hammer, grinning, staring at Holly's chest. Smitty stands, rattling a pair of blacksmith's pincers open and closed, open and closed.

"Tssss," Smitty says, scowling at the Minotaur.

Something singes. Burns.

Biddle gives a slobbery wolf whistle. Holly is more amused than annoyed.

"It ain't been the same since you left, M," Biddle says. "When you coming back?"

"Tssss," Smitty says again. He won't look at Holly.

Neither of them mentions the uniform. The Minotaur is (still) dressed as a soldier. Still ready for dying. Still.

Holly picks up a hand mandrel, a heavy cone-shaped tool from Smitty's forge. It's fitted with a handle and meant for making and stretching iron rings.

"Goodness gracious," Holly says, wagging the thing at the Minotaur. "This is my kind of tool."

Holly laughs.

Smitty doesn't.

"Them ain't toys," he says, looking at the Minotaur.

Tookus steps between the blacksmith and the Minotaur. Faces the man. Grins.

"Bang bang," he says. "Bang bang."

Then the boy rushes away. It's a blessing in disguise. A saving grace. Holly has to follow. Too, the Minotaur. Biddle yammers something as they disappear into the Fruits & Vegetables Competition.

Table after table, in neat orderly rows, what the earth has yielded up lies in obscene display, already judged and ranked. Blue ribbons, red ribbons, Runners-up. The carrot and its promiscuous dangling. The lascivious purple of the eggplant. The cucumber's knobby flesh. The halved cabbage and its furls. The tomato's red cleft. Everything offered up by the clumps of basil. The onion, after all.

"Damn," Holly says.

She takes a closer look at the first-place cucumber. Fingers its blue ribbon.

"Abbigail Zeek," she reads. "Grade 9, Foot-of-Ten High School."

Holly looks at the Minotaur, then past him. Smiles.

"Go, Abby, go," she says.

Holly picks up the prize-winning cucumber. Tookus is at an opposite table looking at jars of honey. The Minotaur can smell everything. The crowd is, more or less, occupied elsewhere. Holly holds the cucumber batonlike, as if she's going to pass it to him any minute now. Her thumb rides along its ridges and over the bumpy flesh. Then she smiles again. Then she takes a very deliberate, very delicate bite from the tip. The give and take of her bottom lip against the waxy green flesh is unbearable.

"Unngh," the Minotaur says. Trespass. Trouble. He looks around.

Holly giggles, pleased with her rebellion, and returns the champion cucumis (minus half an inch) to its place of honor. She winks, still chewing, at the Minotaur, and her breath plows him deeply, takes root.

"Wait up, Tookus," she says.

"Where to now?" she says.

"Let's go over there," she says.

Holly gestures up and over the crowd to a banner that reads, *4-H Animal Husbandry Exhibit.*

"Mmmnn," the Minotaur says. Anywhere. That's the point.

CHAPTER TWENTY-NINE

THE MINOTAUR IS ETERNALLY at the mercy of nonsense: his own and humans'. Sometimes happily so. Other times not. Were he more clear-headed, the Minotaur might balk at the prospect of the 4-H Animal Husbandry Exhibit. But the world is topsy-turvy of late, his thoughts pell-mell, and so it happens.

"This way," Holly says.

"Going to the chapel," she says, giddy with criminality, "and we're gonna get ma-a-arried."

The 4-H-ers are giddy, too. And why shouldn't they be? Head, Heart, Hands, Health. The youth, bright eyed and compliant, buzz about admiring each other's projects, or stand beaming pridefully by their own. There, a banana nut bread fairly radiates wholesome deliciousness. Here, a mechanical apple peeler has littered the floor with beautiful red coils. The maker, the boy in charge, invites Tookus to crank the handle.

They believe, the 4-H-ers. They command a vast roofless room at the Joy Ag-Fest. There are demo chicken coops, an array of rainwater collectors, and a BB gun shooting booth (which Holly steers her brother clear of). Happily steers him here and there.

"I wish we could stay here forever."

She said it aloud. The Minotaur heard it.

Holly put the prizewinner right into her mouth and bit the tip off. The Minotaur saw it. Saw it all.

"Butter butt butt butt butterrrrrrr," Tookus says.

And sure enough, the roomful of butter sculptures is worthy of praise and awe. It's a cold room, locked tight, and the floor-to-ceiling glass walls keep the oglers at bay.

Tookus is drawn immediately to the odalisque, life sized, scantily clad, lying demurely on her yellow slab. And why not?

The bust of a soldier, saluting.

The cow jumping over the moon, both grinning.

A tableful of small vignettes, pastoral and idyllic, though one lass skipping with a basket seems to have lost her head. The Minotaur leans in. There, he sees it, her tiny yellow head. Upside down by the perfect yellow porch steps.

"Look," Holly says. She points across the exhibit hall to the Science of Farming display. "I saw one of those when I was a kid."

What? the Minotaur wonders, but will follow the redhead with or without an answer.

It's a cow. A living, breathing, cud-chewing cow with a porthole in its side. A window into its gut. Holly reads the information poster.

"Cannulated," she says, and looks deep. "It's called cannulated."

The Minotaur doesn't care. There is an explanation of *how* and *why*. The Minotaur doesn't care.

He is jostled and displaced by a troop of Boy Scouts clamoring to see inside the cow.

Two booths over, a line has formed. Tookus steps up, Holly behind him, the Minotaur behind her.

"What is it?" she asks.

There is lots of giggling and eww-ing. The line moves in fits and starts. But soon enough it's visible. The 4-H-ers have set up a calving simulator. Veterinary-school quality. Lifelike. The heifer's four hooves are bolted to a plank base. The heifer's backside is aimed at the gathered crowd, her black vulva all slick and on display, loose and floppy. There is a box of rubber gloves, arm-length and hospital blue. There is a bucket of lube. A rack of pamphlets from Allegheny Community College describes its exciting new vocational diploma in veterinary technologies. There is a line of people (not unlike the lines for the pillories at Old Scald Village) ahead of them and behind—kids and adults waiting to glove up and reach inside the fake cow's vagina.

The Minotaur is not faint of heart. Is not squeamish. But this apparatus strikes close to home. Strikes an ancient chord. The Minotaur closes his eyes, can't escape the field of hyacinth, the craftsman's relentless hammer, his own dubious conception. The Minotaur didn't ask for any of this.

He opens his eyes to see a tattooed boy showing off for his tattooed girlfriend. The boy snaps his glove on with aplomb, strikes a come-hither pose, and lunges in up to his shoulder. A chittering, a chuckling, pulses through the onlookers. The girlfriend isn't sure what to do. The Minotaur either.

"Dumbass," Holly whispers, but she's just as curious as the rest. And when the boy's eyes widen and the look of surprise, or maybe shock, takes over his face, Holly leans in like everybody else.

"Hey!" the guy says. "Hey! Let go!"

He jerks, is jerked, deeper into the heifer's backside.

"Tommy!" his girl says. "Tommy!"

There's a struggle deep inside the fake cow. It's not clear if Tommy is going to win. He looks fierce but worried.

"Mandy!" he says. "Mandy!"

She wants to help, but how? Mandy looks frantic.

"Tommy!"

Tommy is contorting and wrenching his arm. The lube-slathered latex sputters and farts in the struggle.

"Mandy!" he says.

"Mandy!"

And one final time, when it seems as if Tommy is about to lose the battle and be sucked in fully and forever.

"Mandy," he says, yanking his arm free, raising it high in victory, kneeling before the weeping girl, opening his hand, where sits a ring box.

"Mandy," he says, "will you marry me?"

"Good God," Holly says.

Applause. Applause.

A sweet sleight of hand? Farmyard tomfoolery? Who is the Minotaur to judge?

The Minotaur is undone. Flummoxed. Though he'd blame what happens next on more jostling Scouts, the Minotaur steps back without looking. His pant leg snags on something. Maybe a rough edge on a stanchion post; maybe a sharp screw tip overrun by some zealous 4-H-er; maybe even the tooth or claw of a less common beast. Doesn't matter. What matters is that the gray wool of the Minotaur's Confederate trousers is no match for what snags them. They rip from knee to hip, and Holly hears it.

"Oops," she says, kneeling and poking her finger right inside the tear. Breech and probe. Her fingertip there, where thigh meets calf. A fully human place.

It might as well be a branding iron. Tssss! The Minotaur smells burning flesh. No. The Minotaur's mouth waters; he can't help it. She kneels there, red hair parted over her face, red hair hanging down, framing the milk-white tableaux of her breasts. The shirt gapes, reveals the most sacred diptych, reveals the true Eucharist. The shirt gapes, and the Minotaur falls into the abyss. The Minotaur can't help looking. The Minotaur is man enough. The Minotaur is beast enough. The bellows of his lungs fill, and the Minotaur's horns rise toward the heavens.

"Are you looking at my tits?" she says, cracking his moment of rapture wide open. It is not an accusation. There is levity in her claim.

"Come on," Holly says. "We've got to get you fixed."

Anywhere. That's the point.

Holly has a plan. Holly is quick on her feet. Holly parks Tookus at the gates of hell. No. It's just an arcade game.

"We'll be right back," she says, feeding half a dozen coins into the slot, then giving him an entire roll of quarters. "Don't you go anywhere."

"You've opened the gates of hell!"

Tookus purrs with contentment.

"You stay right there, Tooky," she says.

Anywhere. The Minotaur will follow the redhead. Though he has to stoop, bend to one side, and hold his torn pants closed in order to do so. It is late April. Tick tock, tick tock. Time clicks its boot heels and marches on. It is dying season somewhere. But the Minotaur is not dying today.

The redhead takes the bull-man by the hand. By the hand. Takes him, by the hand, out of the Kmart cum Ag-Fest building right down the sidewalk and into the Goodwill next door. (There is a new commotion on the stage, the Sacred Harp having unstrung and departed. The Minotaur hears, he thinks, a feral horn. But the Minotaur has other things on his mind.) The Minotaur goes, but not without trepidation. He is conflicted. About leaving Tookus and moving through the Ag-Fest crowd specifically. About thrift stores in general. The items always seem sticky with the residue of the lives they've passed through.

But Holly is on a mission. Holly, with the Minotaur in tow, charges into the Goodwill, straight past shelf after shelf of porcelain figurines—some animal, some human, some mongrel, most smiling beatifically—past stopped clocks, themed salt and pepper shakers, pots and pans, past all the smells of countless suppers, of closets and cabinets, past generations of tchotchkes come to rest after some final death in the family. She charges ahead, tugging him through rows and rows of orphaned shoes, a line of wheezing neckties, racks and racks of used clothing parsed out by gender (by generation?), then (roughly) size, right to the men's section, as if she's been there and done that before. The Goodwill employee, a creature of indeterminate age and sex clad in an ill-fitting smock, clad in a universe of woe, mumbles something as they pass. Beyond that nobody pays them much attention.

"You stay here," she says, parking the Minotaur at the end of an aisle on one of those low shoe-store benches that require something of a straddle. "No, wait a minute. Stand up."

He does.

She looks him over. Up and down.

"Turn around," she says.

He does.

"Not bad," she says.

"I'm thinking thirty-two, maybe thirty-four inseam," she says.

"Sit down," she says.

He does.

He watches her disappear behind the rows. She hums "What Wondrous Love Is This." He sits. He waits. The aisles are narrow, the racks of clothing full. Try as he might the Minotaur can't keep his horns from slipping into the line of shirts at his back. He can feel the ghosts crowding him.

"Kenny!" somebody calls from across the store, rupturing the moment. "Kenny! Goddamn it, boy, where are you?"

Holly returns with a pair of blue pants draped over her arm.

"They're not gray," she says.

"I think it's time for a change," she says.

"Kenny! I'm gonna whip your little ass when I find you!"

"Mmmnn," the Minotaur says.

"Hold these," Holly says. "I'll be back."

The Minotaur believes it more than he's believed anything in a long time.

"Kenny!" the voice rages behind him.

The Minotaur is about to stand up, to see what's happening, when he hears the cry. A soft tiny weeping. Maybe human, maybe not. Hearing isn't the Minotaur's strong suit. He tries to find the source of the cry.

"These, too," Holly says, returning from her sortie to drop more trousers into his lap.

They're all shades of blue. The Minotaur doesn't care.

"One more run. Hold tight."

The Minotaur holds tight, straddling the low bench, throwing caution to the wind, letting his torn pants gape. When he hears the cry again it's right behind him. Human, most certainly. Coming from beneath the densely packed row of women's pantsuits, sizes thirty-six to fifty-two. The Minotaur angles his head so low that the horns nearly scrape the linoleum flooring. He sees the feet. The Minotaur parts the hangers, and there the boy stands, four, maybe five years old, tears rolling down his cheeks. A thick clump of his curly brown hair is snagged in a zipper. The boy was playing, swaddled in the secrets of the old clothes, then became trapped, and is now being held prisoner by a pair of tweed extra-large pants.

The boy looks up at the Minotaur. Surprisingly there is no fear in his face. The Minotaur knows boy behavior. He understands the desire to burrow, to hide, to root, to creep. He knows, too, the consequences of flawed judgment. Many times over the centuries the Minotaur has been caught unaware in the zippers of the hand-me-downs, the habits, the vestments of strangers.

The boy flinches a little when the Minotaur reaches out, but within seconds the hair is untangled and he is free. The boy grins, then disappears between the rows of pants.

The Minotaur hears the mother greet him.

"Goddamn it, Kenny! Where you been?"

The redhead rounds the aisle again.

"This should do us," she says. "Come on."

"Goddamn it, Kenny! Get back here!"

The Minotaur stands to follow the girl, then feels a tug on his pant leg. It's Kenny. The boy is holding up something for the Minotaur. It's a Minotaur. Tiny. Plastic. Wielding a bloody ax. Well muscled and wearing very little.

"Mmmnn," the Minotaur says.

The boy clearly intends the toy as a gift, so the Minotaur takes it, reaches to pat him on the head.

"Aww," Holly says. "So sweet."

"Kenny," the mother shrieks from the end of the row, "get away from that!"

Kenny smiles then runs to his mother.

"Bitch," Holly says. She winks at the Minotaur. "Ready?"

He's not sure what to expect. He says yes anyway.

The lone Goodwill employee is at the register by the front doors checking out Kenny's mother, who seems to be haggling over every price tag. Holly leads the Minotaur to the rear of the store, to the *Fitting*

Rooms sign. The door is open, flanked on one side by a pegboard wall hung with mismatched crutches and on the other by bookshelves densely packed with pulp novels, pages yellowed, spines cracked and peeling.

"Hubba hubba ding ding," the girl says, and it makes as much sense as the rest of his day, so the Minotaur doesn't question.

They go through the door to find themselves in a narrow windowless room with another door on the opposite wall that opens to the delivery lane at the rear of the shopping center. For the Goodwill this back door serves as the port for all donations.

"Look at all this," the girl says with no small awe. "So much . . . stuff."

Indeed, *stuff*, the donations, nearly fill the room, spilling out through the open door and into the drive. Furniture, electronics, an old aluminum walker sitting atop an old aluminum adult potty chair. Baby goods galore. Boxes of this, stacks of that, all waiting to be processed, to be valued and either priced for sale or discarded. *Humans*. The Minotaur thinks it but doesn't speak.

Holly, distracted, fascinated, pokes around while the Minotaur clings to his several pairs of blue pants. Holly picks up Bronco Bob from a cluttered Formica table. It says so on his cowboy shirt. Bronco Bob is a cowboy doll made of rubber and cloth. Bronco Bob wears boots and jeans and a red bandana. He sits on a plastic bull, the bull's face frozen in a perpetual snort. Bronco Bob sits on the bull with one arm raised high. A thin metal axle runs through the bull's belly and into Bronco Bob's boots at the ankles. The bull is mounted on a post that also runs into its gut and into a faux stone base, and Bronco Bob is upright because of it. An on/off switch is on the bull's haunch.

Holly flips the switch. Bronco Bob is in trouble. Something has gone awry in the circuitry. Bronco Bob starts jumping spastically, furiously, up down up down up down, shrieking manically from a tiny speaker inside his cowboy shirt, "Yee-haw, yee-haw, yee-haw!" Up down up down. "Yee-haw, yee-haw!" Holly startles, laughs, and drops the toy to the floor, where Bronco Bob continues to twitch.

The Minotaur puts his boot down and grinds his foot until Bronco

Bob is still.

"Sorry," Holly says. "I couldn't help myself."

The Minotaur understands fully.

"Are you ready?" Holly asks.

"Unngh," the Minotaur says. He is.

She isn't. The redhead's focus is taken hostage one more time.

"What the fuck?" she says.

She lifts a tattered and mud-colored bath towel from whatever it drapes. It's a display case, a cabinet of three wooden shelves and a glass door, meant to be hung on a wall but leaning instead against one. Practically hidden, intentionally so.

Holly lifts the case and props it on a table. Dust billows. Dust settles. Holly peers in. The Minotaur waits. That's the point.

"Ha!" she says. "They're shitting! Look!"

The Minotaur looks. It's true. The cabinet shelves hold a dozen or so figurines, all squatting with pants down or skirts hiked, all hovering over tiny brown coils. Holly is so excited she can barely contain herself.

"There's the pope!" she says. "And Betty Boop. And Jesus. Michael Jackson. Darth Vader!"

True. They are all there, squatting and defecating.

"That's Marilyn Monroe, I think," Holly says. "But who's that? And that? And that?"

A little brass plaque is tacked to the case's top edge. Holly licks her thumb and wipes the tag.

"El Ca-ga-ner," she reads, then again. "El Caganer."

"I wonder . . . ," she says.

"People are so weird," she says.

"God love a freak," she says.

"We might have to come back for this," she says.

Okay. The Minotaur will come and go as often as she asks.

"Okay," Holly says, and winks. "Stop your dillydallying."

She points to the fitting rooms, three stalls lining the far wall. The dividing panels don't quite reach the floor and leave substantial gaps at the ceiling, but they provide a modicum of privacy. How much more is needed? The door to the first stall stands ajar.

"In you go," she says.

In he goes. Narrow benches span both of the side walls. A cloudy mirror hangs opposite the door; half a dozen wire hangers rattle on a hook when she closes it. Everything is pale white except for her toes. The Minotaur can see them, in all their celestial glory, poking beneath the door. He wonders if she can see his horns overtop.

"Give 'em up," she says, one lean and freckled arm reaching over the door panel.

"Unngh?"

"Your pants," she says. "Give me your pants."

The stall is tight, corral-like. But the Minotaur's balance is good. He drapes the torn trousers over the door.

"These first," she says.

To accommodate the span of his horns the Minotaur stands sideways in the stall. Even so, it is a small balancing act to get them on. He grunts into the task, and as soon as he tugs the zipper up she opens the door.

"Let me see," she says.

The Minotaur stands as still as possible.

"No," she says. "You look like an old man."

She closes the door, and they make another exchange.

"Nope," she says. "Boy Scout if I ever saw one."

The third try gets close. The Minotaur opens the door to the stall himself, clutching at the waistline.

"Not bad," she says, "but way too saggy. Hang on for minute, I'll get you a . . ."

Holly speaks as she leaves the room, so the Minotaur doesn't hear what it is she's gone in search of. He is hopeful. Expectant, even. And a little disappointed when she returns with just a belt. A leather belt. He buckles it.

"Oh, no," she says. "Now you look like a really old-man Boy Scout. Give them to me."

When the door is closed the Minotaur strips down again.

"Wait there," she says through the panel.

Where would he go? The Minotaur is not ashamed of his human side, his man half. But walking around in his underwear, socks, and shoes seems unwise. The Minotaur sits on one of the benches and lets his heavy head lean back against the dividing wall. He hears laughter out in the store; he's pretty sure it's Holly. He sits. He doesn't look in the mirror. He worries briefly about Tookus at the gates of hell. He sits still. He sits. Still. Until Holly returns.

The Minotaur expects a pair of blue pants to appear overtop. But she shoves open the stall door, laughing.

"I love this place," she says. "Let's stay here forever."

"Mmmnn, okay."

"Look!" Holly says with unfettered glee. "I found the best stuff."

Holly comes into the stall where the Minotaur sits. The stall cannot possibly contain her big energy, her real body, all motion and scent. There is no room for the Minotaur to breathe. He drowns willingly. She stands facing him, puts a shopping basket on the opposite bench. Her leg brushes the Minotaur's bare thighs.

"Ta-da," she says, reaching into the basket, pulling out a hand puppet. "It's Picasso! Tooky loves puppets."

Holly parts the puppet's fabric orifice, squints, peers inside. She blows two hard puffs into the opening.

"Oooo," Holly says in a strange accent of dubious origin. "Meester Pablo likes it when you do that."

She puts the puppet on her hand, oohing and cooing in the voice.

"Mmmnn," the Minotaur says, not sure how best to participate in the charade.

"Well, hello there, big boy," the puppet says. "Pablo likes your horns. Much much. Very much."

She reaches out. The little puppet hands stroke the Minotaur's horns from base to tip. First one, then the other. Then again. The Minotaur sits very still, watches her toes, watches the soft paunch of her belly shift beneath her white shirt. Picasso gives him a quick peck on the snout, then gets impaled fully onto a horn.

"Perfect," Holly says, adjusting the puppet's face. "Perfect. And for my next trick . . . "

This time, she has a shiny black sphere and another affected voice.

"The Magic 8 Ball knows all, tells all. Quick, think of a question, but don't tell me."

She upends the plastic ball, and they both watch the die float to the little round window, its answer bobbing gently in the ink-black liquid: *REPLY HAZY, TRY AGAIN.*

"Hmmm," she says. "Very mysterious."

But there was no question. The girl moved too fast for the Minotaur.

"My turn," she says.

She doesn't tell him the question, nor does she share the answer, but she laughs loudly and looks hard at the Minotaur. Holly sets the Magic 8 Ball on the bench opposite him.

"Are you ready for the next?" Holly asks.

"Mmmnn," the Minotaur says.

She reaches into the shopping basket. Hesitates.

"Are you really ready?"

The Minotaur has every intention of answering. He wonders what the Magic 8 Ball would say. He wonders how many freckles her body carries. He wonders when she last bathed.

"Are you?" she asks. "Guess what it is."

The Minotaur is not good at guessing.

"No," she says. "Don't guess. Close your eyes."

The Minotaur is good at closing his eyes.

But the Minotaur is slow, and Holly is eager in her command. She is already unbuttoning and pulling her pants down before she finishes speaking. "Don't guess" comes as the pants are somewhere down her long thighs, their apple white flesh. By "Close your eyes," the Minotaur sees, without meaning to, the absence of panties, the thatch of red hair bursting from between her legs, nothing less than a conflagration. The

Minotaur is good at closing his eyes. He does so.

Rustle, rustle.

"Now," she says. "Now you can look."

The Minotaur is okay at looking.

She stands before him in full nun's regalia. White coif, holy habit, the scapular. She stands, palms up and out, fingers cocked precisely in the gesture of wonder.

"Hail Mary, full of grace," she says in her Picasso voice. "Something about fruits and wombs."

"Unngh," the Minotaur says.

"One at a time!" another voice says, from outside the stall. "That's the rule! Only one at a time!"

The Minotaur sees the thick-soled black shoes of the Goodwill employee beneath the door.

"We got rules," she says.

Her wide splay-footed stance makes the Minotaur want to be nice. To follow the rules.

"Holy Mary, mother of God," the girl says, trying hard not to laugh. "Let me beat you with my rod."

"We got rules," the employee says. "Only one at a time!"

The Minotaur starts to speak, but Holly puts her fingers to his lips. The gesture of declamation.

"My boyfriend," she says, cocking her head upward, speaking over the partition. "My boyfriend's crippled. My boyfriend, he's blind."

They hear the employee grunt. She stays just outside the stall door.

"He's a soldier," Holly says. "A veteran of war. The things he's sacrificed for this country . . . You ought to be ashamed of yourself."

The woman harrumphs. "We got rules," she says, but she says it on the way out of the room.

"Shhh," the girl says to the Minotaur. "I think she's gone."

She takes up the Magic 8 Ball, consults it again, and once again keeps the results to herself. But she seems both surprised and pleased.

"One more," she says. "I've saved the best for last."

"Close your eyes," she says. "Don't look."

The Minotaur listens to nun's habit come off and pool on the floor. He knows those long legs are there, and the rest of her body. Naked and right there. The Minotaur will not look without permission.

"Mind your p's and q's," she says.

"Forgive us, Father, for we have . . . " She laughs. "Shhh."

The stall door opens, then closes quickly. The Minotaur hears her chuckle, rustling into the next incarnation.

"Don't look," she says.

The Minotaur feels her hand under his chin. She lifts his head, his long snout. She steps close. She steps between his open legs, but it is not her naked flesh against his bare thighs. She steps closer, takes him gently by both horns, pulls his face into her body. But it is not her naked breasts that he nuzzles. Then she steps back, out of his touch.

"Now," she says. "Look."

It's a fur coat. Long and brown. Mottled and splotchy. But her red hair, the finch eggs, those green eyes, painted toenails, the body whole, contained by the coat: the beast is stunning.

"Mmmnn," the Minotaur says.

"They've got rules here," the redhead says, smiling. "Forgive us our trespasses."

"Mmmnn," the Minotaur says.

"Close your eyes," she says. "Don't look."

The Minotaur hears her sit on the opposite bench. Feels her still more. The space is cramped. Tight. The Minotaur's eyes are closed. He does not see the fur coat fall open. Does not see her breasts fall into their softness, nor the nipples reach. He does not see her legs part.

"Don't look," Holly says. "They've got rules here."

He feels one bare foot come to rest at his side, then the other bare foot at his other side. The Minotaur will not look at her spread legs. Spread. Him between. Heat and musk, between him and the girl. Her musk, her heat, just there, and everywhere. She presses the soles of her feet against the partition.

"Don't look," she says.

And the Minotaur will not see the wild red hair, the bush burning, swirling, glistening. Will not see her palm ride up the swell of her ribcage, lift and squeeze the breast.

"Ummh," she says.

"Don't look," she says.

And she knows he will not. And he knows, without looking, what business the hands are about.

"Don't look," she says.

It becomes a mantra, a pacesetter. A syllabic coxswain.

"Don't look," she says slowly when the fingers trace the lips, part the folds.

The Minotaur knows this unseen thing. This sweet mutt. A thing both flora and fauna, there, out of sight, so close. He could name it if he had to.

"Don't," she says, "look," when the fingers dip in, tips first, then fully, to find her most private flesh.

"Don'tlookdon'tlookdon'tlook," she says when those two favorite and slick fingertips circle and circle and circle, now right above, now a little lower.

She stops. She stills. The Minotaur wonders if something is wrong, if she heard something, someone. No, she is in motion again.

"Don't look," she says.

The Minotaur hears her stickiness. Hears her inside herself. Holly inside of Holly. The Minotaur feels her fingers at his mouth before he smells, before he tastes. This is what the redhead tastes like. Root and stem, soil and stamen. She tastes of the plow and the rut. Of cloud. Sun and moon. Day and night. The redhead, her pussy, it tastes like the universe. Her fingers there, then gone. The tastes linger. Here, the pussy. Her pussy. There, the still more earthy backside. He knows this. Knows now the taste of her.

"Don't look," she says. "Don't look. Don't . . . don't . . . don't . . . look."

The Minotaur feels the surge as the muscles in her legs contract and spasm. The bird takes flight, the fish breeches, the bull bucks and heaves, everything drips. The Minotaur is drowning. The Minotaur is man enough. He cannot help what rises between his pinioned legs. The redhead kicks at the fitting-room stall, her breath a staccato utterance, a hymn to flesh and blood and bone. Something falls to the floor. The Minotaur hears it roll away. The Magic 8 Ball. It rolls to a stop against a far wall. Aftershocks of her orgasm jolt her body and, through it, the Minotaur's.

Holly sits splayed, recovering, until her breath comes to order. She leans into him, her forehead against the bony expanse between his closed eyes. She kisses the Minotaur lightly on the snout.

"Don't look," she says.

She pulls her legs from around him. The Minotaur listens to her breathe deeply, consciously.

"Don't look," she says, almost whispering.

She stands. The fur coat drops from her body. He listens. She gathers up her own clothing, returns to herself. No longer naked. The Minotaur listens. Every sound drips with her, what? He doesn't know how to name it.

"Don't look," she says so softly that it contains almost no sound.

"Don't look."

The Minotaur hears the hinges protest just a little when the stall door opens, then shuts. The Minotaur sits with his eyes closed. He's okay, there in the dark. He hasn't been given permission to look. He's content enough with the things he can smell and feel and taste. The sweat from her calves along his thighs. Her viscosity, her sweet filth, on his tongue, in the black wells of his nostrils. A pair of crows argues outside. The Minotaur doesn't have to see. Doesn't have to look. The fitting-room mirror bore witness. The Minotaur sits on the bench in his underwear, his modest cock still hopeful. Petulant, even. The Picasso puppet dangles from his horn tip. On the floor the mottled fur rests atop the nun's habit. No longer Holly. A beast in its own right. Asleep or waiting. On the bench where she sat Holly left a puddle of herself. He doesn't have to see it. The Minotaur wonders if he can open his eyes yet. The Magic 8 Ball, having rolled window up in the corner, has the answer bobbing plainly, clearly, in its murk.

CHAPTER THIRTY

THE MINOTAUR TAKES HIS TIME. Sweet time.

When he steps back out into the day, the day has wreaked havoc on the earth. All is charred black. The gibbous moon, in a hissy fit, has upended and poured its moony gall over everything. The Minotaur runs naked—nay, gallops—through the smoldering ash and stump world. Bellowing.

No. That's not it at all. Things have changed.

The Minotaur steps back into the day. The skirmish line. Route. Flank. Retreat. The Minotaur steps into the dog and pony show. The cock-a-doodle-doo swung round and round and round, the tarot deck, the chopping block. There is no difference between the prie-dieu and her scapula.

No. Too much. The Minotaur knows. This is too much.

The Minotaur knows the furnace, the smelter, the bellows.

The Minotaur knows Peter, Peter, pumpkin eater. The titty-twister.

The Minotaur knows the solipsistic eye of Copernicus. Knows pomp and circumstance.

The Minotaur knows the travesty of orbits and gravity, the muckrakers of the universe.

The Minotaur knows a girl made of fire. Of fire. Echo.

The Minotaur remembers that thing. She never did.

The Minotaur stands in the strum hollow. In the wash of the treble drone.

The Minotaur stands on the mountaintop.

The Minotaur always finds himself standing on the goddamn mountaintop.

One goddamnable mountaintop after another. The tide of histories (plural) roiling in the valleys below. Giddy. Giddy-up. The Minotaur stands on the mountain and, with his horn tips, stitches himself to the cloud-heavy sky. The running stitch. The hemming stitch. The basting stitch. The slip stitch. The catch stitch. The backstitch. The invisible stitch.

Maybe the heart is both. Vessel and whole note. Sintered, as he is, by her.

CHAPTER THIRTY-ONE

THE MINOTAUR TAKES HIS TIME, there in the changing room stall of the Goodwill, a late April afternoon. The Minotaur lingers. In the Goodwill, in the goodwill of Holly's tastes and smells. Her presence and absence. He sits in his underwear, his horn tips pressed against the wall panel. One ear twitches. He taps at his brass buttons. He reaches into the coat and rubs at his seam. It's on the move now. Surely. He's half convinced that she'll be gone when he leaves the store. That she was, maybe, never even there.

"Closing!"

The voice breaks the Minotaur's reverie. No matter. It is still his.

A door squeaks. Footsteps. The voice calls out again. "Closing!"

The Minotaur sees her shoes, the thick black soles worn lopsided from her unending drudgery.

"Mmmnn, okay," he says.

He would like to tell her not to worry. He would like to step out of the changing-room stall and put his arms around the woman and hug. But the Minotaur hasn't changed that much. The pants-less bull-man would surely terrify the Goodwill employee.

"Okay," he says again.

The Minotaur puts his pants on. Holly picked them. She must have been there. He looks at the bench where she must have sat. Sees what she left. Must have. Drags a finger slowly through her. Puts the finger in his mouth. Again.

The husk of a beast is piled at his feet. The Minotaur toes it gently to make sure she's not still there, swathed and hidden. The Minotaur picks up the plastic Minotaur. The living Minotaur is not a thief. He pockets the toy anyway. Devmani will love it. He thinks of her full black eyes. The Minotaur is not a thief. He shoves the Picasso puppet into his other pocket. Anyway. Sweet time.

He goes to pay for the pants. At the register something in the $1.00 *Each* bin catches his eye. It's a cap, a gray Confederate soldier's cap. A costume version likely purchased in the Old Scald Village Gift Shoppe. The Minotaur takes the hat, and fortune blesses him again. There's a toy pistol at the bottom of the bin. A pistol with a black wooden dowel for a barrel.

"Th-these, too," he says to the clerk. Tookus will like these.

She bags his purchases. She eyes him up and down. The Minotaur can't tell what she thinks, what she wants. Things have changed.

The Minotaur steps out into what is left of the Ag-Fest afternoon. Yes, things have changed. Not the crowd. The crowd is boisterous still. Nor the ridge line in the distance. The windmills are still there making languid loop-the-loops. But change has come. Surely. The Minotaur doesn't see Holly or Tookus. He does see a young girl in a taffeta dress with a yellow ribbon draped across her chest. *Henceforth Joy Dairy Goat Award 3rd Prize.* A retinue of underlings flocks about her with sno-cones and taffy apples in their little fists and envy in their little teeth. The Minotaur is happy for her.

Where, then, is the change? How will it manifest?

Through the bell of a horn. The Minotaur hears the unbridled blatt and turns and sees them. Sees Holly first and her eye patch second. Ocular? Not the change he expected. Sees next Tookus pounding away on a drum, the boy's spastic motions at last put to good use.

They're on the stage, under the tent, both captives and captors. Roger is there. Jolly Roger, stomping along the front of the stage in tight leather pants with goat hooves and jingle bells sewn from the knees down along the outer seams. Several corseted women flank the stage (one very pregnant), heads high, arms back, boobs up and out. *Titties,* the Minotaur thinks. *I'm a tit man*, he thinks. No. Things have changed. They're nice enough, for sure, and meant to be seen. But the Minotaur has other fish to fry.

The Allegheny Bilge Rats Shanty Choir.

It says so on the yolk-colored poster, right below the grinning skull and crossbones with its blood-red bandana covered in white hearts. Says, too, *All You Have To Be Is Loud*.

And loud they are. Roger has delegated the sousaphone to a skinny boy with more enthusiasm than talent. One man, black clad and tall, churns at a steel-bodied guitar, the metal so bright it catches and reflects all the day's light. There are three, at least, men in full pirate regalia (storied media-rendered versions of pirate regalia, anyway). One pumps away at a squeezebox. Another kicks and scratches at a drumlike contraption made from a washtub, his right hand in a thimble-tipped glove raking and slapping a washboard bolted to an ax handle (which is bolted to the tub). The third pirate just sings, but Lord is he loud! Too, he never takes his eyes off the boobs. All in all there are probably fifteen people onstage (though they sound legion), belting it out. It's a spectacle, for sure. Just this side of cataclysm. And though the modest audience is largely indifferent, gumming away at their plates of fried things, everybody in The Allegheny Bilge Rats Shanty Choir is having a blast. Including Holly and Tookus.

"What shall we do with a drunken sailor, early in the morning!" Roger wails.

His choir rallies, an ocean of noise swelling and crashing down over all. "Hoo-ray and up she rises! Hoo-ray and up she rises, early in the morning!"

Roger says something about shanties.

"They're the work songs and party songs of seafarers," he says.

"They're all call and response," he says. "Sing along if you've got the balls!"

Roger takes a felt tricorn hat from one of the singers and puts it on Tookus. The boy beams. Holly, deep in the groove of the beat, sways and rocks her hips, keeping time with a tambourine. Things have changed.

Roger spots the Minotaur at the back of the rows of picnic tables and raises his hand high.

"Yo!" he says.

Everybody looks.

"Yo, sarge! Get your shanty panties on and get up here!"

So he does.

What's this world coming to?

CHAPTER THIRTY-TWO

IN A MANNER OF SPEAKING.

The Minotaur moves before self-consciousness can hobble him (as it has so many times). Tips his big head forward and lets the weight of his horns and snout carry him right through the crowd and up onto the stage. If anyone gets trampled along the way it's their fault. There, his presence, a half-bull half-man in Confederate soldier dress, is no more or less out of place than the rest.

"Ladies and gentlemen!" Roger says. "Boys and girls! Friends, enemies, and the rest of you scurvy-ridden dogs! The Allegheny Bilge Rats Shanty Choir is proud to present . . . "

Roger whips them all into a frenzy. Holly lifts her eye patch, grins big, jiggles her tambourine in the Minotaur's direction. Jiggles. Tookus thumps away at the drum in perfect time.

" . . . the horniest pirate in town!"

Somebody hands him a shaker egg, and the Minotaur does his best.

"Look at you go," Holly says.

"Horns and all," Holly says.

It might be the weirdest moment of his life.

Up there on the stage, as much as possible off to one side, bodies in motion, tits galore, the Minotaur shakes his little egg. Hears how the impossibly small clicks—Chhkk-chhkk-chhkk, chhkk-chhkk-chhkk—weave in and out of the larger sounds. The Minotaur is not smooth or graceful under scrutiny, is not fluid or rhythmic. Turns out that it doesn't matter. At all.

They sing another shanty. Something called "Whup Jamboree," with the lyric "Jenny, keep your hoecakes warm" driving the song harder and harder. The festival goers, weary after a full day of agrarian revelry, are underwhelmed, but it doesn't matter. The Minotaur does his best, with his little egg, to stay out of the way. He moves his lips, works his tongue. When the choir is at its loudest the Minotaur lets sound escape.

"We're gonna do one more for ya," Roger says into the mic. He gives the Minotaur a slap on the ass, and a squeeze as well. "It's a long-drag shanty," he says. "A purty one."

"Hanging Johnny" starts out slow and never gains speed. The song is glacial in its movement, meant for the long tedious task of raising an anchor from the seafloor. It is hypnotic and stunningly beautiful in its torpor.

"Well, they call me hanging Johnnyyyyyyyy."

"Away, boys, awayyyyyyyyy . . . "

By the end of the song the whole damn crew is shoulder to shoulder, spanning the width of the stage, swaying back and forth. Even the Minotaur. Even the Minotaur.

"Sooooo it's hannnng, boyyyyyyys, hannnnnnnnnnnnng!"

The final note becomes a drone, pulsing and throbbing, harmonies colliding in discord.

Then it's over. The Minotaur's shanty choir debut has run its course.

"We are The Allegheny Bilge Rats Shanty Choir!" Roger says. "We're available for weddings, funerals, birthdays, bar and bat mitzvahs, flea dips, prosecutions, persecutions, uprisings, and outbreaks of all kinds. Look for us on YouTube!"

There is a smattering of applause, but nobody onstage pays attention. It doesn't matter.

Tookus keeps thumping the drum until its owner has to claim it. Tookus wants to stay with the drum, with the beat, in the music. The Minotaur, too, though he wouldn't say as much.

Tookus is getting agitated; he holds tight to the shoulder strap and will not let go. Holly looks anxious. Things with Tookus can turn quickly bad.

Roger comes to the rescue with another shaker egg.

"This one's yours to keep, hotshot," he says to Tookus. "Practice, practice, practice."

Tookus hesitates, then Roger does a little dance and shakes the egg. The boy grins and swaps.

"Chhka chhka chhka," Tookus says. "Chhka chhka chhka."

Turns out, you really can buy "Shanty Panties" at The Allegheny Bilge Rats merchandise table, on display between the Bilge Rats kazoos and the Bilge Rats CDs.

Holly holds a pair up to her hips. "What do you think?" she asks.

She asks the Minotaur.

"Unngh," he says, quaking in his boots.

She buys two.

Roger gives them each a kazoo.

Roger tries to talk them into staying.

"Let's go to my house," he says. "Most of the crew is coming. You can stay the night. We'll sing some more."

The Minotaur is willing. Things have changed.

"This was a blast," Holly says, "but . . . "

All the way to the Odyssey, Holly gushes.

"So much fun," she says.

"So fucking weird," she says. "The perfect thing for Took's last . . . "

"Maybe I should go to music school," she says. "What do you do with a music degree?"

"Maybe you should come with us to Pittsburgh," she says. "All the way."

"Unngh, what?"

"Pittsburgh," she says. "Come with us. Come with me."

Everybody is leaving the Ag-Fest at the same time. The parking lot is gridlocked. The Minotaur's tongue is gridlocked. Always has been. He'd like to say things. To ask things. But words clot against his thick teeth.

"Buckle up, Took," Holly says, but they're not moving for a while.

"Chhka chhka chhka," Tookus says, shaking his egg. "Chhka chhka chhka."

"Take that out of your mouth, Took," Holly says. The boy is chewing on his varnished cow chip.

"Chhka chhka chhka," Tookus says.

"Maybe you should pee before we get on the road, Took," she says. "Do you have to pee?"

"Chhka chhka chhka," Tookus says.

"What do you think?" Holly asks.

The Minotaur thinks he would like to watch her dance again, hear her sing again, see her put those shanty panties on and take them off. He puts his fingertips to his nose. She doesn't know why. He does.

"What do you think, Tooky?" she asks. "We did okay out there, on that stage. On them high seas. Didn't we?"

"Drunken sailllllllor," Tookus sings.

The Odyssey, stalled in its progress, holds an unlikely trio. But the heart and the mind together are capable of untold alchemies. A crow alights above them, on the giant red K of the Kmart sign by the parking lot entrance. Sits as sentinel (the crow, maybe the sign, too), taking names. There, in the passenger seat, the Minotaur comes to conclusions. Hatches, even, a plan, albeit fetal. He will go with this redhead, this freckled and green-eyed redhead named Holly, will follow in the fiery tail of her cometlike presence, anywhere. He will go back to the Judy-Lou Motor Lodge and kiss Devmani Gupta right between her beautiful black eyes. He will thank Ramneek for all the *gulab jamun*, and Rambabu for everything else. Before he leaves the office the Minotaur will touch the Ganesh on its wrinkled brass trunk. It will take the Minotaur no time at all to pack up Room #3, his tools and sewing kit. He'll cross Business 220, walk right into the midst of Danny Tanneyhill's wooden menagerie, and bless the creatures one by one. The Minotaur will wriggle out from beneath the shadow of Scald Mountain, birthed into a brand-new self, and thus transmogrified will lift his bull horns and walk on his man legs through the covered bridge over Stink Creek, walk right into the heart of Old Scald Village, will stand in the door of the Blacksmith's Shoppe and let the anvil's ring wash over him. Will release Widow Fisk. The

Minotaur will sever his ties and gather his wits, climb into the Odyssey, and leave behind this land of plaster Nephilim.

The crow grows impatient on its perch. Caws, retches up a break in the traffic.

"Are you ready, big boy?" Holly asks.

Is she talking to him? The Minotaur chews mindlessly on his fingertip. What will he say? How will he answer?

"Pussy," he says. It's the word closest to his lips "It's called pussy."

Holly laughs.

"Whoa, Nellie," she says.

"Give a girl some warning," she says.

The Minotaur didn't mean to say it aloud. Didn't intend to speak his mind. But having done so, he will accept the consequences. The Minotaur takes the Picasso puppet from his pocket, puts it on the horn closer to Holly.

"Oooo," Holly says in that same strange accent. "You do know how to satisfy Meester Pablo."

Tookus laughs, sings part of a line from a shanty. "Shave his bellllllyyyyyyy!"

Holly grabs hold of the tune. "Shave his belly with a rusty razor!"

The Minotaur takes the toy version of himself and sets it on the dashboard, facing the road. One of them is a charlatan, a huckster. He'll gift the toy to Devmani. She'll like it. The Minotaur takes the Confederate cap and the toy pistol from where he secreted them inside his jacket. Offers them back to Tookus.

"Bang bang bang," Tookus says, happily shooting at everything they pass.

Holly sings. Tookus sings. They all sing. Even the Minotaur. Even the Minotaur.

It is a joyous few miles. Bang bang bang.

"Peeeeee!" Tookus says in the middle of a song.

And as it happens the four staggered hearts of a Love's Travel Stop & Country Store marquee are in sight. The crow may have some hand in the circumstance. The travel center sits at a crossroads in a basin of flat land poked and prodded by the Allegheny Mountains on all sides.

"I told you," she says, pulling the van up to the curb.

The lot and the store throb with busyness, with coming and going. Even inside the Odyssey the Minotaur feels the crackling energy of people not quite where they want to be, not sure they want to go there anyway.

"Unngh," the Minotaur says, prepared to bless and comfort them all.

"Let's get this over with," Holly says.

CHAPTER THIRTY-THREE

OVER WITH.

"Bang bang," Tookus says, and cocks the Confederate cap high on his head.

"Bang bang," he says, taking aim at his sister and the Minotaur.

"Bang bang," he says, taking out an imaginary target.

Tookus shoves the pistol into his waistband and heads for the door.

"Wait up, Tookus," Holly says, following her addle-brained brother.

The Minotaur watches her walk. Sashay. Swoon, Minotaur. Anywhere.

She waits by the entrance, asks the Minotaur to go in with Tookus.

"Keep him out of trouble," she says.

Anywhere. Love's Travel Stop & Country Store, for instance.

The plaza swarms with travelers. And with the food court here, the restrooms there, and the convenience store over yonder, it's ready to meet any need. Mark the hustle and bustle. Slow down, Minotaur. Bless them all.

Most of the food-court tables and booths are occupied. Chitter chatter, chitter chatter. Just people being people. Bless them all. Bless the couples and the families. Bless those traveling alone. Bless the security guard hunched over and eating by himself in a corner booth. Bless the pouty teens and all their piercings. Swoon, Minotaur.

A giant backlit map of the Keystone State spans the eight-foot wall between the men's and women's restrooms. Holly heads for Pittsburgh.

"Be back in jiffy," she says.

"Meet you right here," she says.

"Don't leave without me."

The Minotaur follows Tookus toward Philadelphia.

The boy goes into a stall and locks it. "Drunkennnn sailllllor," he says. "Shave his belllllyyyy."

The Minotaur goes into the open stall beside Tookus and sits down to wait. *As long as it takes*, he thinks. *That's the point.* The Minotaur sits up straight because there isn't room in the stall for him to do otherwise. The Love's bathroom smells of disinfectant and is clean enough, though at the bottom of his stall door, written in Sharpie and upside down, is a little missive about what Minky wants to do to Pooter in no uncertain terms, and with an illustration.

"Hoeeeeecakes warm!" Tookus says. Bellows, really.

The boy is taking a long time. The Minotaur goes out to wait for Holly, for instructions, if necessary. It seems the right thing to do. As soon as the Minotaur steps into the food-court area, Tookus lets rip another lyric. Everybody looks up.

"Mmmnn," the Minotaur says.

The security guard cranes his neck to get a better view. The Keystone State map shines behind the Minotaur. His horns span hundreds of miles. Of course they do. He's in the way. He's blocking the door. The Minotaur steps clear, steps up to the low decorative fencing that delineates the dining area. Two fake plants flank and beautify the trash can. The Minotaur tries to find somewhere to look. Tries to be unobtrusive in his benevolence. Settles on an old man sitting alone at a table right by the trash receptacle. He's ancient, as humans go. A colorless overcoat, colorless pants and shoes. His downcast eyes runny and yellowed. His skin, all his visible flesh, wizened and dappled with liver spots. He mumbles to himself and scribbles on a napkin. Balls it up, shoves it aside into a mound of other crumpled napkins. The ink bleeds through. Nothing is decipherable.

Tookus sings.

The old man looks up and into the Minotaur's eyes. Looks into the Minotaur. The old man wipes his wet mouth on his sleeve, rakes a wormlike tongue across his teeth, rooting in the gums, hisses, and speaks. No, shouts.

" 'Bout goddamn time!"

The old man gets up and shuffles toward the exit.

The Minotaur is rattled. Should he bless this man? This moment? He doesn't know. He turns to the map at his back. Maps make sense. This one, laced by color-coded roads and streets and highways, is almost a living thing. It's like he is looking at the innards, the circulatory or nerve system, of an immovable leviathan. He leans close, listens for a heartbeat. The Minotaur locates himself, his companions, and Love's in a perfect circle alongside a blue artery that splits, then parallels a ridge of the Allegheny Front.

You Are Here.

The red heart says so. The Minotaur wants to believe.

You Are Here.

Here, at the junction of a north-south interstate and an east-west turnpike, at Love's Travel Stop & Country Store. The Minotaur traces the spot. Locates Business 220. Sees without meaning to Joy Furnace, marked plain as day on the map. And called a Local Attraction. It's more than that. Just ask the Minotaur. He decides, then and there, to take Holly and Tookus to see it. To take them into the high stone walls, to be inside of, to share, Joy Furnace with him.

You Are Here.

"Are ya lost, big boy?" somebody asks.

Discombobulated by the old man, the Minotaur can't answer. Off beam, out of joint, shaken, for the moment, anyway, the Minotaur looks into the face of his interrogator. No. False. Insist on the truth. The question was soft. Caring, even. The Minotaur comes about, looks. And finds that she is official. She wears the Love's smock.

"Can I help you find your way?" she asks. Eyes black. Nose thin, beakish.

The Minotaur cannot tell how old she is. Even standing still she seems to flit back and forth. It's hard to see her clearly. But there is no denying her smells. The molt. The twiggy nest's filth. Keratin. The Minotaur is sure he hears the scritch and scratch of talons inside her boots. And is that a trail of blackish down settling around those boots?

"Unngh, no," the Minotaur says. "Thanks, but no."

The Love's employee smiles, a very corvidae smile. "Okay, then," she says.

She swoops through the Employees Only door. As it closes behind her, the Minotaur hears a caw. He'd swear it.

"Caw."

No. It's Holly. She comes out of the bathroom, zipping her pants.

"Hey," she says, "is that boy still in there?"

"Unngh," the Minotaur says.

It wouldn't surprise him at all if Holly were to waltz right into the men's restroom to retrieve her brother. Not at all. She looks about to do just that. Looks at the Minotaur, picks, deliberately, something from his coat, right over his brass button. It's a tiny black feather. Holly holds it aloft on one fingertip. Blows gently. The feather lifts up and away. Holly winks at the Minotaur. 'Nuff said.

"Hurry up, Took!" she calls into bathroom.

"I'm going to get us some water," she says. "And some Tic Tacs. You hold down the fort."

The Minotaur watches her walk away. It never gets old. Steady, big boy, you have a fort to hold down.

A gangly kid in a Love's smock rolls a trash can up to the old man's table and sweeps all the crumpled napkins into it. The security guard stands, slurps the last bit of cola from an extra-large cup. No. The Minotaur sees the truth. Insist on it. The man is not a security guard. He's a game warden. His uniform crisp and green. His shield radiant. His duties? Of and about the natural world. He's pink cheeked. And if he has any hair at all the Minotaur can't see it. See it. The Minotaur sees things in a new light. Everything happens for a reason. Or not. The game warden is there. Maybe he's there for a reason. Maybe, sometimes, the peace and quiet of the outdoors get to the man. Maybe the natural world is too pure, too purely brutal. Maybe he longs for complication. Maybe he gets tired of bag limits and worrying about seven-inch trout. And those goddamn poachers. It's too much sometimes. Sometimes he likes to come inside, maybe, to bathe in the pure artificial light of Love's Travel Stop, to eat bad food and fret over his alopecia. To worry, amid the other worriers, about whether the baby in his wife's belly will be retarded. They wouldn't use that word, but the goddamn ultrasound showed some problems. Bless him. Bless the game warden. Maybe he just needs to think, maybe even to talk, to confess, to tell someone, anyone, about what he did down at the quarry with that Rite Aid cashier. Not because he doesn't love his wife. Not at all. Bless the game warden, who is just scared and lonely, like everybody else. Who just wants someone to tell him everything is going to be okay. Maybe the Minotaur. Bless him.

The Minotaur, undone by Love's, meets the game warden halfway.

"B-bless you," the Minotaur says.

"What?" the man says.

"You are here," the Minotaur says, amazed at the clarity of his claim.

"What?" the game warden says.

"Put him in the scuppers with a hose pipe on him!" Tookus roars from the toilet. And his clarity is magnificent as well.

"What the hell?" Holly says. She's back with a bottle of water in each hand. Practically saintlike.

Then the gunshot rings out from the men's room.

"Fuck!" Holly says, drops the water. One bottle ruptures.

No. It's not a gunshot. It's a firecracker. An M80. But people don't know that. And though stunned and confused by the first explosion, at the second folks dive for cover under the food-court tables or run screaming into Love's busy parking lot.

"N-no," the Minotaur says. It's just a firecracker. It's just Tookus.

Holly heads into the bathroom, but she's knocked to the ground by all the men rushing out. Bless her. Bless them and their ringing ears, their stinging eyes.

"No," the Minotaur says, reaching for Holly.

"Move!" the game warden says, reaching for his weapon. Duty calls. "Move, now!"

"No," the Minotaur says. Everything is okay.

"No," Holly says, struggling to her feet. "It's not . . . He's not . . . "

"What wondrous love is this!" Tookus sings from inside the bathroom.

Comes out of the bathroom singing the next line. "O my soul! O my soul!"

Comes out of the bathroom singing and pointing his toy pistol. "What wondrous love is this! What . . . "

There is a little mouth in the middle of the game warden's fat pink cheeks. It's saying something. But the Minotaur can't hear what. The game warden's gun is pointed and cocked. Sometimes the game warden's wife helps him polish the gun.

It's okay, the Minotaur says. No. Thinks. *You Are Here.* The Minotaur has been here before, right? He can't remember. It's called pussy. No. It's more than that.

Tookus staggers, wide eyed and giddy, singing, into the fray. His fray. He sees the other man in uniform, the game warden. Raises his toy pistol.

"Bang bang," Tookus says.

Holly lunges for her brother, puts her fine body between the boy and the rest of the world.

"Bang bang," Tookus says, looking down the black wooden barrel.

The Minotaur looks at the game warden and sees it in his eyes. The reason. He knows it. The game warden and the Minotaur both know. It is the dying season.

"Bless you," the Minotaur says, his heart pumping.

And what pumps through those human veins is, no doubt, monstrous blood. And in the monster's bloody core there is no denying humanity. Much humanity. Most try to pretend they're different. It's a tiresome chore. On good days the Minotaur knows a few things. Want. Hope. Need. Fear. Hunger. Hunger comes. Hunger goes. The Minotaur has learned that beyond hunger is just more hunger. He is learning to eat the emptiness.

"What wondrous love is this!"

There is an eternity between the pulling of the trigger and what happens next.

You Are Here.

"O my soul! O my soul!"

You Are Here.

There is a perfect little red heart on the Love's Travel Stop map.

Is that Tookus? Is he singing? Is the song perfectly sung?

You Are Here.

The little red heart says so.

The Minotaur believes it.

ACKNOWLEDGMENTS

I WOULD LIKE TO THANK the following for their help (direct or indirect) in bringing this novel to life: Lee Peterson, wife o' mine; the Peterson-Littenburg-Rich contingent in NYC; Michael Griffith for his reliable genius; Nicola Mason and all the folks at *Cincinnati Review* (in which an excerpt of the book appears); Yseult Ogilvie; Anna Jean Moriarty and the folks at ThePigeonhole.com; Ian Staples, Jon Seagroatt, and Bobbie Seagroatt for the creation of *Deathless*; Ian Wilson for his operatic vision; and Penn State Altoona for its ongoing support of what happens in my noggin.

Printed in the USA
CPSIA information can be obtained
at www.ICGtesting.com
JSHW021317120923
48357JS00002B/10